If I was going to save this city, I needed three things: one empty detergent bottle, one magazine clipping of Zoe Saldana as Uhura from Star Trek, and one stolen child.

My gun vanished into my jacket as Isabel Famosa stepped into her kitchen and tossed her keys onto the counter. She froze halfway through the process of removing a green windbreaker. "Who are you?"

"Do you have any electrical tape?" I asked.

She backed into the small kitchen. Going for either a phone or a knife. By the time she returned, I had my badge ready.

"My name's Jessica." A lie, but I wasn't about to tell her or the bureau my true name. "I'm with the FBI. Do you know where your husband is, Mrs. Formosa?"

"The FBI? But you're ... you're not—"

"Human?" She had gone for a boning knife. Nice choice. I hopped down from the chair, clenching my teeth as the movement sent new pain tearing through my leg. Blood oozed through the blue silk tie I had used as a makeshift bandage. Damn troll. I shoved my blonde hair back and hobbled closer, giving her a good look at the narrow pointed ears, the oversaturated blue of my eyes, the deceptively fragile build. "No, I'm not."

—from "Corrupted" by Jim Hines

THE
MODERN FAE'S
GUIDE
TO
SURVIVING
HUMANITY

edited by Joshua Palmatier
and Patricia Bray

DAW BOOKS, INC.
DONALD A. WOLLHEIM, FOUNDER
375 Hudson Street, New York, NY 10014

ELIZABETH R. WOLLHEIM
SHEILA E. GILBERT
PUBLISHERS
http://www.dawbooks.com

First Printing, March 2012
1 2 3 4 5 6 7 8 9

DAW TRADEMARK REGISTERED
U.S. PAT. AND TM. OFF. AND FOREIGN COUNTRIES
—MARCA REGISTRADA
HECHO EN U.S.A.

PRINTED IN THE U.S.A.

Acknowledgments

Introduction copyright © 2012 by Patricia Bray and Joshua Palmatier

"We Will Not Be Undersold," copyright © 2012 by Seanan McGuire

"Changeling," copyright © 2012 by Susan Jett

"Water-Called," copyright © 2012 by Kari Sperring

"The Roots of Aston Quercus," copyright © 2012 by Juliet E. McKenna

"To Scratch an Itch," copyright © 2012 by Avery Shade

"Continuing Education," copyright © 2012 by Kristine Smith

"How To Be Human™," copyright © 2012 by Barbara Ashford

"How Much Salt," copyright © 2012 by April Steenburgh

"Hooked," copyright © 2012 by Anton Strout

"Crash," copyright © 2012 by S. C. Butler

"Fixed," copyright © 2012 by Jean Marie Ward

"A People Who Always Know," copyright © 2012 by Shannon Page & Joseph E. Lake, Jr.

"The Slaughtered Lamb," copyright © 2012 by Elizabeth Bear

"Corrupted," copyright © 2012 by Jim C. Hines

Table of Contents

INTRODUCTION

As one of three children growing up in a small house, it was a constant battle to keep my siblings from getting into my stuff. Eventually I hit on the perfect solution—I appropriated a medium-sized cardboard box and on the top I wrote: *Warning!! Dangerous Polar Bears inside!!! DO NOT OPEN!!!!!!!* Then I placed my most secret treasures inside the box, confident that the warning message would give pause to even the most inquisitive of my siblings.

I knew it wasn't likely that there would be polar bears inside the box, and suspected that my brother and sister knew that as well. But it was *possible*.

It's that sense of possibility, of wonder, that fantasy readers share. Long after childhood has passed, and we've been forced to acknowledge that polar bears aren't generally found roaming the streets of suburban New England, we still enjoy reading what-if stories. What if our favorite myths were real, or we could travel to the stars, or journey back in time? What if . . . ? The possibilities—and the stories they inspire—are endless.

1

Last year, after Joshua Palmatier and I finished editing our first anthology (*After Hours: Tales from the Ur-Bar*, DAW Books, March 2011), we began discussing our next project. Joshua suggested, "What if the fairies hadn't disappeared? What if they were still around today?"

The idea quickly took shape. What if the fae were still here, living among us? Perhaps living in secret, doing their best to pass for human. Or perhaps their existence is acknowledged, but they're still struggling to fit in. How have they survived? Are they outcasts clinging to the edges of society, or do their powers ensure success in the mortal realm? I was excited by the idea, as were the authors that we invited to send in stories. Out of their submissions we picked fourteen fabulous tales—ranging from humor to dark fantasy—that explore how the creatures of fae are fitting into the modern world.

We hope you enjoy.

Patricia Bray and Joshua Palmatier

WE WILL NOT BE UNDERSOLD

Seanan McGuire

"**D**an?" Nimh looked around the employee break room, allowing her eyes to skirt past the slack-faced stockroom workers sitting slumped in their gray plastic chairs. Their cheery green and yellow vests were painfully bright against the industrial beige walls and floor. Not for the first time, Nimh made a note to talk to the store manager about getting some decorations in. Maybe a few cheery posters with kittens and motivational slogans ($4.99, home décor). Those always sold well, so people obviously liked them.

None of the dead-eyed employees were Dan. Only two of them were even male. With a sunny smile and a wave for everyone (stay positive; positivity enhances profitability), Nimh chirped, "Have a fantastic shopping day, everybody!" and turned to leave the room while the workers were still trying to formulate a response. It was always best to leave a situation on a high note.

Dan also wasn't in the stockroom, where some of the

more free-spirited clerks scrambled to hide the poker game they didn't think management knew about (management knew). Dan wasn't in the small dining area attached to the snack bar, either. Nimh frowned as she realized that there were actually no employees in the snack bar. She'd need to notify the supervisors to slip some more coupons into the pay envelopes. Seeing happy workers eating Chikin Chompers™ and drinking Milk-y-shakes™ encouraged customer faith in the menu, and customer faith drove customer dollars.

Nimh was on the verge of giving up her quest when she opened the fire door at the back of the store—the one with the broken alarm the employees thought management didn't know about (management knew)—and found Dan sitting on a splintery old picnic table, his nose buried, as always, in a book. She stepped outside and eased the door silently shut behind her, taking a moment to lean up against the doorframe and just look at him.

She never got tired of looking at Dan. Oh, the rest of the girls in junior management assured her that he was quite average-looking, with his brown hair, muddy hazel eyes, and wire-framed glasses. "You can do better" was a common refrain in the evenings, as they sat around the plastic snack bar tables and slurped Mint-i-licious Milk-y-shakes™. Maybe she could. When you got right down to it, she didn't really care.

They remained that way for several minutes, Dan reading, Nimh watching Dan read. They both jumped when his watch began to beep. "Damn," muttered Dan, reaching for the button that would make the beeping stop—only to jump a second time as he caught sight of Nimh standing up against the wall. "Jeez! Nimh, you scared me."

"I couldn't find you, and then you looked so happy

that I didn't want to interrupt." Nimh grimaced, looking faintly guilty. "I'm sorry. Was that wrong?"

"Only because it would have been nice to spend my lunch break with you, instead of with these two." Dan held up his paperback in illustration. There was a lurid painting of half-naked elf maidens on the cover. "I thought you were on shift until two."

"I got them to shift my shift." Nimh pushed herself away from the wall, giving the book a dubious glance as she walked toward him. "I don't think I'm cut out for chainmail bikinis."

"Don't worry. I like my women black-haired, petite, and fully clothed." Dan slid off the picnic bench, tucking his book into the back pocket of his jeans as he moved to meet Nimh on the no-man's-land between the building and the decrepit outdoor lunch area. "No gossamer elf princesses will lure me from your arms."

"I'm so relieved," said Nimh, not quite able to stop herself from smiling. "Isn't it time for you to go back to work?"

"That was my ten-minute warning," Dan said. "I was planning to track you down and try to convince you to slack off for five minutes before I had to go back to the grind."

"Well, it's a good thing for you that you won't have to do that, since you would have failed. I don't 'slack off.'"

"That's one of the things I love about you. You somehow manage to be genuinely enthusiastic about working at Undermart. That may be a miracle." Dan leaned forward to kiss her deeply. Nimh responded in kind, and both of them were smiling a little dizzily by the time he pulled away. "You always taste like cotton candy. Why is that?"

"Healthy living." Nimh kissed him again before stepping backward, out of the circle of his arms. "Come on. I don't want to distract you and make you late to work."

"Right. Wouldn't want to let Undermart down."

Nimh looked at him with wide, earnest eyes, and said, "That's exactly what I was thinking."

"I know." Dan smiled a little. "Let's get back to work."

Nimh was almost skipping as she led the way inside.

"Dude, what are you doing hanging around with that management chick?"

The words were aggressively delivered, but the nasal voice of the speaker robbed them of the bulk of their menace. Dan sighed, counting slowly to ten before he turned to face his coworker. "Hello, Kyle. How was your lunch? Mine was great. I brought an egg salad sandwich from home."

"What are you talking about?" Kyle scowled at him, eyebrows scrunching suspiciously together. "You been letting that management chick make you drink those Milk-y-shake™ things they sell up front?"

"She has a name, you know."

"Yeah. Her name's 'the Man.'" Kyle paused, a lecherous expression spreading across his face. "Oh, dude, are you sticking it to the Man? You can tell me. We're buddies."

"No, we're not 'buddies.' We only tolerate each other because we work in the same department, and every word you say moves me a little closer to requesting a transfer. I hang around with Nimh because she's my girlfriend, remember? We're dating? People who are dating tend to hang out together."

"So you *are* sticking it to the Man," said Kyle, lecherous expression spreading. "Does she wear that cotton candy perfume in the bedroom?"

"I'll report you for harassment if you don't shut up right now," said Dan pleasantly.

Kyle scowled. "You'd never be banging her if she weren't management. You know Undermart doesn't like fraternization between employees."

"There's nothing in the handbook forbidding it."

"There's nothing in the handbook requiring you to eat that artificial bird crap, either—"

"Chikin Chompers™," murmured Dan, automatically.

"—but you better believe they'll come down on you if you don't do it. She's bad news, man. All them management chicks are. Corporate keeps them in the stores because they make the customers happy, but that doesn't mean they're here to fraternize." Kyle picked up his price gun, brandishing it threateningly at Dan. "Watch yourself, man, or I'll be getting a new buddy, and you'll be getting a promotion."

Dan blinked. "How is getting a promotion bad?"

"Ask one of the greeters that," said Kyle darkly.

He was silent for the rest of the shift.

Nimh was sitting on the hood of Dan's car when he came trudging out of the Undermart, his heavy wool coat almost covering the neon edges of his mandatory work vest. She brightened at the sight of him, enjoying, as always, the way the parking lot safety lights glittered off his hair.

Dan smiled when he saw her, starting to walk a little faster. "Hey, baby. You off for the night?"

"I have morning inventory, but until then, I'm all yours." Nimh slid off the car, opening her arms so that Dan could step right into them. "I missed you."

"We were in the same store."

No, we weren't, she thought, kissed his chin, and said, "I couldn't come see you while you were on your shift. It was lonely."

"That's sweet." Dan raised one hand, brushing her bangs away from her eyes. "Where did you want to go for dinner?"

"Someplace decadent and bad for us," Nimh replied. "How do you feel about the salad bar?"

"Your definition of 'decadent' needs some work, but sure," said Dan. He fished his car keys out of his pocket, holding them up for her to see. "Your chariot awaits."

"Oh, no," said Nimh, looking faintly perplexed. "I like your car much better."

Dan was still laughing when they pulled out of the parking lot. Nimh snuggled deeper in the passenger seat and just listened to the sound of it, wishing, as she always did, that the moment would never have to end. But it would. Moments like this, moments outside the Undermart, always did.

Later that night, after three plates of salad (one with *blue cheese dressing*, and wasn't that the naughtiest thing anyone had ever done?) and half a pitcher of virgin sangria, Nimh nestled under the synthetic cotton sheets ($9.99, housewares) and genuine vegetable lamb comforter on Dan's bed, letting herself breathe in the reassuring salty scent of him as she curled against his side.

"What are you thinking?" she asked.

"That I wish we didn't have to get up in seven hours and head back to our dead-end jobs where we have to work in the same building all day long without seeing each other." Dan pushed himself up onto his elbow, looking at her gravely. He had to squint to do it, but he didn't reach for his glasses. That had been the first sign that he was falling in love with her: when he stopped putting his glasses back on every time they rolled apart long enough to breathe. "Doesn't it ever bother you? The idea that maybe this is going to be our lives? Get up, spend the whole day working at the Undermart, go shopping at the Undermart, go home, go sleep, and wait to die?"

Nimh blinked at him. "No. That doesn't bother me. Why would it?"

Dan hesitated. "Sometimes I don't understand you, you know."

"I know." Nimh reached up one hand, cupping his cheek. "I'm doing the best I can. I just didn't grow up around here, remember?"

"I remember. I just never thought of Canada as being another planet before I met you." Dan sighed. "Honestly, Nimh, are you going to be happy? If this is all there is? Don't you want to run away from here? Because I'd do it, you know, if you were willing to go with me. I'd run away, and I'd never look back."

"It's more complicated than that."

"I know. But I wish—"

Nimh slid her hand around to press a finger against his lips, trapping the wish before it could be fully birthed into the world. "Never wish," she said, with quick urgency. "Wishing is what lets danger into the world."

Dan blinked at her. Then he sighed, heavily, and dropped back to the bed, rolling onto his back as he stared up at the ceiling. "Kyle was asking today about what I was doing with you—or what you were doing with me, I guess."

"What did you tell him?" asked Nimh.

There was a sudden edge to her voice that made him lift his head and frown, seeing the alarm on her slightly blurry features. "That you were my girlfriend. Why?"

"I just . . . I just wondered, that's all. Can we sleep? Please? I'm tired, and it will be morning soon."

"Sure, sweetie." Dan kissed her forehead before nestling himself a little deeper. "Sleep well."

"Yes," Nimh said. "You, also."

Dan turned off the light. His breathing quickly steadied into the long, slow rise and fall of a sleeping man. Nimh remained awake, staring up at the ceiling and beginning to compose the addendum she would have to make to her upcoming report to management. There was no point in trying to omit what she had learned. Management would already know, and would be waiting to learn what she was willing to do to massage the data.

Management always knew.

"Has anybody seen Kyle?" asked Dan, picking up a refill for his price gun. "I've been taking care of the toy section by myself all morning, and I'm about ready to punch his stupid face in if he comes sauntering in here without a damn good excuse for himself."

The clerks he'd been talking to stiffened, exchanging a wary glance before the shorter one—he thought her name was Peggy—said, slowly, "You mean he didn't tell you?"

Dan frowned. "Didn't tell me what? Oh, jeez, don't tell me he finally decided to quit. Please. I have plans this weekend."

"That he was up for a promotion," said the other clerk. He was actually wearing his name tag, identifying him as one of the store's seven or so men named Arthur. He offered Dan a reassuring smile. "I'm sure he's going to be much happier and more fulfilled with his work now that he's doing something truly suited to his skills."

"A promotion?" Slow, terrifying certainty was uncoiling itself in Dan's gut. He did his best to keep it from showing on his face as he snapped the refill roll into his price gun. "Wow. Well, I hope they'll be hiring for his position soon. I can't manage toys by myself forever."

"I'm sure management is on top of things," said Arthur.

"Yeah, I'm sure you're right," agreed Dan, with a fairly sickly looking smile. He turned and left the stockroom, walking quickly back onto the floor. One of the customers in the toy section had managed to pull over an entire display of toy cars, and without Kyle to help, it took the better part of an hour for Dan to get everything picked up and put back where it belonged.

By the time the display was restored to its original condition, it was time for Dan's first break of the day. He slipped back into the stockroom long enough to clock out, then made his way slowly toward the front of the store, where the greeters would be waiting to welcome new customers to the Undermart.

Undermart wasn't the only big-box store to employ their own small army of smiling faces, but they liked to say that they went The Extra Smile™, with greeters who were somewhere between friendly faces and personal shoppers. They would even follow customers through the store if asked, carrying their bags and offering tips about good bargains. Consequentially, the store employed twice as many greeters as any of their competitors, just to keep up with the demand.

The yellow and green vests of the greeters made them stand out amongst the shoppers like macaws in a chicken coop. Dan scanned them quickly, and was just starting to relax when he spotted a head covered in familiar blond spikes. The greeter was too far away for him to be certain, but he still knew. The moment that he saw the way the greeter was standing, the height of him, Dan knew.

Holding tightly to his price gun, like it would somehow defend him from whatever was ahead, Dan walked over to the door and waited until Kyle's customer turned to leave the store. She was smiling broadly, like a little girl who'd just been promised she'd be getting that pony for her birthday after all. Women never smiled after they finished talking to Kyle. Sometimes they threatened to talk to his manager, but they never smiled.

"Kyle?"

"Oh, hello." Kyle turned, a beatific smile lighting his acne-scarred features and turning them into something almost beautiful. "Welcome to Undermart. Can I help you find some wonderful bargains for your home and family?"

"Kyle, it's me, Dan. Your partner, remember?" Dan held up the price gun, waving it between them. "Why didn't you tell me you were applying for a promotion? I thought you hated the greeters!"

"Undermart greeters are here to help you make the most of your shopping experience. We're like Santa's elves, now with Real Super-Saving Action™!" Kyle kept smiling, but there was something strained in his eyes, like part of him wanted nothing more than to start screaming instead. "What are you looking for today?"

"Kyle!" Dan grabbed Kyle's vest with his free hand. The rest of the greeters froze, the whole yellow and green herd of them turning slowly to stare at the man who had dared to lay a hand on one of their own.

Starting to feel like he had made a very big mistake, Dan let go and stepped back.

"Sorry. I guess I just got carried away."

Kyle's smile never wavered. "Anger management videos can be found in our Entertainment section. Or, if your doctor would like to prescribe anti-anxiety medications, you can have them sent directly to our Undermart pharmacy. They got me, Dan. Run while you still can. Maybe you'd like to have a delicious Milk-y-shake™ while you wait for your nerves to settle?"

Dan's eyes widened. "What did you just say?"

"Milk-y-shakes™ are available in six flavors: chocolate, vanilla, mango-banana, strawberry, our own signature Mint-i-licious, and for a limited time only, seasonal Chokka-berry-yum. Try one today!"

Dan took another step backward. Kyle kept on smiling, giving no sign that he understood what he was saying.

Clutching his price gun to his chest, Dan turned and fled.

"Nimh! Nimh?" Dan burst into the upstairs hall—the one most employees entered only under duress or when called to meet with management. He was still clutching his price gun, and was dimly aware that his break had ended five minutes ago. That didn't seem to matter now. Nothing mattered but finding Nimh and getting the hell out of the Undermart, before whatever had gotten to Kyle started getting to them. "Dammit, Nimh, where are you?!"

"Dan?"

He whirled to see his girlfriend standing framed in one of the private doorways, the door pulled almost entirely shut behind her. The air smelled like cotton candy and fresh raspberries, two scents he'd never really associated with corporate management before coming to work for the Undermart.

Before he'd started dating Nimh.

Not letting himself think about what he was doing, Dan lunged and grabbed her hand, yanking her out of the doorway. "Come on! We've got to get out of here. We've got to get out of here now."

"What are you talking about?" Nimh pulled herself out of his grasp, eyes wide and alarmed. "You're acting crazy, Dan. You're still on your shift."

"Undermart isn't safe."

"What? Undermart is the safest place there is!"

"Kyle's a greeter. Kyle didn't even seem to know who I was, and he would never, never voluntarily take a job as a greeter. He was telling me just yesterday that management 'promotes' people who don't agree with them, and now—"

"Dan, I'm management," said Nimh quietly.

"—he's been promoted, and he doesn't recognize me! We have to go!"

"It's my fault they promoted him."

"If we don't leave now, I don't know if we can— what?" Dan stopped, blinking at Nimh. "What are you talking about?"

"You're right, Dan. You should go." Nimh drew herself up a little straighter, smiling despite the tears he could see starting to gather in the corners of her eyes. "Go now. I'll cover for you with the senior managers, but only if you go now."

"Nimh. . . ." Dan started to step forward, reaching for her.

"You're fired," she whispered. "Now get out before I call store security on you."

Dan stood there, stunned, as Nimh turned away and stepped back through the private door, closing it behind herself with a decisive click.

He took the price gun with him when he left the Undermart. Technically, it was theft. He honestly didn't care.

The doors of the downtown Undermart officially opened at 7AM, catering to those early risers and busy professionals who needed to get a leg up on the day. In order to make the opening seamless, delivery trucks and stockroom staff began arriving at 5:30. Dan showed up at 5:45, wearing the employee vest he was no longer strictly entitled to and clutching his purloined price gun like a sword.

"Morning, Dan," said Molly, as he walked past her without clocking in.

"Morning, Molly," he replied, and kept going, heading through the employee level to the management stairs.

He'd thought long and hard after Nimh threw him out the night before, finally concluding that, having been fired, he could go looking for answers without fear of any further repercussions. Maybe a trespassing charge, but that was about it. He kept that thought firmly in mind as he slunk silently into the upstairs hall, heading for the doorway Nimh had retreated through after firing him. Whatever was behind that door, maybe it could give him some idea of what had been done to Kyle.

Dan tested the knob as he dug in his pocket for the nail file he intended to use as an impromptu lock pick.

The door had always been locked before, and the test was more out of habit than anything else. That didn't stop the door from swinging promptly open, revealing the darkened room beyond. Dan stopped where he was, blinking.

"Huh," he said, softly. "OK, then." Pulling his hand from his pocket, he clutched the price gun a little tighter, and stepped over the threshold, into the dark.

The darkness lasted for three steps. Step one, normal dark, with the dim light of the hallway creeping in from behind him. Step two, absolute dark, like there was no light left in the world. Step three, a somehow even deeper dark, one that went on forever and ever, without end. Step four . . .

Step four and he was back in the light. Not the dim light of the early morning Undermart, but the bright daytime light of a glossy green meadow, dotted with garishly colored flowers that smelled like cinnamon and cotton candy. Dan froze, fingers clenching convulsively on the handle of his price gun. A $12.99 price tag popped out of the business end, looking like nothing so much as a ticket back to the real world. He grabbed the tag, affixing it to his vest, and waited.

Nothing changed.

"Dan?"

Nimh sounded querulous, even terrified. Dan whirled to face her, raising his price gun so that it was held solidly between them, and stared. Her normally black hair was a rich shade of plum purple, like she was trying to look like one of the less popular dolls from the Strawberry Shortcake™ toy collection. She had it pulled back, showing the distinctly pointed tips of her ears. Her eyes were a shade of violet only a little lighter than her hair.

Really, if she hadn't been wearing her Undermart uniform, she would have been entirely unbelievable. But no matter how good his imagination was, he could never have imagined anything that clashed as badly as plum hair and an official Undermart uniform vest.

"What the—where are—what are you?!" The questions came out so fast they tangled around one another, becoming a single long, half-coherent demand.

Nimh shook her head, newly violet eyes wide. "No, no, I can't tell you, and you can't be here. Dan, why didn't you run? You were supposed to run." She started to reach for him, despair washing over her features as he stepped back, out of her reach. "I have to get you out of here before it's too late. I love you. Don't you see? I tried to get you away from the store because I love you."

"Too late?" asked Dan. "Too late for what?"

Nimh didn't answer. She just looked past him, the expression slowly draining from her face. It almost wasn't a surprise when the hand clamped down on his shoulder from behind, a hand easily twice the size of his, with fingers that tightened until they hurt.

"Nimue?" rumbled a voice, in something that sounded less like simple speech than it did the movement of rocks deep beneath a mountain. "What is the meaning of this?"

"Hello, Daddy," sighed Nimh. "I'd like you to meet my boyfriend."

Dan didn't remember leaving the green meadow with the impossible flowers. He didn't remember Nimh changing her hair from purple back to its more customary black. And he certainly didn't remember the face of the man behind that massive hand. But most of all, he didn't remember being tied to a chair. He tugged experimentally on the rope that held him down ($14.99, home and garden). The knots held.

Nimh stood in front of him, wringing her hands anxiously. Her eyes were still violet. He seized on that hope. If her eyes were still violet, maybe he wasn't really tied to a chair. Maybe this was just a really, really weird dream.

"Your mortal man awakens," rumbled a deep voice from behind him.

The hope died. No matter how weird his dreams got, they never made him want to piss himself.

"Yes, Daddy," said Nimh. That odd accent of hers was stronger now. Dan couldn't believe he'd ever believed her when she said she was Canadian. Leaning closer, she dropped her voice, and whispered, "Dan, please. I need you to be respectful. Please."

"Or what? You'll kill me?"

"No." Sorrow filled her eyes. "We'll promote you."

Dan was still trying to come up with a reply when the man stepped out from behind him and moved to stand next to Nimh. Then he simply blinked. "Mr. Ronald, the district manager, is your father?"

"You may address me as His Highness Oberon, King of Tirn an Og, ruler of the Lands of the Forever Young," said the man in an imperious tone. He looked somehow wrong in his three-piece suit, too large and roughly-made, like he would have been more at home on a battlefield, bashing his fellow men—or fellow fairies—with large wooden clubs. "You have trespassed upon my domain. For that, the punishments are known."

"Um, not by me, they're not," said Dan. "I didn't even know you had a domain here." He paused, his brain catching up with his mouth. "Wait—did you say 'Oberon'? As in the—"

"Did not my daughter expel you from our hallowed halls? You were given leave to go. You returned."

"Your daughter." Dan's attention swung to the increasingly miserable-looking Nimh. "He called you 'Nimue.'"

"I told you it was an old family name," she said.

"You didn't tell me it was because you were the Lady of the Lake."

"You never asked!"

Oberon scowled at the pair of them. "If you would be so kind as to shut up so I can commence the punishment, I would very much appreciate it."

"But Daddy, I love him!" Nimh wailed.

"I fail to see where that's my problem."

"I think this punishment thing is about to be my problem, so I'm OK with delaying it," said Dan. "Excuse me for being a little slow here, but what's going on? And where's my price gun?"

"Insolent mortal! That price gun is store property!"

"Oh my God, I've discovered Fairyland, and it's full of crazy people," said Dan. "Seriously? This is really happening? You're really real? You're really . . . what the hell is the King of Fairies doing running Undermart?"

"Plastic," said Oberon gravely.

Dan blinked. "Plastic?"

"Plastic," repeated Oberon.

"Plastic," said Dan.

Nimh inched toward him, bending to murmur, "I'd stop saying that if I were you. He can keep repeating it all day."

"If it delays the punishment part, so can I." Dan focused on Oberon. "Why plastic?"

"Plastic enhances our enchantments, comes in a variety of pleasant colors, and is dishwasher safe," Oberon replied.

"Plus, when people are using plastic, they're not using as much iron," said Nimh. "We don't like iron much."

"I remember that from my fairy tales." Dan turned to look at Nimh. "You really love me?"

"With all my heart." Nimh sniffled, wiping her eyes with the back of her hand. "I'm so sorry I let this happen to you."

"This is all very sweet, but it's interfering with his punishment." Oberon started to raise his hands. "At least you find his smile fetching, Nimue. You'll be able to see it each day at the front of the store."

"Wait!" said Dan hurriedly. "Sir, if I may be so bold . . . you're going about this all wrong. Undermart—you opened the store to spread plastic, right?"

"To spread plastic, reduce iron, and get a bulk discount on candy, yes," said Oberon, frowning. "It's remarkable how many M&Ms the Tuatha de Danann can consume in a weekend."

"Um . . . right. I'm just not going to think about that right now, and instead, I'm going to focus on you not melting my brain. Sir—my lord—Undermart does an excellent job of servicing local customers, but you could be reaching a much wider market share if you had an Internet presence."

Oberon's frown deepened. "The Internet thwarts my attempts at domination. Already have the Aol denied my access twice."

Dan did some hasty mental gymnastics before hazarding, "AOL?"

Oberon scowled.

"Right. Right! Well, see, if you don't fry my brain, I can help you with that. I understand AOL. Also DSL, TCP/IP, and lots of other acronyms." Dan managed a sickly smile. "A whole new customer base is waiting for you. And a bigger audience for your, ah, magic plastic."

There was a long pause. Finally, slowly, Oberon said, "I'm listening."

"Dan?" Nimh stepped into the employee break room, ignoring the way conversation died upon her entrance. The staff had become much more talkative since their enchantments were removed (although most of the greeters opted to be re-enchanted at the beginning of every shift, as it reduced the urge to start attacking customers). That didn't mean they'd started liking management. Some things were beyond even magic's reach. Still, it was a fair exchange.

Dan wasn't in the break room. Nor was he in the stockroom, where the poker game was entering a record fifth week (with management's blessing), or out on the floor. She finally located him out back, sitting on the gently rotting old picnic table with a laptop open on his knees.

"Dan?" she asked, stepping out of the building and starting toward him.

Dan raised his head, smiling at the way the sunlight struck glints of purple off her hair. She never bothered with the little glamours anymore when they were alone. She hadn't since their wedding night (one which, sadly, his own parents had to miss; there were no direct flights from Wisconsin to the Isles of the Blessed). "Hey, you," he said.

"Is that Daddy's email?" Nimh asked, boosting herself up to sit beside him.

"It was. Now it's mostly viruses and spam. Is there any way we can convince him to let someone else access the Internet for him?"

"No," she said, and smiled. "Shall we do something decadent tonight?"

"The salad bar it is," Dan said. "Do we have something to celebrate?"

"We're introducing a new flavor of Milk-y-shake™ today," Nimh replied. "I'm not sure what it is, but everyone who's tried the free samples seems to like it. It's pink."

"Probably cotton candy," he said, and leaned over and kissed her.

CHANGELING

Susan Jett

Marisol Martinez crossed her arms and winced. No one had told her that the most painful part of childbirth would be the throbbing ache of her breasts filling with milk afterwards. But then, if there had been a baby suckling, relieving some of the pressure, the pain would not have been so bad. Of course, if there had been a baby, she could have happily endured any pain. But Tomás was dead.

This wasn't supposed to happen, not to her. Stillbirths happened to other women; women who watched Hallmark Specials on the Lifetime channel while smoking a cigarette or slamming back another beer. Marisol had done everything right. And yet with all her worrying about the baby's health during her pregnancy, she had never thought to worry that her son wouldn't survive being born.

When a knock sounded at her door she looked up out of habit, not because there was anyone she wanted to see. It was a nurse, one who'd been present at her delivery and who'd come by since to ask her to donate colostrum and breast milk. Her lilting accent hinted at Gaelic origins, but this was New York. Marisol herself was from Mexico, and two of the nurses present during her labor were from the Caribbean; accents were nothing remarkable in Brooklyn even if this woman's voice rang like glass chimes.

Marisol forced herself to pay attention to the words instead of just the sound of them. "Your milk is precious, you know. If you do nothing it will dry up in a few days. Donating would be a way to honor your son. It might help you get over your loss."

Marisol hadn't slept in two days; everything felt distant and disconnected. She glared at the nurse. "I'll never get over this." Marisol waited until the door closed before turning back to stare out the window.

She and her husband had opted for a private room when they'd had to transfer here from the birthing center. But it was far too big for one woman whose only visitors were hospital employees. She contrasted its emptiness with the busyness of the bedroom back in Oaxaca where her mother had spent her lying-in with Marisol's little brother. Every day, relatives and friends had come to cook and clean and celebrate. Marisol had imagined the same would happen here in New York with Raffe's family. But no one came. Even Raffe had disappeared, sometime during the night. Once everyone heard that Tomás had been stillborn they avoided her as if it were contagious instead of a stupid accident with the umbilical cord. Marisol was just grateful she didn't have to share the room with another new mother. A new mother whose child hadn't died.

And how that nurse thought she could care for someone else's baby was beyond her. How could she give away the milk that should have nourished her son? It belonged to Tomás. And even though he couldn't use it, she couldn't just give it away. They had offered her a decongestant to help dry up her milk, but she had refused. As if the pain of her swollen breasts was penance, as if her suffering could bring him back.

As if anything she did mattered anymore.

She ignored the next knock at her door. If it was Bridget, her midwife, she'd just come in. If it was anyone else, well, Marisol didn't really feel like socializing right now. She knew Bridget wouldn't say the wrong thing. Bridget had advised her to have a C-section when they'd realized Tomás was breech and would have to be delivered in the hospital instead of the birthing center; but Marisol had resisted, afraid of the cost, afraid of beginning this baby's life with a huge medical bill hanging over their heads. It had been a mistake she would regret forever. But Bridget hadn't said a word of recrimination. She was, in fact, the only person who hadn't yet said something so awful that Marisol wanted to scream.

She had loved Bridget from her first prenatal exam. Wild-haired and calm-voiced and perpetually smiling, Bridget looked like a caricature of an aging hippy, her happy green eyes magnified by wire-rimmed glasses. Today though, Marisol saw that Bridget was grieving too, and for the first time she felt as if the tears might finally come. She dreaded an outpouring of sympathetic words, but instead, the midwife demanded, "Who was that woman and why was she here?"

Marisol blinked. "The delivery nurse?" she said. "I think she left a card. She wants me to donate milk to the local bank."

"I swear I've seen her before," Bridget sounded distracted as she took off her glasses and rubbed her eyes. "Wait, Brooklyn doesn't have a breast milk bank. In fact, there isn't one in the entire state—it's practically criminal, but there it is. Where is that card?"

Bridget's face lost color as she picked up the little rectangle of creamy paper. "Corey Gann, here? Oh damn this eye. I should have recognized her. And she thinks she's so clever using her name like that. Of all the nerve! Of all the fucking *nerve!*"

Marisol was too shocked to do more than stare at the woman she had come to regard as a friend, and she half-wondered if all the morphine had left her system yet.

But this was no hallucination. Bridget was as real as she was. Although, until today, Marisol would have believed that her gentle midwife never got angry. Yet here she was: red-faced, sputtering with indignation, and swearing like a sailor.

"You know her?" Marisol ventured, not really caring, but curious despite herself.

"She owes me an eye."

"What?" Marisol sat up straighter in her bed, even though it sent spikes of pain through her abused midsection.

Sighing, Bridget sat down by Marisol's bedside. She took off her glasses and opened her eyes wide. Then slowly, she looked at something off to Marisol's right. Her left eye tracked normally; her right eye did not. "It's prosthetic," Bridget said quietly, pointing at her right eye. "I went to the best oculist I could afford, and it was worth it. Almost no one guesses unless I show them. But I lost my right eye after she hired me to deliver a baby, seven years ago. And now she's back."

"I don't understand."

Bridget started to shake her head, then reconsidered. "You should know, I suppose. She might even—" she broke off and a wild look came into her eyes. "She was at your delivery? You're sure?"

Marisol gave a little laugh. "I remember because she was so pretty. I was so out of it that I thought she was an angel."

"That's the last thing she is. Mari, have you seen Tomás yet?"

Marisol willed her voice to remain steady and kept her eyes on Bridget as the midwife rummaged in her big floppy purse. "The priest was going to let us spend some time with him today. To say good-bye. But Raffe hasn't come yet. I think they're waiting for him."

Bridget took a deep breath and then set a small tin disc on the bedside table before taking Marisol's hands in hers. "You need to see him," she said quietly, "and I can't be here when you do. Because I can't risk her recognizing me. Here—" she picked up the disc and turned it in her hand as she spoke. "I almost forgot I had this, but I kept it to remind myself. I only used it the once, let's hope it hasn't gone bad." She opened the tin, unscrewing the lid like a jar of Carmex. But instead of eucalyptus and camphor, the ointment within smelled of flowers and something darker, like rust or blood. Bridget sniffed it, then shrugged. With her left hand she smeared a greasy film over Marisol's right eyelid. "Whatever you do—*whatever you do*—" Bridget reiterated sternly, "if you see something out of the ordinary, don't say anything. Do you understand?"

"I don't understand anything anymore."

Bridget nodded as if that were the answer she was

looking for. "We just need to know if your son is really dead." Bridget swept her things—including the nurse's card—into her purse and headed for the door. "You have your cell phone?" Marisol nodded. "I'll be downstairs." She turned and walked quickly back to the bed. Cupping Marisol's cheek with one hand she said, "And sweetie, I'm so sorry. Sorry I can't be here now, sorry I wasn't there when it happened. Sorry this happened in the first place. No matter what happens, I'm just so very sorry."

Marisol had enough self-awareness to be angry that Raffe had left her to face this alone. He should be talking to the nurse and the chaplain about this, not her. *I shouldn't be surprised. It's certainly not the first time he's left me in the lurch.* Throughout their marriage he had only ever been really present when it benefitted him. Marisol shook her head. Whether or not her husband was here, she needed to see her son. She had imagined Tomás's face so often that she needed to see it so she could begin to imagine letting him go.

She rang for the nurse.

It was almost an hour later when Marisol heard them at the door. A priest accompanied Nurse Gann, who pushed a covered bassinet. He said some words that were meant to be comforting. Then the nurse removed the receiving blanket and stood back so Marisol could view her son's body. "Can I hold him?" Marisol asked.

It was the priest who gathered up her baby and handed him to her, as careful of his little neck as if he could be hurt by anything, anymore. Marisol swallowed hard as she looked at him, so tiny and still, curled in the crook of her arm. He had dark hair already falling into his eyes. His lips were pursed as if he waited for a kiss. He looked like her and like Raffe. He had all their best features. He looked exactly as she had always imagined he would. He looked perfect.

Irritated by the tears that threatened to block this precious view, mar this too-short time she had with him before they would take him away forever, she rubbed at her eyes. Her right eye stung a bit as Bridget's cream worked its way in, and then the world went crazy.

Nurse Gann glowed like an ember in this dim room, or rather, her presence cast everything around her into shadows despite the sunlight streaming through the window. Tiny dust motes flared around her head into a living crown of flames, lending her glory. What was she doing here? She should be on a catwalk in Milan or Paris, not working the maternity ward at New York Methodist! Father O'Brien misinterpreted Marisol's gasp and put a warmly human hand on her shoulder. Marisol looked down to hide her face, her confusion, and her gaze returned to her son.

Only it was no infant she cradled, but a collection of sticks tied with twine. Marisol blinked furiously, rubbing her eyes again with her free hand. With her eyes closed, she could feel his tiny arms curled on his chest beneath the hospital blanket. She opened one eye slowly—her left eye—and her son's perfectly still face filled her vision. She closed her eyes again and slitted open her right eye, the one that still stung from Bridget's ointment. He was just sticks. Sticks and a crumpled paper bag for a head, crudely marked with Xs for eyes, a slash for a mouth.

"I can't, I can't," she gasped, and the priest was there to take the body from her and lay it back in the bassinet.

"That isn't my baby," Marisol whispered. The priest kissed her forehead and told her that she was right, that her baby was in the arms of Christ. Marisol watched the nurse cover the bassinet that held—what? Her son? A bundle of sticks?

After the priest left, Nurse Gann turned to Marisol and said kindly, "Are you all right? The drugs can make some people see things that aren't there; you can tell me about it and I won't think you're crazy."

Marisol stuttered an excuse. "He just didn't look like I thought he would. I just can't believe this is real."

Nurse Gann patted her arm. "Remember what we talked about. I think donating your milk might help you recover from this." As soon as the door snicked shut behind her, Marisol called Bridget. Feeling stupid for being unable to separate reality from fantasy when presented with her son's very real body, she told Bridget what she thought she'd seen.

"Stay right there. Don't tell a soul. I'm on my way up."

"You're telling me what I saw was real? And that the nurse switched him somehow? That doesn't make any sense. She was never alone with him—there were doctors and nurses coming in and out. Someone would have seen her."

Bridget shrugged. "People will see whatever she wants them to see. It's her gift, it's what she does. Seven years ago she hired me to assist with a home delivery. Which was fine—I'm licensed—though I did think it odd that an R.N. would prefer that. Things can go wrong." She carefully did not look at Marisol. "Still, who am I to judge? Her baby was being carried by a surrogate, who was also going to nurse the baby. I spoke with the young lady quite a bit since she was my actual patient. She loved living in the city. She loved Corey, couldn't wait to have the baby. The delivery itself was textbook, though Ms. Gann seemed paranoid that I'd baptize the baby without her consent."

"You can do that? Did the doctor baptize Tomás?" Marisol's heart clenched. She wasn't religious but she suddenly hoped fiercely that he had. It would mean that he recognized that Tomás had been a person, not merely a tragedy or a statistic.

Bridget winced, then shook her head. She did not meet Marisol's eyes. "I thought you'd want to know, so I asked. The attending physician says he blessed Tomás, but baptism is a rite for the living. I'm sorry, love, but according to his report, Tomás never took a breath."

After a moment, Bridget continued. "Anyway, Ms. Gann also wanted to use her own antibiotic ointment for the baby's eyes. Since she's an R.N., I saw no harm. But I accidentally got a bit in my own eye, and then I saw the most remarkable things."

"Things like dead babies made of sticks?"

"Worse."

"There is nothing worse."

Bridget grabbed her hands and shook them to get Marisol's attention. "Her surrogate—the young lady who seemed so poised and happy? She wept, begging me to help her escape with the baby. Her baby. The baby Corey was trying to steal. She had been beaten. Tortured. There were creatures—not people, but monsters—everywhere. The queen herself—"

"What?"

"Queen Corrigan. The queen of the Fae. Who did you think she was?"

Suddenly tired of whatever game Bridget was playing, Marisol snapped, "My nurse, maybe? First you put I-don't-know-what in my eye, and now you tell me that my nurse is queen of the fairies? Somehow I missed seeing her wings. Perhaps they're in the same make-believe place as my dead son!"

"But that's just it. Maybe your son isn't dead."

"I saw him." Marisol slumped back against her pillows.

"You saw what she willed you to see, what you expected to see. But then with the ointment in your eye you saw the reality. She needs you to give her your breast milk, Mari, your colostrum! The only reason for that is because she has a newborn to feed."

"Why are you saying this—do you like watching me suffer?"

Bridget took Marisol's cold hands and pressed them together between her own warm palms. "Mari—the last thing I want is to hurt you more. But even more to the point, what do I have to gain by lying and what do you have to lose by believing me?"

By the time her doctor gave her a list of the symptoms of postpartum depression and a referral to a psychiatrist who specialized in grief counseling, Rafael had still not arrived to take her home. Marisol left a message on his cell phone, but realized she wouldn't be at all surprised if she got home and found that he'd moved out. Things between them had been shaky before she got pregnant, and she suspected he'd been making things work for the sake of the baby. *Fine. Losing Raffe is the least of my problems. In fact, if he's still there, maybe it's time to ask him to leave.* She sat down on the park bench where Bridget had asked her to wait.

"You'll have to be invited in—we'd never get inside on our own."

"And she lives in the Friends' cemetery? I thought no one could get in there."

"Ironic, isn't it?"

"Because Quakers don't believe in fairies?"

Bridget had grinned at that. "No, silly. Because the Good Neighbors—the Friends—are pulling this off right under everyone's nose." She seemed inclined to go on, but Marisol just shrugged, having lost whatever taste she had originally had for this adventure. She hurt, and felt physically numb with grief and opiates and a lack of sleep.

"I'm so tired, Bridget. I think I just want to go home."

Bridget shook her head. "I know. But this is important. Possibly the most important thing you'll ever do."

"I should have let them do the C-section. I should have listened to you."

"Sweetie, if I could do this for you, I would. But I only have one eye left."

"You said she owed you an eye. Explain."

Bridget sighed. "When I understood what I was seeing out of my right eye, I didn't put the ointment in the baby's eyes. Instead, I baptized her. I got the girl and her baby out safely, but Queen Corrigan caught me at the door. She couldn't stop me from leaving: midwives apparently have some kind of diplomatic immunity—like ambassadors or messengers because we travel between worlds. But Corrigan cursed me to never look upon anything with my lying eye again or something like that. On the way out, a piece of ivy fell across the doorway and scratched my face. By the time I got home, my right eye was red. By the next day it was infected. I lost the eye the next week and nearly died from sepsis."

"Bridget, this sounds crazy. You know that, right?"

"Just go to her. See if it's Tomás."

"And steal him back?"

Bridget nodded. "Once you have him in your arms, she may ask you to give him to her, but don't—no matter how logical her requests, no matter how clearly she makes you believe it's the right thing to do. Once she's been confronted, she cannot take what is not given freely."

"How do you know all this?"

"I developed an interest in learning how their world works." Bridget grinned crookedly. "It's amazing what even a one-eyed woman can learn if she's got an Internet connection and a good relationship with a librarian." More somberly, Bridget added, "Just remember—don't eat or drink anything; and once you have him, don't let him go no matter what. Hold fast."

Marisol shrugged. "This is crazy, you know."

"You've got a knife, and oh—" Bridget filled a clean baby food jar with water from the drinking fountain.

Marisol took it reluctantly. "I'm not religious. Or at least I wasn't. I'm having a hard enough time thinking of her as a fairy. Does this mean that crosses really do keep vampires away?" She laughed self-consciously and then sobered quickly, saying, "Please tell me that vampires aren't real."

"I have no idea about the vampires. But claiming a child has less to do with Christianity than with baptism being a formal human ceremony. We could just as easily perform a bris or a *Namakarana* naming ceremony. Any ritual that claims him for the human world would work. It just so happens that a Christian baptism is remarkably easy and quick. Painless, too, since I assume you don't want to try performing an emergency bris—not that I'd recommend it even if you do."

"This is really weird, Bridget. You know that, right?"

"The world is a strange and wondrous place, Mari. It's what makes it so interesting." She rubbed her eyes under her glasses. "And so dangerous."

Marisol sat on a bench the nurse would have to walk past if she cut through the park to the cemetery. The Friends' Cemetery was one of the oddities that made Brooklyn such an interesting city—she knew the urban legends surrounding the iron-fenced burial ground: it was closed off in the 1950s to keep Montgomery Clift's fans from sleeping on his grave, or maybe from digging it up. She'd also heard that people performed satanic rituals there. In high school, everyone had dared each other to spend the night inside the gates, but no one had ever done it as far as she knew. Of course, no one she knew had ever claimed it was a fairy haunt, either.

This part of the park was peaceful, the tall old maples kept the sun away from her face without affecting the warmth of the day. It was easy to act exhausted, because she was. Tired like she could sleep for days without coming up for air. She put her head down in her hands and wasn't surprised when, a few minutes later, a cool hand fell on her shoulder.

"I thought that was you, dear. Are you all right? I hate that the insurance companies make us discharge you so soon after a labor like that. Do you live nearby?"

Marisol made herself look mildly surprised. "Oh, it's you. No, I'm okay. Well, not okay. But. You know."

Corey pursed her lips and looked off over Marisol's shoulder. Seeming to come to a decision she said, "I live just around the corner; would you like to come in for a cup of tea?"

"That would be nice."

"I should warn you, dear, I have a new baby of my own."

Marisol's heart lurched, but she forced herself to say nonchalantly, "This is Park Slope. More babies than adults."

"It does seem that way sometimes. Not at all like the old days when they were harder to come by."

Corey led the way through an ornamental gate toward an old mansion surrounded by beautiful houses on either side—not the kind of house Marisol imagined a nurse could afford. Not unless her husband was a hedge fund manager. Marisol wondered why she had never seen this block before; she had lived near Prospect Park for years and thought she knew every inch of it.

Then remembering, she squinted her right eye. The front of the house was nothing but a swath of greenery, hanging low over an opening cut into the side of a low hill. She noticed that the iron fence surrounding the cemetery stood ajar, and wondered if the padlocked gate she remembered from her childhood was another illusion. There were no houses anywhere nearby. She blinked again, and once more saw a mansion superimposed into a row of equally grand houses.

Feeling dizzy, she put out a hand and felt the hard edges of the entryway, though she could also feel the cool leafiness of ivy beneath her hand. She closed her eyes and the damp leaves melted away, leaving only the solidity of planed wood beneath her hands. This was more confusing than she'd anticipated. It was hard to separate reality from fantasy, and she had a bad moment when she wondered if she was dreaming this whole encounter. Then her breasts throbbed, aching with unused milk. Her head cleared.

"Is everything all right, dear?"

"Sure, Miss Gann."

"Oh just call me Corey." She held aside a fall of ivy—though Marisol's mind insisted that she stood in a doorway, holding open a tall wooden door. It took all of Marisol's courage to enter, but she smiled and let Corey lead her into this pit in the ground.

Following Bridget's instructions, Marisol set down her purse as soon as they got in the house and took the opportunity to push the tiny penknife from her keychain into the loose soil at the entryway. There was no door to hold open here, not in the reality that the ointment showed Marisol, but Bridget believed it was important, and she hadn't been wrong yet.

The house was grand in an old-money kind of way that Marisol recognized from memories of her grandfather's house in Oaxaca. Antique wooden furniture, glossy and stained dark from generations of polishing. An oddly shaped skull, tiny enough to be from some kind of shrew or vole and decorated with brightly colored beads, lay atop a book. A forest landscape hung on one wall, painted so realistically that Marisol felt she could fall into it and lose herself. A portrait, which resembled Corey, faced the room from over the fireplace.

But the subject's features were harder, sharper around the edges, somehow, than the nurse's. Perhaps it was her mother, or another relative—older, angrier.

Marisol realized that Corey was staring at her as intently as she stared at the portrait. "You have a beautiful house," she ventured, and Corey turned, flashing a smile.

"Please make yourself at home. I'll be back in a moment with our tea."

Marisol looked around the room, smiling wistfully. It really was like being back in her grandfather's hacienda, down to the old colonial-era furniture. There was even a fringe of colorful *papel picado* panels along the top edge of the far wall. Her grandfather used to leave them up for weeks after a party. Heavy cushions slumped invitingly on low couches. She could almost smell the spiced chocolate that her *abuelita* used to serve in little china cups. Sure enough—on a nearby sideboard she saw a chocolate set, complete with a *molinillo*—the wooden whisk shaped like a baby's rattle.

Marisol shivered. For the first time, she truly acknowledged the possibility that she wasn't merely humoring her midwife's slightly nutty whim. *Corey Gann is showing me what I want to see. This would look different to everyone who comes here. And if she can do this, then Bridget might be telling the literal truth. What if Tomás is here? What if he's still alive?* Her heart hurt. She didn't think she could stand the disappointment if he wasn't.

While she waited for Corey to return, she closed her left eye and watched the room grow dim. There was barely enough light coming through the screen of old ivy to illuminate the interior of the cave. She walked to one of the walls and put out a hand. Dry, coarse soil brushed her fingertips, and the tiny hairs of rootlets from trees she knew had to be overhead. Not a cave, but a dugout. A barrow. She peered into the dark corridor where Corey had disappeared and was not surprised to see a glow like candlelight surrounding the woman as she returned, a short, uniformed woman walking behind her, cradling a bundled infant in her arms.

"We have tea, or Mrs. Brown would be happy to bring you hot chocolate if you would prefer."

The short, stout woman brought the baby closer and Marisol smelled something green and fresh, like cut grass. Marisol shook her head. "I'm not all that thirsty, actually."

"You look pale, dear. Would you like something to eat?"

"No, thank you." Marisol braced herself and asked, "May I hold your son?"

Corey eyed her, not quite suspiciously. "Are you sure you want to? It's likely to start your milk flowing."

"That's all right." Bridget had been right. Corey wasn't about to hand the child over easily. Marisol took a deep breath and played the one card she knew Corey couldn't resist. "I should get used to it, if I'm going to donate. You were right, I shouldn't be selfish. That's not how I would have raised Tomás. Where do I go to sign up—or should I just pump at home?"

Corey looked eager and excited. She nodded to Mrs. Brown, who immediately handed the baby to Marisol. "Honestly, I feel bad asking for myself, but rather than donating to a bank, would you consider feeding my son? He really doesn't seem to like formula at all, and I'm not able to nurse him. Besides, breastmilk is best. I'd be willing to pay you for your time, of course. You can pump at home or feed him here if you'd prefer. And if you need a place to stay—I couldn't help but notice that there seemed to be some tension between you and your husband . . . ?"

She was waiting for an answer, but Marisol couldn't look away from the unbelievably beautiful baby in her arms. He had red hair, a brighter version of Corey's deep auburn, and bright blue eyes. *It's not Tomás. Of course it's not.* Marisol rocked him carefully, looking between his face and Corey's. He was warm. So alive in her arms that she ached to keep him, no matter who he belonged to. "He looks like you," she admitted finally.

Corey's smile was radiant. "I think so, too."

With her eyes closed, Marisol took a deep breath and held it, then cracked open her right eyelid. She didn't know if she expected his features to remain the same or not. But when she saw him through the film of ointment, she had to stifle a gasp. The baby in her arms didn't have red hair, nor did he have the perfectly imagined features she'd seen on the changeling in the hospital.

But he was hers. Undoubtedly hers. Black wisps of hair curled damply around his face. Delicate lips, red as a rosebud. Black eyes—no newborn blue here. A strong Aztec nose, just like Raffe's, only tiny and snubbed and perfect. He rooted frantically at her blouse, as if he knew her, knew that she had what he needed.

Mrs. Brown was still a turtled old woman who smelled of cut grass and oregano, but her white uniform had given way to a raggedy dress of leaves and feathers and bits of fur. She grinned sideways as Marisol examined her, then her black eyes widened as she realized Marisol could actually see her. She nodded an infinitesimal nod, and Marisol interpreted that as encouragement. Taking a deep breath, she addressed Corey again. "Actually, he doesn't look anything like you, does he?" She took a step back, away from her hostess. Anger fueled her demand: "Did you really think I'd let you keep him? You didn't even try to make that changeling believable—a bundle of sticks and a brown paper sack? Is that all you thought my grief was worth?"

Corrigan drew back at the force of Marisol's words, but Marisol knew she wouldn't be able to outrun her. She was only a few hours out of the hospital and even just standing here, her belly ached, her breasts had begun to leak, and she felt more than a little shaky from exhaustion as well as adrenaline.

Corrigan's eyes narrowed as she forced a smile. "I keep telling the doctors that putting new mothers on morphine is a bad idea. Someone's going to have a bad reaction one of these days, but does anyone listen to me?"

"No one is listening now, Queen Corrigan." As Marisol spoke, Corey's face eased into its actual lines: much starker, much more beautiful, and much more frightening than she had been before. Now Marisol recognized the woman in the portrait.

"If you won't listen, then what will you do, little girl? Will you run? I can shut my doors against you and you will never find your way out."

"Your door is warded with iron." Corrigan's head snapped around and the smile slid from her face, replaced by something darker. Marisol swallowed and said firmly, "So you can't seal me in. I haven't eaten or drunk anything, nor has my son, or else you wouldn't have needed me so badly."

Corrigan's smile grew tighter. "And who will help you? You are a grieving woman whose postpartum depression has sadly morphed into psychosis." Her eyes widened and her mouth thinned as she promised, "I will make your stay at Kingsboro Psych a torment such as bards could write sagas about."

Marisol could almost smell the industrial disinfectant, see the fluorescent lighting, feel the helpless terror of that future, but she said as calmly as she could, "You have no power over us, unless I give it to you."

"Who told you that?"

Instead of answering, Marisol groped for the baby food jar in her jacket pocket and opened it, unceremoniously dumping its contents over her son's head. Tomás squared his mouth in an outraged wail. She spoke loudly enough to be heard over his screams. "I baptize you in the name of the Father and the Son and the Holy Ghost." Her words crackled in the air, and Mrs. Brown began edging back toward the dark corridor.

Corrigan narrowed her eyes and took a single step toward Marisol and Tomás. "We could help each other, you know. I am a wealthy woman and you have nothing—not even a husband anymore. I could ease your way considerably in this world, if you were to help me."

"By giving you my child?"

"You can have others. I cannot. Let me adopt him, and you never need work another day in your life."

Marisol felt her lips lifting back from her teeth in a snarl. "I may be poor, but I would never sell my baby."

"But what does he have to look forward to with you? Your world is a dark and dismal place. And your man was easy to chase away, you know. He won't be back. This child will always know something is missing from his life—you won't be enough to fill it. Let him stay with me and he will be honored and cared for and beloved by all of my people. It is no small thing to be the son of a queen."

Marisol's breath caught in her throat—who would not want the life of a prince for their child? What kind of a mother was she? Bridget had warned her that Corey would try to talk her into giving him up, but this was more difficult than merely refusing to give up her son; if she took him, she would be taking opportunities away from him. Then she breathed in the fragrance from the top of his head. He smelled warm and human and whatever else she worried about, he was hers. He belonged with her. "I will not."

"If you leave him with me, he will live practically forever, never aging, surrounded by marvels and delights. With you, he will grow old and die. Are you so selfish?"

Marisol looked at the baby in her arms. It was hard to imagine him as an old man, frail and sickly, but she knew it would happen someday. She had watched her grandfather waste away after her *abuelita* died, and had grieved for his death most of her life. Then she looked up, meeting Corrigan's calculating gaze. "We die eventually. But sometimes we find someone to love and have children with—children who carry the best part of us into the future. That's how humans become immortal. A child of mine will value that, for I will teach him."

Corrigan shrugged, as if Marisol's victory meant nothing to her but her lips were pressed thin. "Thrice I have asked and thrice you have refused. May your lying eye . . . no, actually—" her angry expression grew satisfied. "When your son looks away from your face, I want you to know who was able to make him laugh when you could not. I want you never to be able to forget that he spent the first hours of his life with me. Some part of him will always be mine."

A grue ran down Marisol's spine. This was a truer

curse than the infection that took Bridget's eye, but she could not keep silent. In a low voice, she said, "Some part, yes, but not the greatest part. Tell yourself whatever stories you like, *Xana*. But he is mine." Marisol felt the ache in her heart ease as her son pushed his damp head under her jaw. *My son!* She took a deep breath, anticipating Corrigan's next offer or curse. She was ready.

Instead, Corrigan's face softened. "He might be yours, but now that you have seen us, you will be forever caught between our worlds, too. Unless — " From a small drawer in the sideboard she withdrew a tiny round tin, no larger than a wedding ring. Delicately, with the tips of her fingers, she opened it, showing Marisol the faintly shimmering ointment inside. Marisol recognized the smell of flowers and blood but did not reach for it. "Someday, if you wish it, if your world proves to be too much — or too little — for either of you, we would welcome you among us. We can always use more heroes, and despite my current annoyance, young lady, you do qualify. You would be welcome with or without your son."

Marisol shook her head, holding tight to Tomás, savoring the human smell and warmth of him as she continued backing toward the door. "He is human, like me. We need to live in our own world."

"So you say. But remember my invitation." Marisol took one last look around the room that reminded her so strongly of her grandfather, of her life before she came to this country that promised so much and had, thus far, given her so little. Life with the fairies might be nothing more exotic than living in the best place she could imagine. It might be entirely outside of her reality, but it might also feel like she was finally coming home.

She took a deep breath, put her hand on the closed door, and then she closed her eye.

A screen of ivy and thorn barred her way. She hunched her shoulder to shield her son and her own face; but at a word from the queen, it fell away and the sun blazed in, streaming through the trees in a fall of golden light. Tomás screwed up his eyes when the sunlight hit his face, and opened his mouth to protest. But Marisol soothed him, stroking his cheek, which felt as soft and insubstantial as a memory. In her mind, a voice whispered, "Remember," but she did not answer, nor did she turn back.

Bridget waited at the iron gate and pulled Marisol through. "You have him. Oh, dear saints and little fishes—you did it!"

Marisol looked down at her son's face. To both her eyes, he looked the same, human and beautifully imperfect. His brow wrinkled as he stared past her, then he buried his face in her shoulder, searching for the nourishment he needed.

Bridget led them to the nearest bench, and Marisol opened her blouse. She winced as his mouth clamped over her tender breast, then relaxed as his suckling began to ease the terrible pressure that had been building since his birth. While he nursed, his eyes remained fixed on something over her right shoulder, but she did not turn to look, just as she did not reach into her pocket to see if the lump against her hipbone was a tiny jar of ointment she could not recall taking from Corrigan. Instead she watched her son's face, so pure in his intent, so angry in his hunger, so human.

Bridget said, "I'll write you a new birth certificate in

the morning. In the meantime, we should celebrate — it's not every day you beat the Queen of the Fae at her own game."

Carefully cradling her son in the crook of one elbow while he nursed, gulping audibly, Marisol glanced up at Bridget and shook her head. "I haven't beaten her. Not yet. But I will."

"What do you mean? He's here. You did it, Mari. What more do you want?"

"I still have to prove her wrong. I have to make sure he learns what's best in the world, and that he knows how much he's loved, knows I would do anything for him, knows I'll never let him go, never leave him. No matter what."

Bridget grinned. "Sounds like you're saying you have to learn how to be a mother."

More slowly, Marisol said, "I have to make this world worth living in. For both of us." Stroking her son's cheek she whispered in his ear, "Come on, *mi hijo*, let's go home." She refused to look over her shoulder to see what still held her son's interest. She would not open the jar of ointment. She would not look for Queen Corrigan every time her son smiled or laughed in an empty room. She would make a life for them in this world — as good a life as she could create, for as long as Tomás had need of her.

She would not look back.

WATER–CALLED

Kari Sperring

Jenny peered through the eyes of the dead man where he floated in the canal. His body hung just below the surface of the water, entirely submerged save for the bagging fabric of his dirty cargo pants above his knees. His hands drifted on either side, palms upwards in silent exhortation. Her waters had already begun to bloat his body, plumping out the dead tissues, filling all his secret cavities, revealing to her all his petty daily secrets. Last meal: a greasy pasty from a corner shop. Last drink: the cheapest cider. Last sight: nothing. Her long fingers, her filaments and streams could run as they wished through his flesh, but his mind, his memories, were all already fled, poured away with the blood that seeped from the narrow punctures that marred his neck. He lay cradled in her waters and gave her nothing, no fear, no glimpse of soul, no sweet last breath to feed on.

There had always been bodies. Since the first settlement of humans in her territory, men and women had run and walked, staggered and slipped and hiccupped their way into oblivion in her rocking embrace. Of course, in the old days, her range—of control, of weapons, of human compliance—had been much, much greater. Humans were easily lured to wander from the known paths into the softer, hungry areas of her marsh, even in daylight, drawn by the silver flash of fish scales or the green promise of edible weeds. At night, cloud often sucked all light from the low moist East Anglian skies. Sometimes, others amongst the old denizens of the fens would help her, leading victims to her marshes for a share of the spoils in flesh and bone. For long years, she had eaten as she willed, and the humans had feared and honored her, offering to her the first fruits of their harvests (of more interest to the waterfowl than to Jenny herself). She liked their darker festivals better by far, when they offered to her not their planting but the firm flesh and smooth skin of their youngest adults or the trussed bodies of their enemies. She drew them close, wrapped them in her tightest embrace, and savored the desperate sweetness of their final breaths. Good days, rich days, days of regular meals and human respect. Better days by far than these, when her waters were trammeled by concrete walls, the only offerings she received bent bicycles and rusting shopping trolleys and the occasional careless drunk. Their last memories were thin and sour—the haze of alcohol and nausea with only the dimmest film of surprise at their fall. Many lost consciousness before they drowned, cheating her of even that small pleasure. And this man . . . This man held nothing, dead before he ever hit the canal. She had swum up to meet him, hungry for her meal, and found only emptiness and the sour taste of stale booze. Footsteps walked

briskly away from her banks: peering from behind the
body, she caught sight of a hunched figure in jeans and a
long dark coat. Another human had done this, had slain
one of their own kind and used her waters as a midden.
She snarled, sending waves lashing the sides of the canal.

This was her place. Her territory. She would not tolerate another hunter in the lands about her waters.

The New Canal ran through the northeast corner of Fenborough, separating the crush of low-rent red-brick Victorian terraces from the richer tree-lined curves of the
streets around Miller's Park, the proud Gothic edifices of
the university, and the glossy buildings of the city center.
Its banks were mean and muddy, brambles warring with
litter for supremacy behind the twisted hanks of barbed
wire that the council strung here and there in the vain
hope of keeping people away from the towpath. Toward
the east end, where it came closest to the park, attempts
had been made to tidy the path up with woodchips and
rustic benches, in the hope of luring cyclists and walkers.
But there was nothing to see, save the flat waters and the
graffitied ends of the red-brick terraces on the other side.
The woodchips clumped, harboring earwigs and black
beetles and sticking to the wheels of any bicycle or push-
chair that tried its surface. Homeless drunks colonized
the benches, pitching their empty bottles and cans into
the canal when they were finished. Sometimes, these
days, Jenny joined them, pitching herself down on one of
the benches and snagging a can of precious cider with a
skinny hand. They respected her, these booze-worn men
and women. They remembered the old folk-learning, living as they did close to the edge of things. They knew
death all too well, whatever shape it wore, and they

treated it with caution, even while they courted it. They might throw their empties into her waters, but they knew better than to get too close themselves. "I'll drink with you, Jenny," Other Tom would say, "but I'll not dance. Not on your dance floor." Then he'd salute her with his bottle or blow her a kiss and go back to his drinking. Tom knew his limits—and hers, too—and he headed off through the park when the last bottle was emptied to find himself a place to sleep in the warm smelly stairwell of the multi-story car park, in some dark corner in the loading bays at the back of the Alderman Center, or the empty stairwells of the university lecture blocks. They respected her, but they took care never to lie in her arms. It took the casual drinkers, the careless young, to come close to her by night these days.

Yet now, in the cool gray hour that summoned dawn, here after all was Other Tom, floating on the surface of the canal, right on the bend where it turned east toward the lock. She circled him, slowly, watched as the ripples she made played through the ends of his gray hair. He weighed heavy on her, body dense and greasy in her embrace, his taste sour and old. When she ran a hand over his cold face, she felt nothing. His eyes were closed, his husk empty: no last memories, no fear or surprise or regret. Like the last body, his life had been drained from him before he ever entered the water. He had wandered away from the canal shortly before the pubs emptied out, shambling off to one of his dens. Most of the other drinkers had already been gone by then, off somewhere into the concrete and tarmac floors of the city where Jenny could not find them. Other Tom had stayed to finish off his last bottle, and then . . .

She had not felt him come back. The cement sides of

the canal muted her senses. She had withdrawn to the heart of her territory, deep amidst the mud and the weeds, where the first body rested, weighted down by the end of one of the bedsteads. She did not readily give up what was hers, however empty or useless.

Other Tom was hers now, though the taste of his blood was foul in the water. She wrapped herself about him and began to draw him down.

A movement distracted her. In the shadows under the road bridge, something stirred. A waft of stale sweat and rotting fabric and musk, and Martin Jack squatted on the towpath, his ears flat to his skull and his tail pressed low against his side. He alone dared to sleep on her banks. He was of her kind, after all, his black dog shape as wound into human myth as her own haunting of the waters. He gave her a yellow grin and said, "Good eating, Jenny-love?"

"No eating at all, and you know it." Jenny bared her teeth back at him.

"Ah." Martin Jack scratched his belly with a back foot thoughtfully, then twisted to try and reach the small of his back. "Not like it used to be. Men don't know how to make the offerings, these days."

"They don't make offerings at all." She pulled herself up onto the bank beside him and sat, dangling her legs into the canal. "They don't remember."

"They think they chained you, Jenny-love. They built their dykes and their drains and their sluices, and they wrapped you up tight."

"Not so tight I can't catch you." But she did not mean it. They were the last of their kind, her and Martin Jack, the last holdouts against the tide of human indifference. She'd never thought to make a friend out of such as he, but in these hungry days, the fae made common cause where they could. "Not that you'd be more'n a mouthful of bone and hair."

He nodded. "I'd choke you, Jenny-love, take you with me to wherever we go." He sighed, looked at the body. "Somewhere other than him, I'll bet you. I hope he went to the good place. He'd earned it."

Jenny shrugged. She wasn't sentimental about the drunks. They were her things, like the ducks and the waterweed. There were always more, if one or two of them wandered. She wasn't made to care for humans, not as anything more than prey. Whereas Martin Jack . . . It was the shape of him, she sometimes thought, that rangy hound form, which bound him to men. Oh, he'd lead them into trouble if he could, but over the centuries his canine heart had learnt to love them. The men and women washed up by life to drink on the canal banks were his flock, his charge, his chosen few. Now, he slumped, brows knitting.

Jenny didn't care for him either. It wasn't her way. Yet, somehow, she found herself asking anyway. "Did you see what happened?"

He shook his head. "Couldn't. There was a wrong smell." His head drooped even lower. "I should've been watching."

She sniffed, experimentally. Dank water and tar, a drift of yeast from the city brewery. The faintest trace of something else, something sharp and metallic, perhaps wafting from one of the old cars parked along the other side of the road. She wrinkled her nose. The new ways that had drained her fens and concreted them over worked to dim all her senses. Nothing smelled good to her any more. She pointed at the body with her toe. "Something emptied him. Cheated me."

"Men have always killed men."

"Not like this. No memories left. Same as the last one."

"He was a kind man. He shared his sausage rolls with me."

That was of no use to Jenny. She stretched her skinny arms over her head. "Better sink him before some human sees him and starts prying."

"Don't want to lose your treasures?" But Martin Jack's heart was not in it and the taunt fell flat.

She began to sink back down into the canal. As the waters reached her neck, he said, "Wait."

"What?"

"I wanted . . ." He shifted, uncomfortable. "Let me smell him, Jenny-love. See if that wrong smell's there, too."

Water was the enemy of scent. Martin Jack knew that as well as she did. And she owed him nothing. But she wound herself about the body, let her waves wash it to the edge just below him. He shook himself, craned out to sniff at the wet form. She caught the scent of him, warm and ashy. Where he touched the body, dry dark patches formed, sent hot shocks through her. She shuddered, setting the body jouncing and water splashing up onto the towpath. Martin Jack started backward, spitting and shaking droplets from his face and head. "Not fair, Jenny."

"You burned me."

"Not me."

The two fae stared at one another. Jenny wrapped her long thin fingers into Other Tom's gray hair. She said, "Wasn't this one. He was just a man."

"He smells wrong too. Hot wrong."

She couldn't sense that. But the emptiness ... She said, slowly, "Men always kill each other. Throw each other away. But they don't ... they don't drain memories. They don't leave a trace, not like this."

"There was a human ..." Martin Jack frowned. "Sort of a human. Smelled ... smelled different."

Different was bad. Jenny closed her arms about Other Tom's body and pulled him down to her heart without another word.

The first men who strived to steal land from the marshes had labored with wooden shovels and buckets and small smelters to carve out ditches and to bend strips of iron to bind the edges of sluices. It had been easier by far in those days for Jenny to stretch herself out through the soft earth beneath their withy-built huts, to poke and push and insinuate a way for her waters into the shallow foundations, to overflow and undermine the manmade banks. Her reach extended for mile on mile, dictating the path of roads and the shape of settlements. Once, her hold had run underneath every square inch of Fenborough, from the stones of the old fort to the undercrofts of the oldest university buildings, from the muddy pastures where men kept their goats to the edge of the chalk ridge that sloped away to the south. But men always had new tricks, new skills with which to outmaneuver her. Inch by inch, they pushed at her, and, inch by inch she retreated. Yet the ground on which the city rested remained porous: every other year, the canal overflowed its banks somewhere and had to be resisted with sandbags. Out in the fields surrounding the canal, pumps and sluices still labored to keep the soil dry enough to farm.

In her bed of silt and mud, Jenny could hear them working. And in the streets of the city itself, waters lifted from her hoard and cleansed somewhere to the east flowed in earthenware pipes under the tarmac and cobbles to feed the faucets and valves of the buildings. Its flow was a distant tingle under her skin. If she listened really hard, she could hear its voice trickling through the layers of stone. Everywhere humans chattered and clattered, thumped and thrummed and thrashed through their short lives, scattering pieces of themselves as they went in snatches of conversations. She could not get a grasp on them; they slipped away from her too fast to hold. *There was a wrong smell.* . . . She reached out through her waters for a sense of that wrongness, of that hunger that had ripped all the memories from Other Tom and the first victim. Something in this town hunted where she should. Something in this town had cheated her of her rightful harvest of memories.

Two days and a night had passed since she had found Other Tom's body floating, emptied out. The drunks were anxious and skittish, pacing and cursing as they drank, and scurrying off to their various lairs long before sunset. Under the bridge, Martin Jack brooded. The traces of the smell choked him, left him shaking and nauseated when he had tried to pursue it over ground. So much for his flock. It was up to Jenny to find the hunter. Find it and stop it, whatever it was.

The university lay at the heart of the city, its buildings crowded close together in a knot of twisting streets. Once, it had stood on a small island in the midst of the marsh, rising a scant five or six feet above the rest. It had been a monastery in those days, a close-packed hive of men in rough robes who fished for eels in the waters, muttering grim prayers to keep Jenny away. A demon, they had called her, a hell-spawn sent to lure them into sin and death. She had felt no remorse when the distant king of men sent his soldiers to drive them away, and had set up the university in their place. Students were easier prey by far, easy to lure with lights and smiles and hints of mystery. Jenny had fed well in those days, while the university outgrew its original boundaries and spread into her margins. Her fingers reached into its cellars and the lower corridors, and few were those who tried to bind her with holy signs or iron bars.

Now, she followed the faint trail, squeezing through pipes and conduits, eavesdropping at drains. It was hard to track, through the layers and layers of stone, but inch by narrow inch she pulled herself after it, around the park and past the fine houses, under the shopping center and, at last, into the basements of the university. Here, men fought off the dark and the dank with harsh neon and so-called water-resistant paints. But the buildings were old, built before the days of damp-proofing. As Jenny passed under the foundation, it called to her. Tendrils of damp wound their way up through the old walls, settled into the frames of windows, behind cupboards and wood panels, under the worn linoleum that covered the floors. She stretched out, relief shivering through her, and set herself to listen hard.

The humans were everywhere, huddled in groups about benches and tables, poring over screens and slabs, glass jars and books, gossiping and chattering and ranting at one another. Their feet drummed on floor after floor, rattled up stairwells. Their breath filled the building in hot clouds. Her fingers yearned toward them, hungry to taste their busy, petty lives. In a small side room, a

plump young man bent alone over a tank, adjusting fine
paddles that made waves in the water it held. It would be
so easy to creep up on him and pull his head down to her
embrace. She could feel the beat of his heart, trembling
in the fine veins just below his skin. Her right hand began
to slide slowly through the pipe that linked the tank to
the main.

With an effort, she pulled herself back to the task in
hand. She could come back for the young man later, now
she knew the way. But first ... first she had to find the
one who dared to hunt her territory.

Martin Jack's wrong smell was stronger here. She followed it up through a line of damp that climbed its way
up the inside of a stairwell, traced it through the warm
living roots of the ivy that blanketed the outside of the
building, sealing her waters inside. She peered through
the rotting wood of window-frames, slid about drain-
pipes, found herself at the last snug between the ill-fitting
panes of a dormer window. The room beyond was tiny,
little more than a cupboard, and made smaller by the
mass of machinery that crowded it. It reeked of hot
metal and wire, ozone and sweat, and old, dried blood.
The smell and the burn that had lingered about Other
Tom's body. Jenny shuddered. This was it, this was where
her rival laired. This was his den, his sanctuary. She shook
herself and oozed out through a crack in the frame.
Droplets of water pocked the floor as she pulled herself
together.

The place was a shambles. Objects covered every surface: papers, wires, empty mugs and cartons, small heavy
boxes that hummed or flashed or beeped. A metal trolley under the window held a jumble of blades and bowls:
underneath it a bin was filled with blood-stained dress-

ings. She sniffed, started back, choking. Blood, yes, blood that conjured for her the shapes of Other Tom and the first victim. The blood of another, also, young and strong and not quite right. A syringe lay beside a small vial. When she reached out for it, heat swirled from it. Not cold iron, nor yet a thing blessed by some human holy man, and yet it held something of the quality of both. Whatever that vial held, someone had imbued it with a vital faith. She pulled her hand back. The whole room was wrong, filled with a hunger that she did not understand.

Notes were everywhere, scribbled onto the piles of paper, scrawled across the walls in thick black lines. Jenny had absorbed human script long ago, from the early days of votive tablets to the sodden pages of old newspapers thrown into the canal. But these words made no sense.... *initial results suggests payments to test subjects would be better made after the conclusion of the experiment, to cut down on interference by alcohol.... Effects of drunkenness may be transferable: more data desirable.... Preliminary research indicates disturbed vision may be due to poor positioning of the chips as subject seems not to be suffering such effects despite alcohol intake.... Excessive bleeding on insertion still proving a problem in some cases. Subjects' memories cloudy. Cleaner and healthier subjects might be preferable to further research, but as yet can see no way to avoid inconvenient questions. Materials still unstable: unsafe to test on students.... Query: should seek further training on insertion work?* Jenny shook her head. None of it made any sense to her. What kind of creature hunted with words and needles and strange uncanny faith? It was nothing of her world, of that she was certain. And if it was human, it was of a kind she had never known before. She had grown insular since the concrete walls had pinned her waters back into the bed of the canal. She needed to know more about how humans had changed.

She needed to talk to Martin Jack.

"They're trying to explain the world." Martin Jack sprawled on the edge of the towpath, the remains of a fish supper that he had dragged out of some litter bin spread out on the gravel beside him. "They want to know how everything works."

Head and shoulders out of the canal, Jenny propped her elbows on the top of the cement surround and let herself float. She said, "That's what the monks did and the priests with their churches."

"Yes. . . ." Martin Jack sounded unsure. "This is different. They call it science. They make things, measure things. It's called experimentation. I hear about it from students, sometimes. The girls talk to me when I walk them home."

Jenny shook her head. He did not change. For all his fearsome reputation as a harbinger of doom, the black shuck still felt the need from time to time to accompany lone women through the streets until they reached their homes, trotting beside them like the meekest pet dog and wagging his tail in delight at the attention. She had suggested once that he lead them to her instead. She could use the nourishment. He hadn't spoken to her for seven years. She had never understood his affection for humans. It served no purpose.

Now, however, was no time to twit him about it. She needed what he had learnt from his regular contacts with humans. He said, "There are all sorts of different kinds of experiment. Sometimes they explode."

"This isn't about explosions. This is about memory and needles and blood."

"Ah. That's called psychology." Martin Jack's jaw dropped in a grin. "The porter at the big gray round building told me about it. He said they study how people go mad till they go mad themselves."

The hunter might well be mad, if Jenny was any judge of human insanity. The bodies of the two victims still lay in her mud: she could feel them like a sore that she could not quite reach. She said, "We have to stop it."

He nodded. She went on, "You could go to the room, scare them like you used to. Curse them to die soon."

"They have to believe." His ears drooped. "These days they just chase me out with a broom or throw things at me."

Jenny belonged to the water. That was where her strength lay. Away from the core of it, the canal, she was weak. But Martin Jack didn't do human-shaped. He was a dog, pure and simple. She shifted, sending ripples rocking into the far bank. She didn't like where her thoughts were taking her. She said, "One of your people, the drunks . . ."

"No." There was a growl to that.

"We need bait. I can't do anything to the hunter unless he comes here. And he comes here with bodies."

Martin Jack snapped his teeth at her and despite herself she pushed back from the canal's edge. The shuck's eyes glowed wild and red. She said, "Someone has to go . . ."

"You go." He rose to his full height, heavy head hanging down toward her. Backlit by the moon, his shadow stretched out over the canal, long and sinister. Jenny shivered.

The drunks were not her problem. They were flotsam,

nothing more. She tolerated them in the hope, one day, of a good meal.

It was not for humans to hunt on her territory or deprive her of her prey. She sighed. "All right. I'll go."

"Would you like tea?" The hunter cleared a heap of papers off a chair and offered it to Jenny. "I can fetch some from the tearoom. There are biscuits, too." She smiled as she took a stool beside one of her flashing machines. "They should be pretty fresh."

Jenny did not want to take anything from her, however it was offered. Her earlier offerings had been more than enough. The taint of them was still within her, would remain until they rotted away to bone. This room reeked of that wrongness and of the tang of human fanaticism. She sat down, straight-spined and said, "No. I don't want those."

She had pictured the hunter as a man, someone broad and muscular and marked by the chase, like the villagers who had lived in her marsh long centuries before, who had fought and killed one another in their wars over cattle and fresh water and cast their enemies into her embrace. She had expected a warrior, an adversary out of human legend. Instead ... The hunter was an angular young woman with lank brown hair and a pinched face. The bones of her wrists stood out below the grubby cuffs of her white coat. From time to time, she rubbed at an angry-looking mark on the side of her neck. Her shoulders hunched: even on the tall stool, she did not seem menacing.

Now, leaning forward, she said, "You know what my research is about, yes? You saw my notice in the free paper?"

Jenny had no idea about that. But she nodded anyway. The hunter went on, "I'm exploring the nature of
emotional response at a very basic level. I'm listening
intently to your feelings, if you like." She rubbed again at
the cut on her neck. "It's really very simple and very,
very safe. I'll insert a micro-chip into you, near to a major
nerve clump. It's linked to one I have myself—you see,
it's really safe, I've been chipped for months. And then
I'll be able to feel what you feel. Do you see?"

It was more human talk, like the chants and mum-
blings of the monks. Her words thrummed through
Jenny with the same disquieting rhythm as church bells.
The room was full of it. Her fingers quivered, yearned
toward the safe damp space within the walls. The hunter
was still talking, chattering on about vital knowledge and
medical breakthroughs. Jenny rubbed at her own throat,
feeling the fine skin begin to heat and tingle. The hunter's voice droned on, ". . . of course, there is a payment,
but the contribution you'll be making to science by itself
is something—"

Jenny interrupted her. "Just do it."

"What?" The hunter stared, her eyes too big in her
thin face.

"I don't care about that." It was hard to talk, the
stench of belief in the room was so strong. "Just do whatever it is."

"You have to sign the waiver."

"Yes." Jenny swallowed. "Whatever you say."

"Are you taking something?" The hunter's brows
drew down. "Drugs can interfere with my results. I
thought I made that clear in my advert."

"No drugs." Jenny licked her dry lips. "It's too hot. I
don't like that."

The frown remained, but the hunter slid from her stool and opened a crowded drawer. She thrust a sheaf of papers into Jenny's hands. "You need to sign this at the bottom, and then on the next page." She fished a pen from a pocket and handed it over. "Here." Jenny made a mark where she was told, imitating the smears that the water made of newsprint. The hunter took the papers back without looking at them and dropped them onto one of her piles. She crossed to the metal trolley. "It's a really simple process. You won't feel a thing." She turned, a wedge of cotton in her hand. "I'll just clean up the site and then I'll inject you." Something cold dabbed at Jenny's neck, just to one side of her spinal column. She fought not to flinch at the closeness of the hunter. Next, surely, would come the blood and then . . .

Something darted into her neck, thin and bitter and burning hot. She tasted hunger and excitement and a violent sense of righteousness. Her eyes blurred: for an instant she was two Jennys, the one on the chair and another, an awkward earthy self filled with need and ambition. Images flashed by, men smirking as they passed, laughing behind their hands.

And then there was only the darkness.

The car engine woke Martin Jack, coughing to a halt scant feet from where he slept under a bench. He opened his eyes. It was maybe two hours before dawn: the orange street lamps still burned, but the windows of the houses were dark and silent. A door opened and closed with a slam, wafting that thick sense of wrongness towards him. He whimpered, pressed himself hard into the comfort of the ground beneath him. Wrong and wrong. Almost twelve hours since Jenny had gone on her mission and now this. He could smell the canal, thin and empty without the familiar green scent of her. His street people had come late and left early, huddling together over a bottle of ginger wine and half a pack of cheap cigarettes. He had wanted to follow them back into the center of the city and sleep curled against warm flesh.

He had promised Jenny. He had promised to help. But Jenny had gone away and not come back and the waters held no trace of her. The footsteps grew louder. They were heavy and uneven, counterpointed by a thick low drag and the catch of ragged breathing. He pulled back into the darkest part of the shadows. Along the towpath came a scant figure, bent over and laboring, with something lumpy wallowing in its wake. The wrongness billowed out from it in rich waves. Martin Jack gagged, felt his body tremble. Too much belief, grown sour through frustration and need. He pulled his ears down and peered out. There was only him, now, to defend what was left.

The figure came to a halt by the side of the canal, seven or eight feet away. Martin Jack fought back a whine that wanted to surge from his throat. The figure straightened, wriggling its shoulders and rubbing at its back, then bent again to pull at the lump at its feet. A waft of dampness rose, damping down the wrongness for a moment. Damp and green and familiar.

Jenny?

Slowly, unwillingly, Martin Jack began to creep forward toward the two shapes. The figure—it was a human woman—tugged and prodded at Jenny, who lay limp and crumpled on the towpath. Martin Jack froze. Jenny was strong and cunning. Nothing had ever caught her, not the ancient warriors, not the monks, not the men who drained the marsh. Jenny was the waters; she had been here before all those others and she would be here long after they had turned to ash.

Huffing and straining, the woman pushed Jenny's limp form forward over the gravel. Toward the concrete lip of the canal. Toward the waters ... The whimper forced its way out, loud in the still night. The woman turned, something glittering in her hand. Released suddenly, Jenny's body slumped back and one of her arms flopped over the edge into the water. Ripples jounced and scurried. Out in the center, the water began to churn.

Martin Jack growled low in his throat and jumped.

Water rushed through Jenny, ran cold through her veins, beneath her skin, surging and grumbling, driving the heat back and back. Her body hung heavy, flaccid, unresponsive to her commands. Her spine ached: at the base her skull something burned, blinding her with pain. She coughed and felt the water fill her lungs. Her arms thrashed out and the water welcomed her, pulling her down and down. Its long chill fingers pried her apart, flushed out the fear, tightened on the flame in her throat. Her body bent and she toppled sideways. The water—her water—caught her and held on, tight and close and homely. It wrapped her, gripped her as it dug deep under her flesh to tug away the taint the hunter had left under her skin. She cried out, and the waters echoed her. She uncurled and found herself home.

Her waters were angry. She wound herself through them and let that fill her to her limit. In the midst of them—in the midst of her—something thrashed and flailed and flapped. She swam up slowly to investigate. A mouthful of dog hair, stale and chewy: she spat that out and swam on. A long pale limb, thin and bony, wrapped in dirty cotton. The rush and thunder of a heart beating too fast in panic and alarm. The tang of fear and the sweet, sweet flow of living memory. In the heart of her waters, Jenny smiled as she wrapped herself about the hunter and drew her down and down and down.

She was very hungry.

THE ROOTS OF ASTON QUERCUS

Juliet E. McKenna

"**M**ora is late with her leaves again." Gamella stood with her arms folded tight across her bosom.

Fraina longed to ask what exactly Gamella expected her to do about it. But of course, she knew the answer. Go and talk to her. But why was she always the one expected to go and talk to Mora? She knew the answer to that as well. Because hers was the closest oak tree to Mora's own, out here on the edge of the grove.

"Where is she?" Fraina stroked her own tree's rough bark and felt the deep thrum of his irritation. He didn't much like Gamella at the best of times and definitely didn't welcome her agitation when he was settling down for winter's sleep.

As usual, the other dryad seemed oblivious to the oak tree's mood. "Up aloft. Where else?"

Where else indeed? Fraina need not have asked that question either. After so many uncounted seasons living together in this grove, there was little that the dryads didn't know about one another. There were no quirks or foibles among their little group that didn't rub someone up the wrong way. Mostly annoying Gamella, if truth were told.

"I'll go and talk to her." Fraina stepped inside her tree and rode the surge of life-giving water to his topmost twigs. She walked out onto the coppery leaves gently swaying in the wind to see Mora sitting in her own tree's crown staring up at the sky.

"May I join you?" Fraina called out.

"What?" Mora looked around, startled. "Oh, yes, of course."

Fraina stepped across the emptiness separating the two trees. Mora's tree welcomed her with a shiver of affection. There was no sign of him sinking into an autumnal doze, as was evident from his bright green leaves.

Mora grinned at her. "I take it Gamella's been nagging you to come and nag me?"

Fraina reflected, not for the first time, that Mora had a fine instinct for tension and who was causing it, notable in a dryad who spent so little of her time associating with the others.

"He is the only tree still in summer foliage." Fraina patted the nearest sprig and smiled as Mora's tree creaked amiably at her touch.

"We'll get round to changing that soon." Mora was unconcerned.

As ever, Fraina was baffled that any dryad could have so little apparent interest in managing her tree in accord with the seasons and the weather. Fraina loved taking care of her oak and of every living thing that enjoyed his shelter, from the tiniest insects to the biggest birds.

"What do you suppose that is?" Mora was staring upwards at something flying so high that it was barely more than a bright speck. It was steadily drawing a white line of wholly unnatural straightness across the crisp blue sky.

"I've no idea." Fraina wasn't much interested either. Now that the dragons were long gone, with all the perils that trailed after them, she only came aloft to tend to her tree and its denizens.

"I think it's a human thing." Mora was still gazing upwards, fascinated.

"Then it has nothing to do with us," Fraina said flatly. "It will be wrought of iron."

The other dryad stopped staring at the sky and looked at her instead. "What's the matter?"

Fraina hesitated before answering. "There was a dog."

She had always liked dogs and horses too. They reminded her of her tree: loyal, trusting, uncomplicated in their enthusiasms and affections. But nowadays horses and dogs alike saw the fae so seldom that their reactions were hard to predict.

Fraina held up a blistered hand. "I was trying to soothe her but I didn't see the iron studs on her collar. It was my own silly fault."

Dryads had long since learned there was no point in lamenting humankind's obsession with the iron that all the fae abominated.

But Mora wasn't listening, looking out across the grass instead. "Who is that?"

A man was striding along the footpath that the dog walkers and horse riders used, cutting across the pastures surrounding the grove, which was now hemmed in with hedgerows planted by humans quite some time ago.

"What is he carrying?" Fraina was mystified. The man

had an armful of yellow poles and a heavy black bag slung on his back.

"Let's find out." Mora stood up and vanished to slide down through her tree's sapwood to the ground.

"But he's not alone!" Fraina called out, alarmed. Two more humans were coming over the crest of the hill, similarly burdened.

She leaped back to her own tree and slid downward, apologizing as she went for such unseemly haste. Her tree bathed her in his reassuring love before opening his bark to allow her to step out onto the grass.

"What is she doing?"

To Fraina's relief Gamella had gone off in search of someone else to harass. Adleria was watching Mora walking along the footpath.

Ordinarily humans couldn't see a dryad. Now that Mora chose to reveal herself, she had fashioned herself an outfit like the dog walkers of this season: sturdy shoes, blue trousers, a rustling coat over a fleecy shirt.

Fraina was surprised to see how adept she was at doing that. Of all the dryads in the grove, Mora spent more time than anyone in her ethereal form, a shifting image of naked femininity, roundly ripe of hip and breast, soft and welcoming.

"What are they doing?" Adleria persisted. She favored a more constant form; long hair rippling to her shoulders and a high-waisted, round-necked gown. That was the dress she had worn when the young curate had fallen in love with her, pausing in the grove as he walked from the village church over the hill to the hamlet beyond the river, always wearing his long black coat, white linen bands and wide-brimmed shallow-crowned hat.

He had a passion for natural philosophy, so he had

told her, noting down all the details of the trees and the flowers, the beetles and birds in his leather-bound notebooks. Adleria had even gone to see him preaching in the church. The humans asked so few questions in those days that mere mention of a mother visiting cousins in the next town was readily accepted.

But the young curate had grown old and died in the way of human men and the humans who came after him had put iron railings around the church. The last time that Fraina had walked that way, she'd seen the church roof had long since fallen in, only the stone walls still defying the winters.

"I don't know," she belatedly answered Adleria.

They stood together and watched as Mora walked up to the first man. Fraina noted she was staying a prudent distance from the poles he carried, so those must be metal.

The man held the bundle upright and then pulled the poles apart, to set up a bright yellow tripod. Crouching to open his bag, he took out something with a single shining eye and fixed it firmly on the top. His companions were opening their own bags and taking out shallow black boxes that unfolded rather like the long-dead curate's book.

They couldn't hear what Mora was saying or what the man was telling her. His companions didn't pause in their activities and it wasn't long before Mora was heading back to the grove.

Fraina shifted from foot to foot, impatient. Now that the humans had seen her, Mora must stay in that form until she was out of their sight. She had to walk every step of the path rather than ride the gentle breezes which a dryad could summon with a flick of a finger.

"What is it? Who are they?" Vaseya stepped out of her own tree just as Mora reached the edge of the grove.

"They are surveyors," Mora scowled. "He says there's to be a road built through here."

"A road?" Adleria asked cautiously. "Is that so very bad?"

"It is," Mora told her, forthright. "This isn't a stone and gravel road like the ones your curate walked. They will scour away the grass and earth and lay stones and layers of tar before fencing the whole thing in with metal."

"Why would they do that?" Adleria was alarmed.

"Because they won't be riding horses or having horses draw their carriages." Vaseya looked grim. "They will be riding in their automobiles, those things that I told you about, all wrought from metal. That's what they need such roads for."

She had fallen in love most recently of all the dryads, with a young man who came to the grove seeking healing and peace. He'd told Vaseya of a great war in a distant land, where men had drowned in mud if they hadn't been killed by devices which he called guns, hurling deadly showers of metal bullets. If the men escaped the guns, other evil contrivances had thrown still bigger missiles. Those burst into myriad lethal steel splinters to slice innocents into quivering shreds.

Gamella and a good many of the other dryads had decided there was no hope for humanity after that. They'd avoided the dog walkers and everyone else ever since.

"That won't be very nice." Adleria's lip quivered. "To have such a thing so close to our grove."

"It's worse than that," Mora said bluntly. "The road

won't run alongside our grove but straight through it. He says our trees will be felled."

Fraina was still watching the vile humans as the dryads listened aghast to Mora's news. As the entire grove shook with their trees' anger, she saw the box with the glass eye tumble off the top of the yellow tripod. One of the men with the folding black book or box things looked up at the sky, apprehensive.

"What are we to do?" Adleria cried.

"Where are we to go?" Vaseya wasn't inclined to panic but Fraina could see the terror in her eyes.

That frightened Fraina. Vaseya knew better than most what the humans had made of the world, from talking to her wounded soldier. There was metal everywhere now, in the most unexpected places. Getting her soldier out of his clothes to make love to her on the summer grass had been quite a trial, with all the buttons and zips that would so readily raise welts on her skin.

Adleria looked around, hunted. "Where do you suppose the nearest forest is? Do you suppose—" She gazed at the dead stump of the fallen oak by the river.

"Lusita was old and her tree older still." Vaseya's voice shook. "Besides, she was a hamadryad. Truly, she was," she insisted.

"She never said." Adleria scrubbed a tear from her cheek.

"Would you?" Fraina didn't expect an answer. Who among them would admit to such frailty? Dryads outlived their trees, tending a new sapling when their first beloved companion finally succumbed to the cycle of nature. Hamadryads were bound to the acorns of their mother's tree. When the tree they were given to died, so did they.

"Gamella says that Lusita had already left before her tree began to fail," Adleria persisted. "She says that one of us should have borne a daughter to take care of it."

That had always been the custom, whenever a dryad had left in search of a new home. A tree used to such loving care could not be abandoned.

"Let me guess?" Mora said sarcastically. "Gamella would have done her duty for the grove? What if she was wrong? Then we'd be stuck with her daughter fretting and whining because she didn't have a tree of her own."

While the humans were content to leave the grove's mature trees well alone, they persisted in uprooting any saplings long before they were tall enough to benefit from a dryad's care. So they had all given up bearing children a long age ago. No one was prepared to send a daughter wandering when they had no idea if she could find a tree before she withered and died.

Nor could they rid themselves of the likes of Gamella, for the sake of the grove's harmony. In days gone by, if a community of dryads agreed that one of their number was too discontented, too disruptive, the offender would be asked to leave. She could wander through the trees that had cloaked the land until whatever tormented her was left far behind, or until she had learned some humility. Once the wanderer found peace with herself, there would always be a community of dryads to welcome a new sister.

"I miss sex," Adleria said wistfully.

"Me too," Fraina nodded, glad of the change of subject.

It had been such a pleasant pastime, whether or not she had any intention of bearing a daughter for the grove or a son to send out into the human world.

Her own beloved—bringing his pigs here so long ago

to eat the fallen acorns each autumn—he had been lucky to have a few copper pence in the purse tied inside his jerkin and the only iron he ever carried was the little knife on his belt, readily discarded. Fraina had no problem undoing the horn buttons on his shirt and the linen ties securing his hose as he pushed her homespun skirt up her silken thighs.

Sleeping out under the stars, such youths could easily be persuaded to share their blankets with a beautiful stranger. When they woke up all alone, they would either believe it had all been a wondrous dream, or just cherish their delightful secret in silence, lest they be mocked as a simpleton.

"Never mind that," Vaseya snapped, exasperated. "Where are we to go?"

"I have no intention of going anywhere," Mora said tartly. "There must be some way to stop them."

"A troll?" Adleria said hopefully. "Boggarts?"

"Don't be a fool," Gamella stepped out of her tree on the far side of the grove. She looked at Adleria, scathing. "When did you last see a troll? And what would anyone want with boggarts? Filthy little beasts. What are you talking about anyway?" she demanded.

"The humans want to cut down our trees," Adleria wailed.

"What?"

If this hadn't all been so serious, Fraina would have been meanly delighted to see the panic shattering Gamella's arrogance.

"Not all of them will agree to this," Mora asserted.

"What difference will that make?" Gamella recovered in an instant and now sought a target for her fear and anger. "What do you know about it anyway?"

"More than you." Mora waved a hand and the grove was suddenly filled with voices.

Adleria screamed while Vaseya ran for her tree, pressing close to his bark. Other dryads appeared, standing half inside their trees, half out.

"What is that?" Gamella shrieked.

Mora waved her hand and the din ceased. The dryads stood in stunned silence while the grove rang with the harsh calls of alarmed blackbirds.

"That," she said calmly, "is radio. It's a human thing. They talk about all sorts of things using devices to send their words through the air to each other. If you listen, you can learn all manner of things about their lives."

That must be what she did up aloft, Fraina realized, sitting in her tree's crown for days at a time.

"Their lives?" Gamella was even angrier after being taken so unawares. "We care nothing for them!"

"We should," Mora said bluntly. "They are of this world and so are we and they have mastered it in ways which the fae never could. If we wish to live on according to our own needs and customs, we must understand theirs."

Gamella shook her head in absolute denial. "We do not—"

"What has this to do with the road?" Fraina couldn't recall ever interrupting Gamella before but all at once, she was wholeheartedly sick of the other dryad's bossiness.

"There are still humans who love the wild places and the trees," Mora assured her. "They won't want to see our grove cut down. We must find out who they are."

"How?" Adleria quavered.

Mora smiled at her. "We talk to the dog walkers and the horse riders. They'll be able to tell us."

"Talk to them?" Prina stepped out of her tree. "Reveal ourselves?"

As Fraina recalled, Prina hadn't shown herself to any human since she'd fallen in love with a young man with flowing black curls who'd hidden in the grove for fear of the enemies who he'd called Roundheads. While he'd been camping among the trees, he'd written Prina lengthy poems and sung her intricate songs, which the dryads had all enjoyed.

"What do we say to them?" Adleria's voice strengthened, though her tree was still shaking as though a high wind pummeled his branches.

Mora considered this. "The first thing we must ask is whether there's an alternate route for the road."

Gamella pounced. "And if there isn't?"

Mora was more than ready for her. "Then at very worst, we persuade the humans to insist a new grove of saplings is planted a short distance away so we won't be without a home."

"But our trees—" Fraina laid her hand on her beloved oak's bark and felt him stir with agitation. Disquiet rustled through all the trees and she saw her own grief reflected on her sisters' faces.

All except Mora's. She looked ready for a fight, willing to take on a troll if such a beast might stray across her path.

"Come on." Her eyes were bright with challenge. "Or do you want to start coaxing your trees into a deep enough sleep that they won't feel the humans' axes?"

Fraina saw her sisters found that prospect as unthinkable as she did.

Though Gamella wasn't going to let Mora have the last word. "We cannot—"

"Shut up, Gamella." Nalfina stepped fully out of her tree. "Show us how these humans dress nowadays, Mora, and how we can listen to these voices on the breeze."

"They will ask us who we are," Adleria said hesitantly, "and where we are from. Humans always do that."

She was right, Fraina knew. The days were long gone when a dryad's son could walk for a turn of the moon and then present himself in a village, looking for work and offering a tale of seeking his fortune with the blessing of his family in some distant county which these locals had barely heard tell of.

Once he had proved himself honest and hard-working, a village would soon welcome such a son as one of their own, to live a long and healthy life by the standards of his father's blood, if all too fleeting by a dryad's measure.

Mora grinned. "Tell them you're from Hawbury and then ask where they're from. If they say they're from Hawbury too, ask whereabouts. Whatever their answer, say that you live on the other side of the town. It's not like it used to be when humans lived in the village by the church. There are so many of them now that they can't possibly all know each other."

So that very afternoon, all the dryads dressed themselves in the same garb as Mora: the sturdy shoes, the blue trousers and a fleecy shirt with a rustling coat to ward off the rain. All except Vaseya, but once she had shortened her hair and frosted it with gray, her tweeds proved perfectly acceptable, especially to the older men walking their dogs.

It felt most peculiar to Fraina to be so far removed from the grass and the trees, with such clothing shielding her from the wind and the occasional spatter of rain from the gray clouds now scudding across the blue sky. These people were supposedly coming out here to enjoy the beauties of nature. But humans were very strange. The dryads had always known that.

Strange, but as it turned out, oddly passionate about preserving the oak grove.

"It's an absolute disgrace," the horse rider told Fraina. "There's no good reason why the bypass can't follow the old railway line on the other side of town. Except that the developers want to open up more land for housing."

"Of course." Fraina nodded sagely and hoped this nice woman in the green coat didn't see how little she understood. She really must start listening to these radio voices of Mora's.

"He's perfectly safe," the woman remarked. "If you want to pat him, go ahead. I can see you like horses."

"I do." Fraina smiled but couldn't see how to stroke the glorious chestnut's neck without getting too close to the iron rings and buckles of his harness. It was such a shame.

"We need to gather as much evidence as possible," the woman continued briskly, "to put before the planning enquiry. Any evidence of special scientific interest hereabouts and as much proof as possible of the history of this right of way." She gestured with her short whip, indicating the path through the fields.

"History?" Fraina knew that's what the humans called everything that went before their own short lives.

"The more, the better." The brisk woman gathered up her horse's reins. "Well, we'd better get on. It's a bit chilly to keep the old boy standing here. Will we see you at the town hall meeting opposing these wretched plans?"

"I'm not sure." Fraina smiled apologetically.

"Do try and make the demo," the woman urged as she rode off.

Fraina watched her go, still sad that she couldn't have petted the horse. Then she hurried back to the grove. "Adleria?"

"Yes?" Even in these uncouth clothes, Adleria looked winsomely beautiful as she stepped out of her tree.

"Your curate, what was his name?"

"The Reverend Quintus Norris," Adleria said promptly.

"Did he ever mention anything—" Fraina paused to recall the horsewoman's words correctly, "—of special scientific interest in our grove?"

Adleria thought for a moment. "He was very taken with our slipper orchids and the fritillaries."

"So was my soldier, and he wrote about them too." Vaseya appeared beside them. "I've been talking to a gentleman who's going to look for his diaries in the library at the university. Apparently that's just the sort of evidence they need, to persuade the planning authorities to send the road another way."

Fraina looked at her in awe.

Vaseya grinned. "No, I don't know what all that means either. But you know how devoted the humans are to writing everything down."

Fraina nodded. They had all done it; Adleria's curate, Vaseya's soldier, Prina's poet. Perhaps it was because their lives were so fleeting. If they didn't leave such records, who would know that they have ever lived?

Adleria had grasped the essential point. "So if we can show them where those plants still bloom, that should make a real difference?"

Vaseya nodded. "And the butterflies and just about anything else."

"Quintus used to study at the university." Adleria smiled mistily before looking bright-eyed at Vaseya. "Could your new friend look for his notebooks there?"

"I'll suggest it." Vaseya nodded.

"And they want to know how long the footpath has been here," Fraina remembered. "Oh, by the way, does anyone know what a demo is? Because there's going to be one, apparently."

"We had better ask Mora," Adleria said uncertainly. "Here she comes."

"With a human." Vaseya froze like a deer scenting trouble on the breeze.

"We should hide." Fraina was abruptly convinced of it. "Let Mora handle him."

Adleria's chuckle was surprisingly earthy. "She seems to be doing that well enough."

The others vanished and Fraina stepped inside her own tree. Feeling his unease, she did her best to soothe him as Mora and her companion reached the grove.

The two of them sat down, their backs against Mora's tree. The young man was very good looking, Fraina observed. As handsome as any lover a dryad had ever brought to the grove.

Adleria slipped into Fraina's tree, pressing close beside her. "Do you suppose they—"

"He certainly wants to." Vaseya joined them too.

"By all means, step in." Fraina's half-hearted rebuke died on her lips as the young man wrapped his arms around Mora and kissed her long and deeply.

"There seems to be much less metal in clothes these days," Vaseya observed.

But Mora still pulled abruptly away.

"I'm sorry, I'm sorry," the young man said hastily. "I just—"

"It's okay." Mora's smile reassured him with the allure that came as naturally to dryads as the leaves came to their trees. "But what have you got in your pocket?"

"What?" The young man hastily searched his coat. "Sorry, my penknife." He held out a folded blade. "Did it—"

"Never mind." Mora waved a hand. "Just keep it away from me. I don't approve of metal."

"You don't approve?" The young man was bewildered.

"Metal, oil, mining. It all damages the earth." Mora smiled, still more seductive.

"You're really hardcore." The young man seemed impressed. "Vegan?"

"What do you think?" Mora grinned.

"Vegan?" Vaseya looked at Fraina and Adleria, baffled.

"Hardcore?" Adleria was completely at a loss.

"I've no idea what he means." Fraina wondered if Mora understood these strange words. Her smile was sweetly confident, as though she and the young man shared a secret. Of course that could just be Mora bluffing. She did seem very good at that.

"You say your group's called The Friends of Aston Quercus—" the young man hesitated.

"Aston Quercus Medieval Village." Mora pointed over the hill toward the ruined church. "It's a very important site and really should be scheduled as a monument."

"What is she talking about?" Adleria was still more bemused.

"History," Fraina guessed promptly. "The humans want to know everything that's gone on in this place."

Vaseya looked askance at her. "We can hardly tell them what we know."

"Quintus's notebooks should help," Adleria said hopefully.

"Perhaps they can find out something from the church's graveyard. We must suggest that to the dog walkers and horse riders." Though as Fraina recalled, the engraving on the few remaining stones was worn almost to oblivion. Still, these humans must have kept records.

Aston Quercus had been the name of the village where her loving swineherd had lived. All that remained of his cottage was one of the lumps and bumps rising in the field beyond the church, the long-dead hearths marked by flourishing clumps of nettles.

Adleria nudged her elbow. "She's kissing him again."

"We won't let them cut down these trees," the young man said breathlessly as he pulled reluctantly away some while later. "Even if we can't get them to change the plans, we can set up a camp here, break their chainsaws with nails driven into the wood—"

"No!" The dryads' collective gasp of horror sent Fraina's tree into a frenzy of rustling leaves.

While the young man looked up, startled, Mora looked straight across at the three of them and scowled.

"Wow, I thought a branch was about to come down." The young man tried to cover his embarrassment with a laugh.

Mora looked upwards. "Not today."

"You really know about this place, don't you?" The young man was intrigued.

"So will you get all your friends involved?" Mora shifted closer, pressing against him. "Here and in London? Can you get the story on the radio and in the papers? It really needs to go national."

"We'll see it go viral." The young man promised her fervently. "Look, can I ring you? Email?"

Mora shook her head. "I don't have a phone or a computer."

"Totally off the grid?" The young man marveled. "Right. But when will I see you again?"

Mora leaned forward to kiss him. "At the demo. I could do an interview there?"

"OK. And after?" he asked hopefully.

"Maybe." Mora's smile promised untold delights.

"What are they talking about?" Vaseya wondered.

"I really have no idea," Adleria said helplessly.

"Mora seems to know what she's doing," Fraina observed.

She never did find out exactly what a demo was. Mora did invite her, saying it was a gathering to oppose the planned road, but Fraina really couldn't bring herself to mingle with so many humans at once.

So she sat in the crown of her tree and searched the radio voices just as Mora had taught her. Finally she lit upon Mora's own voice, eloquent and impassioned. The dryad talked about the ancient woodlands so brutally stripped from the lands and how vital it was to save these last precious remnants.

Hearing Mora's voice, all the trees shook their branches in fervent agreement. Their golden autumn leaves fell in thick showers. Looking down, Fraina saw all the other dryads in the grove looking up with desperate hope.

Mora's young man came to the grove regularly after that. Her tree swiftly colored his leaves with autumn's hues and shed them to make a soft bed in the sheltered hollow of his roots. Even though the weather was growing colder, the young man and Mora would make love swathed in long woolen coats, their ardor burning all the hotter for such constraints upon it.

One afternoon, while the two of them were occupied, Fraina slipped out of her tree and carefully borrowed the mass of folded sheets of paper which the young man had brought with him. Of course he couldn't see her, so she had to make it look as though his paper was blowing away, not being carried by some unseen sprite.

She hurried to the far side of the grove and spread the sheets on the fading grass. Whatever was in here must be important. Mora was rewarding her young man with sensual enchantments that few living humans had ever enjoyed.

"What's that?" Adleria appeared beside her.

"A newspaper." Fraina was proud of knowing that now. "It's a human thing."

"Oh, poor thing." Adleria stroked the white expanse sprinkled all over with blackness. "It was once a tree."

"I know." Fraina had just about got used to the lingering echoes of the paper's mistreatment, pounded and crushed between great iron rollers. This was a far cry from the paper which the curate and the poet had used. "But see, it can tell us so many things."

As she ran her fingertips across the words, the paper eagerly gave up their meaning.

"The Hawbury Bypass Campaign has successfully persuaded the County Council to adopt the western railway route rather than risk the considerable environmental damage that the Aston Quercus option would entail. The proposals for the establishment of the Aston Quercus Country Park have also won council endorsement and will be presented at a series of public consultations before the end of the year."

"But what does that mean?" Vaseya had joined them.

"It means that we're safe." Fraina looked up at the oak trees and smiled.

Mora was late with her leaves again, when the spring arrived. No one said anything, not even Gamella.

TO SCRATCH AN ITCH

Avery Shade

Autumn Sky knew that there were three rules she must never forget. One, don't tell anyone what her daddy was. Two, if she ever got an itch between her eyes, she couldn't scratch it, but had to tell her parents right away. And three, always, always try to behave like any other normal little girl her age. The first was downright silly (why anyone would care that her daddy was a weatherman was beyond her), the second was pointless since she'd never had such an itch, but the third? Well, out of all their rules, Autumn thought the last was the most important . . . and the hardest to follow. Yes, her hair was a deep sort of chestnut red, yes, her eyes were a bright sky blue, and yes, she did tend to spend more time hopping about in the air than planted firmly on the ground, but she also thought that if her parents had really wanted her to act normal they should never have given her such a ridiculous name.

She thought their expectation that she live up to the

boring simplicity of normalcy was a grievous edict when burdened with such an unusual name. More than once in the past she'd asked her parents why, if they wanted her to be normal, they had named her such an outlandish name anyway? It was their response to this that convinced Autumn she had no hope of ever being normal. Parents were supposed to know everything. But they never had a good answer for her—"your mother has a streak of the whimsy, pumpkin," was not a good or logical answer when you were touting normalcy—which just convinced her that her parents must be abnormal too.

"Abnormality breeds abnormality, that's what Aunt Elana always says." Speaking to no one in particular, or perhaps more truthfully, no particular "person," she bent down to brush her fingertips over the delicate petals of the newest member of her family. A gerbera daisy. Orange, with the sweetest fringe of rosy pink on the outer edges. The colors hadn't reached their full potential yet, as the petals had just unfurled far enough to be considered blooming, but the kiss of sun-burnt pink already present carried with it the potential of a masterpiece.

She stepped back, softening her gaze so that she could take in the whole rooftop garden. The mix of colors, scents and shapes was a masterpiece all its own. Better than any of the stuffy portrait paintings her cousin Arleen could do.

Yes, her newest baby was going to fit in just perfectly.

She frowned, fingering the frilly fringe on the shirt her mother had made her wear to school that morning. Okay, maybe it wasn't exactly normal to think of her plants in terms of "children" and "family" but that's how she envisioned them and how she cared for them, too, so that's what she would call them. Normalcy be boogered.

Boogered. That was normal. She'd heard James say it at school just last week and James was the epitome of a typical boy, least that's what her second grade teacher Ms. Banks always said. Besides, lots of girls her age played family with things like stuffed animals, Barbies, or even little plastic spring-hinged balls called Zoobles. If they could pretend that such inanimate objects were "alive" and "real" then why couldn't she attribute personalities to her plants?

Apples to oranges, Autumn. Our plants aren't toys.

"True," she agreed, nodding her head sagely.

That settled, she tucked her eyelet skirt up under the back of her knees and knelt down, humming softly as she lovingly topped off her potted children with fresh soil. Being up on the roof meant they were exposed to the elements that habitually erode away the top layers, so it was a constant battle to keep their delicate roots covered.

With the warm midafternoon sun beating down on the back of her head, she had gotten most of the way through the first two tiers when the strangest thing happened. And that was saying a lot for a kid who had trouble with normal to begin with.

Her scalp began to tingle.

Not the I-need-to-take-a-bath kind of itchy-tingle, nor even a someone's-behind-me tingle (she got those all the time and this was most decidedly not it) but an obscure from-the-inside-out tingle that made her brain squirm as if being tickled in her skull and her hair threaten to leap right out of her scalp. Even though she knew the tingle was caused by neither of these, she found herself twisting around, searching the flat rooftop with her gaze.

Nothing, of course, but the tickly itch was just as present

as before, worse even as she stood staring past the lip of the roof. Sun, blue sky, city skyline—wait, was that a faint smudge? She squinted her eyes and sure enough, there, in the distance, marking the edge of the sky like the smear of charcoal on a painters sketch, were the most ominous bulk of clouds she'd ever spied.

She gasped, leaning forward instinctively to shield her prized gerbera daisy. If those clouds broke over the city, her daisy would never survive a storm such as that, nor would her violets, or her freshly sprouted sweet peas, or her lilies. And that wasn't even to mention her young cherry tree, sitting proudly in its new pot, the first blush of blooms upon its limbs. The wind would tear the delicate blossoms right off and then . . . then. . . .

Tears began to leak from her eyes, running twin paths down each cheek. She knew she could bring in most of her plants. Her mother might sigh and huff and mutter as she helped Autumn drag them down to the apartment, but the cherry tree?

She looked at the proud little tree, measured how much it had grown since last summer. At least six inches, and that was only in height. In that pot? Even if both her and her mother lugged and tugged there was no way they could get it inside and down the stairs without risk. In her mind's eye she saw it tumbling down the stairs, pot smashing, soil scattering, limbs snapping, blossoms and leaves shredding. Autumn wailed just imagining such a travesty.

Leaping up, she raced across the rooftop garden, throwing skinny arms around the navy-glaze pot. "Don't worry. It's not going to happen. I'll save you."

The cherry tree shivered, its little leaves rustling, the branches rattling, and the blossoms blushing as they bobbed in the still perfectly calm sunshine.

It had heard her!

A breeze swept up, grabbing one of Autumn's chestnut curls, tossing it into her eyes.

Or maybe not.

Her head was beyond tingling now. Needle pricks raced across her scalp, and though her brain seemed to have ceased its squirming it had started an all-out attack from just behind the eyes. That, combined with the not-so-innocent, warm little breath of a breeze did something to her that had never happened before. Autumn, got really, really mad. Not crazy-mad, or Joey-Berchoni-calling-her-a-dork mad, but the furious sort of mad. The shoot-fire-from-your-eyes kind.

She glared at the clouds, wrinkling her nose up in what her mother called her grumpy face, and waggled her finger at the brewing storm. "Go away!"

The cloud rolled closer, unperturbed.

"Go away!" Autumn jumped up, stomping her foot as she jabbed her finger toward the south. "You can go there for all I care, but you are not coming here!"

As she said this, the all-over tingle in her head condensed down to a ball of achy-itchy pain right behind the bridge of her nose. Autumn gasped, closing her eyes as she dug at them with the heels of her hand. Even through the pain, a horrible thought occurred, one she quickly discarded. This could *not* be the itch her parents had been talking about, absolutely could not. This wasn't an itch, it was a really, really bad headache.

Oh stop, oh stop, go away, go away, go away.

And then as suddenly as it had come, it went, bursting like a firecracker in her head: a quick burst of light followed by a *fzzzz*.

When Autumn was sure the last little spark of the

strange headache was gone she straightened, blinking her eyes. Warily, she looked around. Frowned. It seemed strange and somehow not right that nothing had changed while she'd just had the weirdest experience in her life. Cars still honked at each other down on the streets below, her little garden sat unharmed, and there was not a cloud in the sky to mar the warm spring day.

Wait . . . not a cloud in the sky?

She reached out, curling her hand lightly around the cherry tree's trunk. "That was . . . weird," she told it. And definitely not normal. And right now she wanted nothing else more desperately than to be normal.

Autumn took three long deep breaths, trying to make logic of what had just happened. Her strange headache was gone, along with both the squirmy tingle and the storm. The coincidence of those events could not be ignored, but to think that she had anything to do with the storm's disappearance?

"Silly. I'm being silly. Lots of people get tingles or achy limbs or even headaches when there is an approaching storm front. My headache's gone because the storm is gone, right?"

She turned to her garden for confirmation. Their beaming blossoms smiled back at her. Pleased with their assurance, she smiled back. And because it was so important to keep them happy, she pulled out her watering can and started the first of what would be a number of trips down to the apartment for their filtered water.

"But why, mom? Why can't daddy be here to tuck me in?" Autumn tried. She really, really tried, but she couldn't seem to stop the quaver in her voice nor the trembling of her lip.

TO SCRATCH AN ITCH

Her daddy always tucked her in, the nighttime routine always the same. First her mom would come in and sing; her pure voice as sweet and soothing as the goodnight hug and kiss she gave her at the end. Then her father would come in, with a book tucked under his arm and a promise not to fill their daughter's head with nonsense as he passed his wife at the door. He'd shut the door, his angular features stiff and serious as he waited the required five seconds to make sure her mother had gone away.

And then they'd look at each other and smile their conspirators' smiles. Her father would sneak across the room, discarding the stuffy old storybook on the night-stand before stretching out on the bed, his back to the headboard, his legs crossed, and pull her up against his chest so she could listen to his heart as he whispered to her some fantastical story of fairies and unicorns and mermaids and monsters. And then, after, would be the tuck-in. She loved her daddy's tuck-ins. They made her feel safe and loved and, well, perfect.

Autumn could have lived without the story, but not the tuck-in.

"Darling," Autumn's mother soothed, brushing her cheek with her knuckles. "Your daddy is a weatherman."

Autumn rolled her eyes thinking that must be the most unhelpful explanation ever.

Her mother chuckled, tucking the sheet up tight around Autumn's chin. "That means sometimes he has to go where the weather is."

Autumn thought real hard about that. So hard she could feel her skin bunching on her forehead. Her mother wasn't making any sense. The weathermen on TV never went anywhere. OK, maybe sometimes when there was a huge storm. But most of the time they just pointed at those silly maps on TV, which weren't really maps but green screens that the weathermen had to pretend had real pictures and maps and charts on them.

Daddy had never been on TV. Not in front of those silly maps and not in the middle of a big storm. He said it was because he was more of a "behind-the-scenes guy." Which made her wonder, would a behind-the-scenes guy really have to go away to track a big storm?

A shiver of worry ran up her spine. She didn't want her daddy in the middle of a big storm. People got hurt. People *died* in big storms.

"When is daddy going to be home?" Her voice was definitely quivering now. She didn't care.

Her mother looked down at her with serious grown-up eyes. Autumn could tell she was debating her answer. She was not only taking too long but she was gnawing her lip again. Mom did that a lot when she was worried or unsure. Autumn really hoped it was the latter.

Then her mother smiled, bending down to tickle her as she delivered another kiss. "Don't worry, darling. Daddy should be home sometime tomorrow."

But it wasn't tomorrow, nor the next day. Three days and lots of lip-chewing on her mother's part later, Autumn dragged her backpack up the stairs to her apartment and pushed the door open. It had been a terrible day. James and Joey had been relentless in their teasing and Jessica? Argh, could a girl be any more perfectly normal? Who really cared if Autumn liked using big words and so what that she didn't find some stupid square sponge funny? Nope, she didn't feel one ounce of bad for telling them that they had been brainwashed by pop culture and had the intellect of said sponge.

Autumn had stomped halfway across the living room

before she saw him. Her daddy, sprawled on the couch, eyes closed. With a thud, she dropped her book bag and leapt, flinging herself across her daddy's massive chest. He grunted, but then chuckled, his arms tightening around her like bands of steel as he returned her hug. And quite a hug it was.

Maybe if she held on tight enough he would never disappear on her again. If not, then at least it might make up for all the hugs he'd missed while away.

A large hand came up, stroking down the back of her head. "I missed you too, pumpkin."

"Where were you, daddy?"

"There was quite a storm to the south of here. I had to go and check things out."

Autumn pushed up, looking down at her daddy. "To the south?"

He nodded, his wide eyes narrowing. "Why, pumpkin, did you—"

"Evan?" They both looked around at the sound of her mother's voice. She stood in the doorway to the kitchen, a steaming cup in her hands.

"Ah! Thank you, Gwen." He sat up, shifting Autumn over to his side as he reached for the cup, wrapping his large hands around the stoneware. "This should hit the spot."

"Still cold?"

He sighed. "It was quite the storm."

Autumn's mother cut her gaze to Autumn, then back to her husband. Whatever message was being sent between the two of them must have been more obvious to them than it was to Autumn because her daddy cleared his throat and turned to her with a smile plastered on his face.

"So what have you been doing while I've been away, pumpkin?"

That was all Autumn needed. She began to fill her daddy in on all the wonderful things that had been happening in her garden while he was away. How her cherry tree had blossomed and her sweet peas were growing so fast they'd started to curl around the fourth string and her gerbera daisy . . .

"You have to see it daddy! It's so pretty and it has three blossoms on it now. I hoped it would get one or two this year but I never expected it to grow so fast."

"I did." He grinned, pinching her cheek. "You have the magic touch, pumpkin."

"Evan."

They both looked at her mother. Another wordless message passed between her parents. Autumn couldn't fathom what it was so she shrugged and went back to talking. She really wanted to share her flowers with her dad. He always loved her garden and was so impressed by how she made them all fit together like a master's artist palette, everything working in harmony to create a beautiful blending of colors. That's what he said, always following it up by, "You're the genuine thing, pumpkin. Someday you're going to put your old man to shame."

It used to disturb her, that last bit, but that was before she'd asked her teacher and Ms. Banks had explained that to put someone to shame meant that you surpassed them in skill. Autumn didn't think it could ever really happen (her daddy was the best daddy ever and good at positively everything) but it made her proud to think that he thought she was going to be even close to as wonderful as he was someday.

"Daddy, do you want to come up and see my garden?

At least half is blooming now and I switched some things around so that—"

"Autumn," her mother interrupted. Autumn twisted to look at her mother who was still hovering nearby. "Your father is tired. Let him rest."

Autumn looked back at her father, for the first time noticing that his beautiful golden skin looked sallow, his handsome face looked drawn. Worry warred with disappointment. She didn't like that her daddy was so tired looking, but she still wanted to show him her garden.

"Maybe after your father has a nap he can come up."

Autumn chewed on her lip. What had her daddy been doing that he was so tired? Was the storm that bad?

Her mother cleared her throat. "It is a hot, dry day. Do you need to water your plants?"

That had Autumn springing up. It had been hot. Nearly a hundred degrees at noon, which was totally unheard of in early May. Most of her plants were hardy enough to make it until tomorrow but there were a few . . . she looked back at her dad. For some reason she didn't want to leave his side. It was silly, but she couldn't help but fear that he might disappear on her again.

"Ah, pumpkin, ease that worry from your brow. You are my sunshine. And like one of your precious flowers, I promise I'll be here awaiting your return."

Her daddy was so smart to understand her so well. She bent down, smacking a sloppy kiss on his lips and then spun and raced for the roof stairs.

Autumn tiptoed down the stairs leading from the roof to her apartment, her precious cargo clenched tightly in her hands. The afternoon had passed, as had a quiet dinner with her mother, and still her daddy had slept on the couch. He did manage to rouse himself to tuck her in, but there had been no story, and as soon as he was done he'd stumbled off down the hall to his bedroom. This morning, her mother had said he was "run down" and "sleeping in" and that Autumn "shouldn't disturb him."

Autumn didn't like it but she understood. It was like that time she'd gotten that awful tummy bug and afterward she'd slept for almost two days straight before she felt better again. Her daddy hadn't been sick, but it was obvious that whatever he'd been doing for his job had tired him terribly. She'd decided that "run down" was a kind of sickness and was determined to help him get better as fast as possible.

Which was why she was bringing him her gerbera daisy. She just knew having it beside his bed to look at would cheer him up. And her daddy said that a smile was one of the best cures in the world.

Autumn reached their front door, slipping inside. Her backpack weighed down her shoulders like a guilty reminder of what she should be doing. Heading to the bus stop. It would be okay though. She'd just leave the gerbera daisy on his dresser, slip back out, scoot down to the back entrance of her building, and cut through the side street to catch the bus at its next stop. And because of her efforts, by the end of the day her daddy would be up and about and ready to go to the roof to look at the rest of her garden.

She hadn't made it past the tiled foyer when her parents' voices drifted down the hall to her, her mother's voice pitched with worry and her daddy's . . . well she'd never heard her daddy sound like that. All hard and angry and . . . scary.

"Whoever he or she is, they're an idiot. The council is

not going to tolerate this sort of blatant display of power. The moment the *bean-sídhe* tracks them down it will be the end of their fool life."

There was a stretch of silence then the sound of something smacking into something else. Like a fist into wood.

"This is exactly the kind of thing that we can't have! With how efficient technology is today, with no plausible explanation for such an extreme shift, incidents like this could expose our entire race. Do you have any idea what could happen then? The kind of mad panic that could ensue?"

Autumn held her breath. She didn't know exactly what her daddy was talking about, only that he'd taken on the same kind of urgent tone he used when he spoke to her about the "big three rules." But how those rules could have anything to do with other races and councils and power . . .

Daddy is talking like the people in his stories are real. Autumn inched another step closer.

"Do you suppose it was a mistake?" her mother asked. "Perhaps someone newly come into their power and unused to handling such a large storm?"

"By Danu, I wish that it were, but no. A newly fledged youngling would not be able to divert such a widespread weather pattern. The power needed to shift the jet stream and then create a pressure bubble to keep it there? We still haven't been able to re-establish the natural patterns and that's with both me and Avril working on it."

"Is that why it's been so hot the last few days?"

"It's all we can do to keep the temperatures down to livable levels." There was a pause. "If this doesn't break, we're looking at one of the worst heat waves ever."

"And then what?" Her mother's voice trembled with worry. Autumn felt a corresponding sink in her tummy. She waited for her father's answer breathlessly, her lip clamped tight between her teeth.

"People could die. No. People *will* die if we don't. . . ."

Her father kept talking but Autumn didn't hear. She gasped, the pot slipping through her numb fingers. She watched, time seeming to slow, as her prize gerbera daisy plummeted to the floor, the pot smashing on the unforgiving tile. Dirt heaved up and spread in a ring. The daisy bounced, petals shaking violently in the explosion, the blossoms splitting and slumping down on the mound of dirt and terracotta shards.

Not me. Not me. It was chance the storm went away when she told it to, she assured herself.

"Who's there?" A door banged open. Hurried footsteps.

But what about the headache? Was that a coincidence too?

"Autumn?"

She lifted her head from the destruction at her feet, eyes wide as she gazed at her father. His edges were blurry, like looking through the funky old glass at her Aunt Elana's Victorian house.

She looked back down at the flower at her feet. It laid limply, one blossom bent awkwardly on its stem. The others crushed under the settling dirt.

She'd killed it. She'd told the storm to go away. She'd . . . she'd . . . .

"Pumpkin. Honey. . . ."

She jerked her gaze back up again. Saw her daddy easing down the hall, his hand outstretched like she was a cornered dog that he was trying to soothe. Her mother was less than a step behind, her hand clenched around daddy's other arm.

Daddy. Her daddy could fix anything.

But not this. Her daddy couldn't fix this.

With a cry of dismay she spun around, pushing through the apartment door. She ran. Faster than she'd ever run, her feet hardly touching the treads as she disregarded the slow elevator and bolted down the stairs instead. She heard her mother calling her. The heavy footfalls that told her daddy was chasing her. Whimpering, she shrugged the heavy backpack from her shoulders and ran harder, taking chances, leaping down half-flights of stairs.

She thought it was hopeless, that her daddy would catch her and then he'd find out that she . . . that she'd. . . .

No, no, no. Not me! Coincidence. Just a coincidence.

Behind her, her daddy shouted in surprise. There was a loud thud, then a long exclamation of words strung together that she'd never heard her daddy utter before.

Her backpack, he must have tripped. And now he would be really, really angry with her.

Choking back a sob, she ran down the last flight of stairs and burst through the back door onto the street beyond.

"Autumn? What are you doing here?"

Autumn choked back a sob, just one in a long string of them, and raised her swollen face from her knees. A trail of snot dripped from her nose to the soaked edge of her skirt. Embarrassed, she swiped it away, hoping that James hadn't noticed. Bad enough James had caught her crying. She bet James never cried. James was too much of a *boy* to cry.

She looked up at him, saw the horrified look of disgust on his face, and had to fight the urge to stuff her head back in the crook of her bent knees.

"Aw, man. Have you been crying?"

Well, duh, she thought, jutting her chin out defensively. Though defensive or not, it never hurt to be polite. "Hello, James."

"Yeah, hey." He scratched the back of his head, his mouth twisting up funny as his gaze drifted away from her, scanning the empty park they were in.

Autumn looked around, too. It wasn't the best place in the neighborhood. The playground equipment was old, the grounds overgrown with weeds and shrubbery that had a tendency to both catch and provide shelter to an assortment of trash. The majority of the mothers and children in the neighborhood utilized the new park three blocks over near the Baptist church. But this had been the only place she could think to go. The other park and her school were completely out of the question if she didn't want to be found.

"Aren't you going to tell me what *you're* doing here?" James asked again, his attention settling on her once more.

"Maybe." She straightened her legs, brushing out her rumbled skirt. "You going to tell me what you're doing here?"

"Skipping."

Her mouth flopped open. She gave a furtive glance around.

"Skipping? As in . . . hooky?" She whispered the last, as if uttering the evil word would bring the hounds of hell down upon them. She knew James could be a bit of a troublemaker, and he certainly loved to tease her—

pulling her hair, calling her names—but playing hooky from elementary school? Unheard of.

He shrugged, wrapping his arms around his chest. "Yeah, so? You got a problem with that? Miss I'm Not in School Either."

Autumn hung her head. That's right, she was as bad as James was. No worse. She'd . . . She'd. . . .

"I ran away," she mumbled.

"What's that?"

She lifted her head back up, meeting his gaze. "I said I ran away from home."

His head jerked back and he rocked onto his heels. "Why would you do a stupid thing like that?"

"I have to." She stated this bravely, ruined it by sniffling.

"Ah, man. That bites." He took a step closer, plopped down beside her. They sat together, legs stretched out alongside one another's for a while, when he spoke again. "You don't seem to be running very fast or very far."

"I don't know where to go," she admitted.

"Well, if you're going to do it right, then you should find a better hiding place than this. This is one of the first places they'll look."

"Not the first."

"Not the last though."

She had to agree with that, albeit grudgingly. It might not be one of the top three places, but she didn't doubt James was right: this wouldn't be far down on the list.

"Do you want help?"

She blinked, twisting her head to stare at him. How could he be so casual about her running away? How could he be so calm as he offered to aid and abet her?

She nibbled her lip, looking at him. He seemed just

like any other normal boy their age, maybe an inch taller than her, skinny from play and games. She knew that though he liked sports, he had an oftentimes clumsy streak, and frankly, neither his curly mop of brown hair nor the dirt-brown eyes did anything to set him apart from his classmates.

Yet he seemed so brave and grown-up, and he obviously hung out on the streets enough to know more than she. All of a sudden, a completely disobedient and insane thought crossed her mind. She leaned in, her mouth just inches from his ear, and whispered, "My daddy's a weatherman."

He twisted to look at her, his brow drawn tight together as he eyed her oddly. "And that's why you're running away?"

She shook her head in exasperation. "No, not because of that. I'm running away because I scratched 'the itch'."

At least she thought that was what she'd done. It hadn't exactly been an itch, not really, but the more she thought about it and the more she applied it to what she'd overheard, she knew that's what she had done.

"Ah." He nodded knowingly. "You got in trouble."

Frowning, she crossed her arms across her chest. She'd just told him two of the top three big secrets her family had and that was the answer she got? "No, not yet. But if they find out what I really did. . . ."

She trailed off, gulping down the funny lump in her throat. It was jagged and hard and even more bitter than the coffee her mother had let her have a sip of once.

He tipped his head, his brown eyes steady on her. She knew he wanted her to tell him what "scratched the itch" meant, but she couldn't. She practically hyperventilated just thinking about it.

"I killed my gerbera daisy," she exclaimed in a poof of breath.

His face crunched up.

She looked down at her feet, seeing again the pile of broken pot, dirt, and limp blooms. "My plant. It was just a baby plant."

He was silent for long time. Autumn pleated her skirt, un-pleated it, ironed it down. He swallowed, and then said, sounding amazingly loud compared to the nearby street noise, "I killed my goldfish last summer. Overfed it. I felt terrible."

Autumn was careful to keep her gaze down in her lap. She suspected that for James to admit that he'd felt such genuine emotion was akin to her revealing her family secrets. She was sure of it when a few seconds later he snapped out, "So, do you want that help or not?"

Did she? She remembered the last scene in her house. The conversation she'd heard, the broken pot on the floor, the strange look in her parents' eyes as they approached her like some sort of wild animal. *And they don't even know what I've* really *done yet.* What would they think of her when they knew that she'd . . . she'd. . . .

She choked back a sob, hiding her face in her hands. She practically jumped when a hand came down on her shoulder, patting it awkwardly.

"Hey, it's okay. If you just want to go home. . . ."

She leapt up, rounding on James. Her small hands fisted with fear, fury, and frustration at her sides. "I told you, I *can't* go home!"

James stared up at her, his expression saying it all. She must look crazy.

Taking a deep breath, she worked hard to unfurl her hands, wrapping them around her tumbling tummy instead.

She glanced around, up at the sky. Noon. "You, uh, said you could help?"

James stood, brushing off the seat of his jean shorts. "Yeah. I know a place you can hide out. Best of all, no one ever goes there."

James "knew" a place?

"Oh. OK. Good. That sounds . . . good," she replied. Though to her own ears, it sounded anything but.

The moment she saw the place that James suggested she hide, she knew he was right. No one would go here—because no one would want to. Down at the far end of an alley, behind an abandoned building and tucked in the corner of a crackled and pothole ridden parking lot, sat an overturned garbage dumpster. It had been tipped over and wedged against the building behind it, thereby making the only way in or out via the one side of the "top" that wasn't crushed up against the crumbling wall. It would have been a vagrant's dream, except for two things: the rusted-out delivery truck that sat behind it was obviously not going anywhere, which meant you couldn't move it to make the slim opening bigger, *and* it stunk worse than a skunk.

Autumn stood. Transfixed. No . . . *horrified* as she stared at her new home. She couldn't live in that. She was used to fresh air and fragrant flowers. Not stinky, rotten-garbage skunk smells.

She tried breathing through her mouth—ugh, she could taste the stench. She didn't even notice that James had run ahead of her until he called.

"Come on!" James motioned with his hand in a come-hither gesture, urging her on. "I've brought a few things here. Got the inside set up kind of cool."

His eagerness did nothing to alleviate the weight

crushing down on her chest, squeezing her lungs. She dragged her feet, but followed him across the parking lot. With a numb sort of detachment she watched as he wiggled his body inside the slim crack between building and dumpster. A moment later a light flickered on and a beam shone back to illuminate the opening better.

As if this could get any better.

James twisted the light, the glow casting his face in an eerie kind of scary-movie shadow. "Come on, Autumn. It's not that bad once you get inside. Even got an air-freshener in here."

Cautiously, Autumn poked her head in, and immediately drew back. Stink aside (clean-mountain-mist did nothing in the face of that kind of smell), she couldn't get over what she was doing.

She shouldn't be here. She didn't want to live in this hot, stuffy metal box that smelled of rotted garbage. Just thinking about it made her skin crawl, her spine tingle, and her feet twitch. The thought of trying to sleep in that thing when she could be at home in her canopy bed, her babbling water-fountain bowl on the dresser soothing her to sleep, formed a funny twisty knot feeling in her chest. And of course, thinking of her bed got her thinking about her mother and how sweet her voice sounded when she sang to her at night. And Daddy—her lip trembled—if she stayed here she'd never hear another one of his fantastical stories. He'd never tuck her in again, either, pulling the covers to her chin as he told her how it was his way of hugging her all night long.

This place, this dumpster, was not home. She couldn't sleep here. Couldn't even force herself to squeeze her body in there.

Couldn't do it. Wouldn't.

"I want to go home!" she blurted, feeling childish, no babyish, in the face of James' obvious worldliness, but yet . . . yet . . . not really caring.

The light switched off. A moment later James squeezed back through the opening, his gaze steady as he looked her over from head to toe. Then he nodded and said, "I thought you might." As if her desire to go home had been a given, as if he'd known all along that that is what she'd do.

Autumn wondered how he could possibly have concluded that when even she hadn't known until now. An hour ago, no, two *minutes* ago, running had seemed the only option. But now?

Daddy can *fix anything.*

She believed it. Had to believe it. Because the alternative was unthinkable. Besides, her parents loved her. She knew they did. How many times had they both told her that no matter what she ever did or said that nothing could change that? True, she suspected they hadn't been thinking about something as awful of what she'd . . . what she'd . . . what she'd. . . .

"What's wrong, Autumn?"

Autumn sucked in a deep breath, the brown spots receding from her gaze. She tipped her head up to meet James' worried gaze and swallowed. "I don't know how I can go home. I don't know how to tell them about what I did."

There. It was out. Her worst fear was realized. Admitting she'd done something so horribly wrong. Admitting she hadn't lived up to their expectations. That she'd shamed herself.

James waved his hand. "Ah, that's easy."

She leaned in, gripping his arm eagerly. "You know how?"

"Sure. Just spit it out. Like a loogey."

Ugh. She dropped her hand. He was such a *boy*. That wasn't an answer. It was stupid and simple and . . . might work.

Running her tongue over her top lip she considered it. Tried to envision just blurting it out. *"Mommy, daddy, you know how you told me I should always try and act normal? How I should tell you if I ever had an itch?"* No. That wasn't quite right. *"Mom, dad. I was up on the roof and my head felt all tingly and then I saw this big cloud . . ."* Better, but not quite.

"Ah, jeez. You're thinking again, aren't you?"

She bristled, planting her hands on her hips. "Is there something wrong with thinking?"

"Only when you overdo it."

Autumn started to open her mouth to retort but he shushed her, his gaze rising meaningfully at the sky.

It was getting dark. And far past time to get home.

She looked around, tried to remember how they'd gotten there, and realized she had no idea.

"James? I don't remember how to—"

"No worries. I'll show you the way."

And he did. The two of them half-walked, half-ran through the streets. Autumn suspected he went so fast so that he could be rid of her as soon as possible. Or maybe he was just doing it so she couldn't slow down and "overthink" things again, but she didn't care. The closer and closer she got to home the less and less worried she became and the less and less she could even recall how angry her daddy had sounded when he'd tripped over her backpack in the stairs. She still feared what their reaction might be to what she'd . . . what she'd. . . .

She drew a deep breath through her nose, tried again. What she'd *done* when she'd "scratched the itch."

There, she'd thought it. Next step was just to come right out and say it. Which she knew now that she would, because she also knew that even if her daddy was as angry with her as he'd seemed to be with the "idiot" who'd chased away the storm, he wouldn't stop loving her. So knowing that, it was on feet of anxiousness and not anxiety that she finally flew through the front doors of her apartment building.

She was halfway through the front lobby when she skidded to a stop. Unable to go on. Something was wrong. Something was. . . .

"James!" She spun around, saw that he'd stopped at the door and was about to take the steps down out of the lobby.

"Yeah?" He took a hesitant step forward, his head tipped questioningly.

This was the problem. Somehow things with James didn't feel finished. She wasn't sure how to fix it, but. . . .

She raced back to him, reaching out to grab his arm. "James?"

"Yeah?" He sounded more annoyed now than curious.

Her cheeks heated and she dug her toe into the runner in the lobby, ruffling the oriental design. "Thanks for, um, bringing me home."

She took a peek up at him. He dropped his obvious annoyance long enough to give her his own pink-cheeked smile. "You're welcome."

She hurried on; afraid he'd leave before she could finish that something that needed finishing. Whatever it was. "And thanks for offering your hiding place. It was really nice, even if I didn't end up needing it."

"No problem." He jerked his shoulders up and down. "And don't worry about not digging my hide-out. I don't think any normal girl would."

And there it was. What she had to tell him. She straightened, bracing herself for the revelation, sure it was going to be a real shocker. "James?"

"Yeah?" he asked, hesitantly this time.

"I'm not a normal girl."

His face twisted into a scrunch, his gaze seeming to measure her words, and then his mouth split in a big grin, and he nodded. "Good."

"Good?"

"Yeah," he shrugged. "Good. Who would want to be normal anyway?" And with that he turned and bolted out the door.

Autumn stood, watching the swing of the closing door to the street. All of a sudden a smile took over her face and she spun about, her feet skipping as she raced up the stairs for home. *Who would want to be normal anyway?* She'd never thought of it that way.

CONTINUING EDUCATION

Kristine Smith

"**W**here the hell have you been?"

I looked up from my laptop to find Jerry Pope standing in the classroom doorway. "What?"

"Oh, Lee, no—I didn't mean—" Jerry swore under his breath, his moonface the same beet red as his polo shirt and shiny with sweat. "I thought you were Sheryl. You've both got that blonde short kinda—" He mimed fluffing his hair and tucking it behind his ears. "You know."

"Yeah." I stood, cracked my back, took a swig from my water bottle. "And I'm wearing jeans and a turtleneck and she's wearing a corduroy dress and is about six inches taller and three sizes smaller than I am. Other than that, we look exactly alike."

"Look, I'm sorry, OK. Have you seen her or not?"

"Not since lunch."

Jerry waved to someone down the hall. "Lee hasn't seen her either." He threw his hands in the air. "We're presenting our case study in a half hour, and she has the slide deck."

Oh boy. Now I knew why Jerry's sharp edges were on full display. "That's Derivatives with Ashford?"

"Yeah, that bitch. We're first out of the box, and if we're late, she docks us half a grade like we're in goddamn kindergarten." Jerry paced a tight circle. "We were supposed to meet Sheryl downstairs to do a run-through, but we've searched every room in this damn building and there's no sign of her." He bounced on the balls of his feet like a sprinter warming up, then took off, deck shoes squeaking on the linoleum.

"Good luck." I stepped out into the corridor, and waited until he vanished around the corner. "You'll need it." I refilled my water bottle from the fountain across the hall. Returned to the classroom and my desk by the window, and looked out in time to see Jerry hustle across the street, Lorne and Pat on his heels. Three balding thirty-somethings in polo shirts and khakis talking, or in Jerry's case, yelling, on their smartphones. *Desperately seeking Sheryl.* I watched them trot up the narrow street, then make a hard right at the corner and head in the direction of the library.

I had never taken a class with Ashford—she taught finance track and I studied management—but I had heard stories. "Are you late to your meetings in the real world, Mister Pope?" I took a stab at the woman's nasal singsong. "Then I expect you to arrive in time for mine." Poor Jerry. He really should have known better. Sheryl Quade had earned a reputation for dependability over the past year—you could depend on her to let you down. She missed assignments, skipped classes, and never pulled her weight in group projects. During one Saturday

night get-together, she admitted that she had only en-
rolled in an MBA program to meet people. At the time,
no one had believed her.

"We do now." I rested my forehead against the window, and felt the soft heat of the early fall sun through
the glass. Looked out over the short street lined with red
brick buildings, copper roofs gone antacid green with
age, as the sales pitch from that never-quite-forgotten
television commercial drifted through my head. *Tired of
your job? Stuck in a rut? Come build a new future at the
Old Campus of Monckton College.*

And so we came, the bored and the ambitious and the
confused, in search of that crumb of knowledge, that secret handshake, that would turn our lives around. Monckton went out of its way to make it easy for us, their older
students. Online classes were the rule, with only one
weekend a month spent on a quiet, wooded campus that
looked like something out of an old movie.

Get the degree, Lee, my ever-helpful managers told
me. *Can't get anywhere these days without it.*

Maybe you'll meet someone, my ever-helpful friends
told me. *It's been two years, girl. It's time.* I touched my
left hand, still weighted down by a gold band that was no
longer there. Tried to recall details of projects that had
consumed me only twenty-four hours before, and realized that I couldn't even remember my network passwords.

What the hell am I doing here? I stared out at the
bright fall sky until my eyes watered, then returned to
my chapter on viral marketing.

Marketing wasn't a favorite subject, but I muddled
through the four hours of quiz and lecture and breakout

session. The instructor's name was Magory, a wrinkled walnut of a man with the scant remains of a brogue. He had once owned a chain of landscaping companies, according to the faculty directory. Now, he paced back and forth in front of a roomful of doggedly rapt adults, the sleeves of his overlarge sweater flapping as he gestured like a conductor and tried to impress upon us how quickly an idea could snowball once planted in a single mind.

I had taken my usual seat by the window, and glanced out every so often at the fading day. The classroom overlooked a picnic area that we had claimed as our own during the summer. It stood deserted now, a rise of still-green lawn dotted with red-berried shrubbery, shaded by a surround of oaks. The umbrella tables and chairs had been stored away for the winter, leaving a pair of stone benches the only furnishing. As the sun set, the gold light of dusk filtered through the leaves, casting the scene in sepia. The place looked older than old now. Ancient. Timeless.

The side of my face tingled. I turned to the front of the room to find Magory watching me. He made no comment about my inattention, but continued to lecture, eyes glittery as flint.

"All it takes is one. If you remember nothing else I tell you, remember that." A corner of his mouth twitched. Then he flipped off the lights and tried to turn on the VCR, struggling with it until Neil took pity and helped him.

"Modern times." Magory stood to one side and shook his head, the technically challenged old timer, and waited until Neil inserted the tape and got the thing going.

*   *   *

The following Saturday morning, I ran into Jo Tate in the coffee shop. Like me, she had settled on the management track. Unlike me, she braved the occasional foray into the world of finance, which this semester meant Ashford's derivatives class.

"It was horrible." Jo hugged her coffee cup. "Sheryl never showed, and Ashford just let them have it in front of everyone. I mean, they tried to wing it, but what could they do? Sheryl had everything." She dug through her handbag, pulled out a bottle of ibuprofen. "'Failure to plan,' Ashford said. 'Failure to anticipate.' You know how red Jerry's face turns when he's pissed? I thought he was going to have a stroke right there at the podium." She shook out a couple of tablets, tossed them back and chased them with the last of her orange juice. "I didn't see him at the dorm last night. Every Friday, he checks in by 7:30, then stakes out a table in the break room and works until all hours, but last night I didn't see him."

"Maybe he couldn't get in until this morning. He's got a crazy job." Jerry had never been my favorite classmate, but he had only been at his company a few months and had a fresh divorce under his belt besides. I may not have liked him much, but I felt sorry for him. "We have the same class this morning. Keep an eye out."

"We all have crazy jobs." Jo looked around the coffee shop, filled wall-to-wall with continuing ed students forcing carbs and caffeine in preparation for 8AM classes. "No, I bet he quit. I wouldn't be able to face anyone here ever again if Ashford chewed me out like that."

As if on cue, the door opened and in walked the dreaded Ashford, followed by another instructor. Hawthorn, his name was, a tall, pale counterpoint to his companion's rounded brunette bustle. The sea of bleary-eyed bodies parted before them as they made their way across the room, leaving lowered voices and sidelong glances in their wake. They slipped through gaps in the crowd to the counter, snagging the attention of one of the clerks and placing their order before anyone could complain. Assuming anyone would.

"Must be nice to live in a world where lines are for other people." Jo shook her head. "Eight more weeks of her royal highness." Her eyes widened as Ashford turned, cup in hand, and fixed on us. "Oh, shit. Incoming."

Ashford maneuvered to our table, Hawthorn at her shoulder. "Ah. The quiet ones." She set down her coffee and grabbed a handful of sugar packets out of the serving dish. "Every time I see you, you are in a corner, watching." Ripping sounds punctuated every word as torn paper and sugar crystals scattered across the tabletop. "Or looking out a window, dreaming." She shot me a look and her eyes reminded me of Magory's, tiny, dark and stone-like, the whites barely visible. "Kincaid, I believe. Lee Kincaid." She nodded to me. "Hawthorn here has told me something of you."

"Really?" I looked up at Hawthorn, met eyes the clear green of the edge of glass, and wondered how he could have learned anything about me. He taught special topics, industrial espionage, Ponzi schemes and scandals of various types, and I had never taken a class with him.

"Magory likes you," he said, answering my question. His voice was deep and quiet, barely audible above the din.

"That's good to know." I felt my face heat, broke eye contact, ripped pieces off my bagel just to have something to do with my hands.

"Is that any good?" Ashford pointed at my plate. "What kind is it?"

"Cinnamon-raisin." I glanced at Jo, who bit her lip and stared at her coffee. "Toasted. With butter."

"I must try that some time." Ashford stood next to an empty chair, yet made no move to sit. She looked older than she sounded, older than she behaved, and had taken no pains to cover the years. Her sallow skin bore no trace of make-up. Her clothes were dull, gray trousers and a plain blouse, the only hint of color an odd necklace of red and pink beads. "I thought I might see you in Derivatives with your friend." She nodded toward Jo. "I want more females in my classes. Instead, I have males who all want to be multimillionaires by midterms."

"You have Sheryl." I fielded a blank look. "Sheryl Quade. She's in your class."

"She has dropped." Ashford sniffed. "She will not be back." She sipped her coffee, frowned, then grabbed the last sugar packet and dumped it in. "The talents of some are better applied elsewhere." She tried her coffee again, shrugged, then turned and headed for the door.

"Good morning." Hawthorn nodded, then followed after her.

"I don't know where in hell they find them," Jo said as soon as they were out of earshot. She gathered up empty packets and dropped them in the bowl, then swept off the spilled sugar. "They must work cheap."

I watched Hawthorn step off to one side as Ashford stopped to harass another unlucky soul. He scanned over the heads of the assembled with occasional glances toward the door, raising his head as though sniffing the air.

Then he looked back over his shoulder at me, and at

that moment I knew how the deer felt when the wolf met its eye.

Eventually he smiled, breaking the spell. Ashford beckoned to him, and he followed her out of the coffee shop like a pale shadow.

"I think Hawthorn must have worked in security." I tried to eat my bagel, but nerves still had me by the throat, and I pushed it aside.

"I'm not saying they don't know the subject matter." Jo pulled a packet of wet wipes from her bag, and went about cleaning her hands. "But you have to admit that they lack people skills. I mean, isn't that something they're supposed to teach us, and not the other way around?" She checked her watch, and sighed. "If you had told me on the day I graduated that ten years later I'd be going through the same old crap all over again, I'd have said you were crazy."

We dumped our trash and headed outside. The morning had dawned cool and gray, the air heavy with hair-frizzing damp. Jo pulled an elastic band from her jacket pocket and bound her mass of black ringlets. "I checked the weather in Atlanta this morning. 70s and sunny. Tell me again why I left."

"Hypothermia slows the aging process." We walked down the tree-lined street to our building, and climbed the four flights to our classroom because the elevator was out of order yet again.

"I don't see Jerry." Jo stood in the doorway and counted heads. "He always sits in the front row and he is not here."

We took our seats, and readied for four hours of Management Principles IV. At the stroke of eight, our instructor entered. Alder, a tall, pale, willowy woman, who looked enough like Hawthorn to be his twin. Funny that I never noticed it before.

That evening, the gang went to dinner at an Italian place off-campus. I begged off, claiming a day job crisis, but the truth was that I just didn't want to go. I knew they would pick over every bit of gossip they knew about Sheryl and Jerry—Sheryl had also recently gone through a divorce, and was worried about being laid off—and I didn't want to hear it. Restlessness had claimed me, and I needed to walk. Needed to clear my head.

She has dropped. She will not be back. Ashford's words about Sheryl kept looping through my head. That clipped, cool voice of hers.

"Bet you know what happened, don't you, highness?" I left the dorm, and walked up one tree-enclosed street and down the next. There weren't many people out and about, but I felt safe enough. Had my phone in my pocket, and my car keys in hand. *Never go anywhere without your keys*, my late father had always told me. *Good for fighting off all kinds of things, keys are.*

I thought about my father as I walked. I thought about a lot of things. The night held a bite, an early taste of winter. There was no wind to speak of, and fog laced the air. I had worn the wrong coat—leather isn't worth a damn in the cold—and I shivered as the damp chill seeped through. I couldn't tell where I was. I had never learned the campus street names and all the buildings looked alike, amorphous smears of black that loomed on either side.

Then I saw a couple of patches of paleness in the distance, which resolved into stone benches as I moved closer. I had arrived at the picnic spot. The low hill.

I stuffed my hands in my pockets, wished like hell that I had worn a decent coat. The air felt even colder here, the fog heavy enough to mist my skin and drip from the leaves. I ducked into a building entry and was about to go inside and grab some paper towels from the bathroom when I heard voices from the direction of the street. A man and a woman, arguing.

I hid in the shadows and squinted into the murk, picked out the shapes moving toward me. The woman was tall and very slim, her coat belted tightly and her hair hidden beneath a brimmed hat. The man stood half a head shorter, his leather jacket zipped to the neck, a backpack dangling from one shoulder.

"I don't believe—I let you talk—me into this." The man struggled to keep up with his companion, his breathing rough, chubby legs moving like pistons. "Couldn't we just do an extra paper? Clap erasers?" Then the muted light of a streetlamp washed over him, and smears of color snapped into sharper relief.

"Jerry?" I stepped out of the entry. "Jerry!"

Jerry Pope stopped short and stared at me, his mouth agape.

"Where have you been?" I trotted down the sidewalk toward him and his companion. "We all thought you dropped out." At that moment, the woman broke into a run, dashing across the street toward the rise. She tried to skirt the light, but just enough touched her to illuminate her face. "Sheryl?" I ran into the street. "Where the hell have you been?"

Jerry bolted after Sheryl, and together they darted toward the rise. I charged after them, the soles of my shoes sliding on the slick pavement, the damp grass. "Wait for me!" Just as I came close enough to grab Jerry's coat, I slipped and fell, my face mashing into the cold wet. I scrambled to my feet just as they disappeared behind the shrubbery. Heard a sound like the slam of a door. Circled to the rear of the rise and found—

—nothing. No one. I hunted through the surrounding trees, then returned to the rise. Perched on the edge of one of the benches and listened for any sound, the crack of a twig or muffled voices or the wheezing of a man unused to running. But I heard nothing except the steady tick of dewdrops on leaves, and the pounding of my blood in my ears.

"I know you're out there." I rose slowly, turned, stared into the fog, straining for any hint of movement, color, or shape. But I saw only a world wrapped in gauze, silent and pale.

I'm losing my mind. I shook my head. *No. I saw them. I did.* And then they vanished as though they'd never been.

I remained atop the rise for over an hour, hunting for any proof that I had seen Jerry Pope and Sheryl Quade. But I found nothing, no convenient dropped wallet or information-laden phone. Finally, I gave up and descended the slope, inching sideways to keep from skidding. Made it to the bottom intact, and started up the street. Saw something at the far end, and stopped.

It began as a curl in the mist, a pearlescent gleam, which darkened to a shadow, tall and slim. Then the fog split like a curtain being swept aside, and Hawthorn stepped through the gap. He said nothing, made no move to come closer. He just watched me, hands tucked in his pockets.

"I saw them." My voice rose and fell, wobbling from whisper to cry, buffeted by something that I couldn't see.

But I could sense it, oh yes. It brushed the hairs on the back of my neck, touched my fingers. Spoke in my ear, a language I had never heard before and couldn't understand.

All the while, Hawthorn remained still and silent, watching me. Then another wave of fog swept across the road, and he was gone.

By the time I got back to the dorm, Jo and the others had returned from dinner and had staked out a corner of the lobby. They had dragged every available chair and couch to form a circle, and huddled in conversation like conspirators planning a coup. They all turned to look when I entered, took up where they left off when they realized who I was.

"Day job crisis solved?" Jo patted the empty chair next to hers. "Saved you a seat."

"I can't. I need to get some work done." I ducked into the stairwell before Jo could question me further, took the steps two at a time. Hurried down the hall as though the devil himself was at my heels, keyed into my room and slammed the door so hard the wall shook. Backed into a corner and stood, shivering and hugging myself as delayed shock took hold.

"Knock, knock?" The door opened a crack, and Jo peeked inside. "Are you all right?" She looked at me, and her eyes widened. "No, you aren't, are you?" She stepped inside and closed the door. "What's the matter?"

"I'm okay. I'm just . . ." I forced myself to move into the middle of the room, even as I longed for the solid press of brick and plaster at my back. "Sometimes I wonder what the hell I'm doing here. Why did any of us come here? You can't go a mile in any direction in Illinois without tripping over an MBA program. There's the University of Chicago. Northwestern."

"Our companies wouldn't pay for UC or Northwestern." Jo sat on the edge of the bed. "And I hate to sound cruel, but could any of us have gotten into places like those? We're not exactly the movers and shakers here. We just want that piece of paper."

I walked to the window, twitched aside the curtain. The dorm overlooked a yard bordered on three sides by trees, rendered dark and solid as a prison wall by the night and the fog. "I just think there's something wrong here." I pressed my ear to the window, and heard the faintest rise and fall of a voice. It spoke the same weird language I had heard on the hill, and even though I couldn't understand the words themselves, this time I knew what they meant.

Come out, come out—we know where you are . . .

"Lee?" Jo got up and walked over to me. "You're spooking me, you know that?" She tugged me away from the window, then gripped my shoulders. "When you walked into the lobby, the look on your face. It was like you had seen a ghost. Did something happen?"

I started to speak, then stopped. How could I describe what I had seen without sounding crazy? Who the hell would believe me? "I'm just tired." I massaged my forehead. "I have a headache."

"Is it allergies? I have some meds that will knock you out for the night." Jo left, returning soon after with a glass of water and a pill bottle. "Take these. Get some sleep. I'll meet you in the morning for breakfast." She shook a couple of tablets into my hand, then patted my shoulder. "Maybe take a hot shower. They always relax me."

"I will. Thanks." As soon as Jo closed the door, I

locked it, then tossed the pills in the trash. Opened my laptop, and ran every kind of search on Monckton College that I could think of. What did I hope to find? A history of student disappearances? Evidence that the campus had been built on some ancient native burial ground?

Go to bed, Lee. Whatever was out there, I didn't want to face it in the dark. Better to wait for the light of the morning. All would be clearer then.

Slowly, eventually, the tension eased, leaving me yawning, exhausted. I didn't even bother to shower or change into pajamas. I just took off my jacket, stretched out on my bed and closed my eyes—

Come out!

I dragged my pillow over my head, and tried to shut out the voice. So high and light. If bells could talk, their speech would ring as these words did.

Come out, Kincaid! Now!

I struggled out of bed, knees weak and heart stumbling, and crept to the window. My hand hovered near the curtain. As much as I wanted to open it, did I really want to see what called to me?

Come out! Time for class to begin.

I pushed the curtain aside. The fog had thickened so that it flowed and swirled before my eyes, but I could pick out Ashford standing in the middle of the yard. She wore a raincoat as red as the beads she had sported that morning, and held a tray covered with a cloth.

Come out, Kincaid. Her lips never moved, yet her voice sounded clear. *You know you want to learn. You know you want to see.* She held the tray up to me. *I have what you seek right here, quiet one. In a few minutes you could know everything.*

I let the curtain fall and backed away from the window, images of what the tray might contain flitting through my head. I had watched too many horror movies growing up. The visions weren't pretty. *Jo*. I had to get her. She had to see this. I needed a witness. I felt like Alice, asked to believe impossible things, ridiculous things.

But as soon as I grabbed the doorknob, I stopped, and pressed my ear to the panel. Heard the barest footfalls in the hallway just outside. Child-light steps, back and forth.

Come out now!

I went to the desk and collected my car keys, then looked around for anything else I could use as a weapon. The twin bed consisted of a mattress and box spring on a metal frame, but I would have needed tools to pull it apart. The dresser and desk were built from wood.

I checked the closet. Instead of being bolted to the wall, the metal clothes pole rested in notches cut into a wooden frame. I pulled out my clothes and tossed them on the bed, then lifted out the pole, which turned out to be hollow but heavy nevertheless. I swung it back and forth, like a batter warming up. Strode to the door and flung it open, stepped into the hallway and saw ... no one.

"I'm losing it." I had strung perfectly normal events together, and spun an impossible tale. Sheryl and Jerry simply hadn't wanted to talk to me, for whatever reason. So they ran away from me and hid in the woods. And Hawthorn had simply gone for a walk. Was it a crime for an instructor to go for a walk?

But what about me? Explain me, Kincaid. Ashford's strange lilt, goading me, mocking me.

"I can't explain you." I slumped against the wall. "I don't think I want to."

But you've come this far. Laughing words, bright as coins, sharp and cool as winter. *You may as well come outside and learn the rest.*

"Maybe you're right." I returned to my room for my warm wool coat. My gloves. Muttered a prayer from my childhood, even though I doubted it would do any good. Hefted the clothes pole, dented and rough with rust. "I'm coming." I knew she heard me. I felt her smile.

Ashford still stood in the middle of the yard, the dim safety lighting encircling her. She laughed when she saw me. "I knew you couldn't stay away. I knew!" She started toward me, tray in hand.

I swung the clothes pole. "Stay away from me!" I stepped forward and swung it again, struck the tray and sent it flipping through the air, its contents scattering. Thick circles the size of my fist, with holes in their middles.

Then their smell hit me. Toasty. Buttery. Cinnamon and sugar and the yeastiness of fresh bread.

"Bagels? Are these bagels?" I picked up one of the halves that had rolled near my feet, felt the warmth through my glove, and flung it aside. "What the hell do you think you're doing?"

Ashford backed away each time I moved, her eyes on the pole. "They were a present. So you would join my class."

"I can't join your class. The add date's past."

"I could arrange it." Ashford's shiny pebble gaze moved to my face. "I can arrange anything. I have power. I am very powerful." She picked up one of the bagel halves, brushed off water and bits of leaf. "I can free you

from this world. No one will even know you've gone."
She held out the bagel. "Take it. Eat it."

I could see flecks of dirt stuck to the butter, which had
already solidified in the cold. I should have been re-
pulsed, but instead, my mouth watered and my stomach
rumbled and all I could think of was the saltiness of the
butter, the spicy taste of the bread and the softness of the
raisins. I reached out—

—then stopped as the clothes pole grew warm. I
looked down at it just as bits of rust flaked off and floated
to the ground.

"Put it down." Ashford's voice rattled against my ears,
its bell tones gone flat. "You tried to strike me with it.
That was evil of you. Put it down."

A few more flecks of rust peeled away, revealing shining silver metal beneath. Ashford's voice sounded harsh
now, a spoon banging against a pot, all beauty vanished.
"No. No, I think I'll keep it."

Ashford straightened quick as a cat and circled me,
taking care to stay just out of reach of the pole. "Evil.
Evil and cruel." Her fingers curled like talons. "Put it
down. I order you—"

"*Ash.*"

Ashford and I turned as one toward the voice. It came
from the shadows along the side of the building, a sound
soft yet firm. The warning growl of a wolf.

"What did I tell you?" Hawthorn walked out into the
circle of light. He wore no jacket against the cold, only
jeans and a heavy shirt, and the mist had matted his silvery hair into a skullcap. "That's not how we do things
now. We do not lie. We do not trick. This isn't a fairy tale."

"From the time of my father and your father, and
their fathers before them, and their fathers before them,

it was how we did things." Ashford glared at him. "It is what we are."

"Not anymore." Hawthorn looked down at the scattered bread, and sighed. "Are you all right?" He glanced at me, then back at the mess on the ground. "You look a little shaky."

"Just a little?" I stood aside as he picked up the tray and the cloth that had covered it and stuffed them in a trashcan.

"The animals can have the rest." Hawthorn joined Ashford in the middle of the lighted circle. "Do you want this one?"

"I don't know." Ashford regarded me sidelong. "I thought her quiet, but she doesn't listen."

"We want willing students, not slaves." Hawthorn met my eye. Then his green gaze moved down to the clothes pole. "And she understands. Without being told, she knows. There's memory there, from the time of her father, and his father before him, and his father before him. That is what we need. The old and the new, together." He continued to watch the pole as he spoke. It seemed to fascinate him, like tinsel draws a cat. "You're a Kincaid. Your family came from the old land."

"You heard her—" I pointed to Ashford, but I didn't know what to call her. Doctor Ashford? Professor? Your Highness? *Ash, like the tree.* "You heard her say my name in the coffee shop." My voice shook. Every time Hawthorn spoke to me, he implied he knew more than he let on. I didn't like it.

"Kincaid." The clothes pole didn't affect his voice as it had Ashford's. It still came soft, steady, persistent. "It's your father's name. You took it back after you and your husband—"

"*Yes.*"

His head dipped, and maybe it was an apology. Then he turned his attention to Ashford, who stood, arms folded. "Go back to your office, Lady. Leave this one to me."

Ashford let her arms fall to her sides. The top of her head barely reached Hawthorn's shoulder, yet at that moment she exuded just as much power. "You dare—"

"Yes, I do."

Ashford studied him for a time. Then she looked at me, and a smile played at the corner of her mouth. "Very well." She walked across the circle of light, and vanished into the dark.

Hawthorn finally turned to face me. "If I might have some of your time, Lee Kincaid?"

I looked at the dorm, counted up and across until I picked out my lighted window. Part of me wanted nothing more than to go back inside, burrow under the covers and sleep, forget any of this had ever happened.

Then I looked down at the pole. It had grown almost too hot to hold, the metal free of rust and as silvery as Hawthorn's hair. "All right."

"You don't need that, you know." For the first time, he sounded the faintest bit nervous.

I gripped the pole harder as again my father's voice sounded in my head. *Always have your keys with you.* But this time, I remembered the rest of his warning. *Always have some iron in your pocket.* He had told me it was for luck, but that had never made sense to me. Now, finally, I understood. "I think I'll hang onto it, if it's all the same to you."

Hawthorn hesitated. Then he gestured for me to join him.

We walked in silence. The chill had worsened, working its way through my coat, my gloves. Hawthorn's shirt had gone dark with damp and clung to his skin, and I shivered at the sight of him. "Aren't you cold?"

He shook his head. "It's refreshing." He closed his eyes for a moment, and breathed deep. "Like a plunge in a winter stream."

I waited for more, but he fell silent again, eyes fixed straight ahead. "I get the feeling I'm supposed to ask questions and you'll answer, but that's not really fair, is it? I don't even know where to start."

A hint of a smile. "I think you do."

"No, I really don't." A car drifted down a cross street, the driver hunched over the wheel and watching us. What drew his attention, Hawthorn's soggy appearance or my choice of walking stick? "One of yours?"

Hawthorn shook his head. "We can't drive."

I waited. Then I took my phone from my pocket, opened the browser, and keyed in *fear of steel iron metal*. Paged through the links to websites about steel markets and fears of strikes and commodities pricing until I found the link to a page that I knew to be the right one, even though this was the 21st century and we didn't believe in such things anymore. "The fae fear iron." I read for a time, then put my phone away. "Tall fae. Short fae. Light. Dark. Fae, fae everywhere."

"But yet you don't believe?"

"When I was in my room, I heard Ashford's voice in my head. Just as though she stood next to me, even though I knew she was out in the yard. It sounded lovely, until this started to work." I raised the pole, but when Hawthorn moved away from me, I lowered it. "You're here at Monckton because it's an old, out of the way place, all brick and wood and trees." I pointed to one of the buildings. "But there's iron in those, too."

"Not as much." Hawthorn's step had slowed to a stroll. "And what iron is there is covered by good wood and stone and plaster. The desks are wood."

"And the doorknobs are brass." We turned a corner, and I recognized one of the buildings I had passed earlier. "We're going to the hill, aren't we? If we'd turned left instead of right at the corner, we'd have gotten there faster."

"You seem to like to walk. I like to walk. I didn't think you'd mind." Hawthorn whispered, yet every word rang loud and clear.

My cheeks warmed, and I gave thanks for the dark. I quickened my pace, rounded another corner, and saw Sheryl and Jerry standing atop the hill at the street's end.

"It's better if you hear it from them." Hawthorn backed away from me. "Anything I would tell you would just be words. It's a big decision. You need to be sure."

Before I could ask him what he meant, Sheryl bounded down the hill toward us.

"Lee!" A grin split her face, and she radiated something I had never sensed in her in all the time I had known her. Confidence. Joy. She hugged me, as bouncy as a five-year-old on her birthday.

"I think this is the first time I've seen you smile." I looked past her to Jerry, who approached more slowly. "You finally found her."

"Yeah." Jerry shuffled up to us, hands stuffed in his jacket pockets. "That I did." He nodded at Hawthorn as if he were anyone else. A colleague. A classmate. A human being. "The rest is a sort of a blur, but I'm adjusting."

"Please tell me what's going on." I herded them down the sidewalk, away from Hawthorn. "Ashford tried to bribe me with bagels."

"Did you eat one?" Jerry frowned when I shook my head. "Then you're not committed. That's how it works. When you accept something from them, they have you. It's like a contract."

"You have to come live with us. It's wonderful." Sheryl twirled, her skirt billowing around her. "It's another land. Guinevere and King Arthur and the Lady of the Lake."

"Folklore major. Minor in anthro." Jerry jerked his head at her. "In case you couldn't tell."

"Oh, shut up." Sheryl bent close. "Ashford said she'd give us a second chance to do the presentation. But we needed to give something in return."

I looked back at Hawthorn, who stood some ways off next to an oak tree. He might have even been talking to it. His lips moved. "What exactly are you supposed to give?"

"Time." For the first time in my memory, Jerry looked thoughtful. "Our knowledge of being human. Some of them—" He laughed. "They're bored. Looking for something else. Excitement. Purpose. And there are corners in this world where they've found they can fit in, like here, and they want to learn how to fit in better. And that's what they need us for. To help them learn. To learn ourselves."

Sheryl patted his shoulder. "He's come so far in just one week."

"I'm not an idiot—I can see what's in front of me." Jerry looked at his watch. "We need to get going. There's a dinner, and we have to be there. First thing you learn is that they're picky about their rituals." As Sheryl ran ahead, he hung back. "Are you coming? It's not a bad place. Kinda like here, but the light's a little different."

He lowered his voice. "And right now it's just her and the guy who runs the candle store in town, and that's a little too much woo-woo for me."

"Jerry. You've gone to live with the fairies. You couldn't get much more woo-woo."

"Yeah, well." He watched Sheryl pirouette across the hill. "Food's good. Kinda starchy. They like cheese." He pondered for a moment. "Rugby. They play something like rugby. They like to have humans around because if there's a dispute, we can referee. We're impartial. They're like Cubs fans versus Sox fans once they get going." He shrugged. "It's not your everyday extra credit project. But I think I could get to like it. For a few weeks. Couple of months." He headed back up the street. "Maybe a year." He broke into a trot. "Hey, beats the shit out of the old 8 to 5!" He stopped to wave good-bye. Then he joined Sheryl, and together they walked behind the hill.

I saw a flare of light, a reflection on the fog, as though someone opened the door into a brilliantly lit house. Then it went dark, and I waited until I heard footsteps from behind. "You pick the ones who are having trouble here. The ones who don't belong. Who won't be missed."

"The ones who search for something they can't find here." Hawthorn drew alongside, bringing with him scents of moss and fresh cut grass. "Who can learn from us, and give something in return."

I breathed deep, felt the calm spread through me. No one had yet used the word *magic*, but wasn't that what this was? Hope, and the promise that there was still some wonder in the world? "They don't have to solve their problems. You give them a place to run to."

"We offer respite. Is that a crime?"

I thought for a moment. "Not sure if I consider Ash-ford respite."

Hawthorn smiled broadly, the skin at the corners of his eyes crinkling. "She spends most of her time here." His expression softened. "I, on the other hand, return quite often." He quieted, and a sense of waiting hung between us.

"I need to think about this." I backed away. Then I turned and walked back up the street, away from prom-ise, and hope, and magic. It took all the strength I had not to run.

By the time I got back to the dorm, animals had cleaned up the bagels. I returned to my room, put the clothes pole back in the closet. The steel had grown cold, smears of corrosion already marring the mirror finish. No more fae to trigger its power. No more wonder.

I sat at my desk, booted up my laptop, began reading the next day's assignment. Told myself that I would fix my life myself, solve my own problems. That anything I left behind would just be waiting for me when I returned.

Respite.

I called the company's 24-hour IT line, and got new network passwords. Logged into my work email account. Sixty-four messages since Friday afternoon, half marked URGENT.

Is that a crime?

I read the first message four times before it sank in. It was my turn to chair the monthly managers' meeting, and there was an agenda change I needed to make im-mediately. The usual life and death.

The old 8 to 5.

I got up, stretched my legs. Dug my coffeemaker out of the closet. I had just started adding coffee to the basket when I heard the voice drift through my head. Infinitely calm. Patient. And a little sad.

It's magic for us too, you know.

I went to the window to find Hawthorn standing in the yard, looking up at my window, hands in his pockets. "Stop reading my mind."

He shrugged. *It's what we do. You would have to get used to it.* He smiled. *Or you could learn to block it. Or you could learn to do it, too. The education goes both ways.*

The coffeemaker gurgled, and the thick aroma of the brew filled the room. I filled my mug, then wandered to the desk and stared down at my laptop. The display had gone into standby, my latest screensaver drifting in and out of focus. A forest scene, the foliage thick, impenetrable, a thousand shades of green. I thought about Sheryl's smile and Jerry's quiet understanding. Had they changed? Or had they rediscovered what they once had been, and found a place where they could be that way again?

I stared at the screensaver as the time ticked away and my coffee grew cold. Then I closed my laptop and shoved it into my shoulder bag. Threw in some makeup and a change of clothes. A couple of books. My coat. The clothes pole, I left behind. I didn't need protection any more.

I went outside to find Hawthorn waiting for me. He held a plate with a half a cinnamon-raisin bagel, toasted and buttered, and I ate it on the way. There was no great flash of light when I bit into it. No lifetime's worth of eldritch knowledge tumbled into my head. It was just a step forward, the first of many.

"The bagel of commitment." I held up the last bite, then popped it into my mouth. "To be followed at some point by the cheese danish of understanding." And I laughed like Sheryl had.

Hawthorn frowned. "Are you all right?"

"No. Yes." I quickened my pace. "I'm fine."

The hill came into view. It looked different now, the colors altered, like Jerry said they would be. Shades of green that I had never seen before, blended with blue and silver and gold. When we circled around to the back, I saw the opening, its faint outlines visible in the grass. Amazing how I could have missed it before. It seemed so obvious now. I started toward it, then stopped when I felt spreading heat in my coat pocket. I took out my car keys, and placed them underneath a rock.

"I'll watch them for you." Hawthorn stood off to one side. My gatekeeper. My guide. "Are you ready?"

I nodded.

The door opened, and I stepped inside.

HOW TO BE HUMAN™

Barbara Ashford

Is there anything more pathetic than a menopausal faery?

Yes. A menopausal male faery. Leading a motivational seminar for humans. At the New Rochelle Radisson.

For two hundred years, I had thrilled audiences with my interpretations of Lear and Othello, Hamlet and Brutus. Now I was instructing them in the fine art of How to Be Human™. A 21st century Charon, a fairy ferryman, guiding them across the River Shticks to the Wonderful World of Self-Actualization.

"True is it that we have seen better days."

But at least my new audiences loved me, too. Two hundred people filled the Empire Ballroom, shining faces lifted to mine like flowers seeking the sun.

Except Penny, my magenta-haired personal assistant. She was leaning on the wall by the display table, mouth agape in an enormous yawn.

Focus, Finn. You've got magic to do.

I could not afford to become distracted. My recent seminars had been marred by minor slip-ups: the occasional lapse of concentration; the momentary flash of impatience; the errant surges of power that shorted out electrical devices, set off sprinkler systems, and—on one memorable occasion—catapulted several members of the audience into orgasm. But I was on track today. In the groove, in the zone, in the money.

My gaze swept the Empire Ballroom. Rapt expressions—check. Heartfelt nods—check. Tears glistening on flushed cheeks . . . yes, it was time to wrap up my Sermon on the Self-Help Mount and send them off with some well-chosen platitudes.

Blessed are the cheese makers, indeed.

I detected an uneasy shift in the collective bliss, an unexpected spike of confusion. I shot a quick glance at Penny. Her mouth still hung open, but now she was gawking at me.

Dear gods, had I spoken aloud?

Something prickled in my armpits. Sweat. I was sweating like a human.

The overhead dome lights began to flicker. Heads tilted skyward. Murmurs rose from the crowd.

I was losing them!

I wrestled for control of both my power and my audience and desperately ad-libbed, "Monty Python's *Life of Brian* offers us many moments of pure silliness."

Heads jerked back toward the dais. Tentative smiles blossomed on a few faces.

"But the movie also teaches us an important lesson . . ."

"Do you want what's in the box or what's behind the . . ." No, you idiot. That's Monty Hall, not Monty Python. Think! You chose the name Phineas for a reason.

The lights returned to their normal brightness, and I smiled with renewed confidence.

". . . and that lesson is: always look on the bright side of life."

The appreciative chuckles offered new proof of Barnum's perspicacity: there really *was* a sucker born every minute.

Right. Time to get back on script before my glamour eroded completely. Serious expression. Firm nod.

"Our time together may be ending, but the journey has just begun. Hold on to the openness of mind and heart and spirit that brought you here."

It's easy if you buy my CD: How to Be Human™. On sale today for only $14.95.

"Embrace your higher self."

It's easy if you consult my How to Be Human™ daily affirmation cards. Business, Love, and Self-Esteem sets only $9.95 each. Boxed set—$26.95.

"And remember our five touchstones."

A graceful wave of my hand and the phrases I had been drumming into their empty heads since 10:00 A.M. promptly appeared on the giant projection screen behind me:

*H*alt Hurtful Habits.
*U*nleash Your Potential.
*M*anifest Your Possibilities.
*A*ffirm Your Transformation.
*N*urture Your New Self.

Utter drivel, of course. But sprinkle it with a little faery dust and they lap it up.

"Lord, what fools these mortals be!"

"Maintain the unshakeable belief in your power to fulfill your destiny. And when you stumble—as we all do . . ."

Cheese makers, anyone?

". . . just pick yourself up, dust yourself off . . ."

And sign up for my advanced weekend seminar: How to Live Human™.   •

". . . and proclaim to the world that you are a glorious, accomplished, authentic human being!"

I flung out my arms as if to hug the whole sorry lot of them. Braced for their reaction, I barely winced when they leaped to their feet, applauding and whistling. When I was young, the turbulence of human emotions merely fed my power. Now, I had to shield myself to prevent such displays from overwhelming me.

I descended from the dais, cringing inwardly as I accepted the clumsy embraces of my fans and made approving noises about their "transformations." My senses reeled from their aroma, that oh-so-human tang of sweat and excitement and flesh. A depressing reminder of my own mortality. True, I would never suffer the indignities of physical aging. My flesh would remain firm, my hair black and glossy. But as my power waned, so would I. Until I simply . . . faded away.

The tales never mention that when they describe my kind as ever-young. Or the humiliation of leaving your clan to spare your kinfolk the unpleasant spectacle of your final passage. Why else would so many fae abide in this world? Not because of some fatal attraction to humans as the tales would have it. But those, of course, were written by humans. What did they know?

My spirits rose when I spied the hotel's special events coordinator hovering in the doorway. Elena? Helena?

Something. My memory was becoming as unreliable as my power.

I freed my arm from the claw-like grip of a portly woman wearing an "Ask Me How to be Human™" T-shirt and sauntered across the ballroom.

As soon as I'd met Elena/Helena/Something, I'd decided to invite her to my room tonight. I was always keyed up after a seminar, and sex provided a relaxing antidote. I'd learned long ago to avoid liaisons with my personal assistants. And certainly, there was little about Penny to tempt me. She was as alluring as a rack of antlers. Too skinny, too young, too many piercings in far too many places. And that dreadful hair.

Elena/Helena/Something, on the other hand, was exactly the kind of woman I enjoyed: attractive in a vaguely Caribbean way, conservatively dressed in a charcoal business suit, black hair tightly coiled in a bun, friendly but not overtly sexual in her manner. There was little sport in seducing a willing human. The challenge lay in chipping away that initial reluctance. A little power, a little charm and her skirt would be up, her panties down, her long hair veiling my face like a dark waterfall, and heigh-ho, Silver! Away!

My smile grew more intimate, my gaze more compelling. I could sense her growing interest, smell the delicious musk of feminine desire.

To my dismay, that fragrance triggered a precipitous surge of power. Before I could suppress it, Elena/Helena/Something was standing very close, clinging to my arm, wetting her lips with a decidedly gristly-looking tongue. Her strident laughter grated on my ears and her incessant head-tossing set her four hoop earrings and my nerves a-jangle.

Silently cursing, I reined in the power, thanked Elena/Helena/Something for all she had done to ensure today's success, and fled, leaving Penny to pack up the merchandise.

I hurried up the wide carpeted stairs to the lobby, then followed the fire stair up four flights to my floor; after my humiliating performance with Elena/Helena/Something, I simply couldn't endure the prospect of being trapped inside the elevator's steel cage.

Safe inside my room, I stood before the window, uncomfortably transfixed by my reflection in the glass. I looked so ordinary in my black jeans and pale blue cashmere sweater. I might actually *be* a man.

"O, that way madness lies; let me shun that."

Turning off the lights banished my reflection if not my melancholy, and allowed me to enjoy the beauty that was nighttime New Rochelle: the white glow of passing headlights, the warmer patchwork of lamplight from nearby apartment buildings, and the multi-colored brilliance of a CVS pharmacy, an Enterprise Rent-a-Car, and a Taco Bell.

I yanked the drapes closed and turned the lights back on. A cool shower refreshed me, as did the four pints of milk I had stocked in the small refrigerator. Far too restless to retire for the evening, I considered a brisk walk to the Long Island Sound. The fresh air would soothe me. And that open expanse of water. There might even be a park. Any small patch of green would do.

But that was impossible. There were other fae in the city. Young ones. I'd sensed them when I ventured outside during the lunch break. The last thing I wanted was to encounter fae adolescents. They could be so cruel, flaunting their ripening power to humiliate the old.

Gods. In the course of an hour, I'd shrunk from mighty Charon to Betty White. I, who could have been as great a violin virtuoso as Paganini, as dazzling a pianist as Liszt, as acclaimed an actor as Gielgud or Olivier or Booth. Edwin, of course, not his hapless brother. I would have eclipsed them all if not for the need to conceal my power.

A need that had inhibited my ascent as a pabulum peddler as well. I could never aspire to the heights—or the speakers' fees—of a Wayne Dyer or a Zig Ziglar. Finn Shepherd was doomed to play the straw-hat circuit of self-help, not Broadway.

The curse of the fae—always to skulk in the shadows. But not, I vowed, in a hotel room.

I strolled through the lobby without attracting more than a passing glance from the few people I encountered. The pretty gay boy playing the grand piano brightened as I approached, and I lingered to listen to his rendition of "You Do Something to Me." But when he segued into "Send in the Clowns," I dropped a five-dollar bill into his porcelain dish and headed to the bar, hoping for more interesting fare in the City Martini Lounge.

Instead, a collection of paunchy middle-aged businessmen clustered around the central bar. In the adjacent seating area I saw a man and woman on what appeared to be a dismal first date and two fortyish women with big hair and embattled faces who assessed me with the narrowed eyes of desperation.

And Penny.

She fixed me with her annoyingly direct stare as I threaded my way through the maze of impossibly small café tables and climbed onto the stool opposite hers. I glanced quickly at the drinks menu, shuddered at the list of specialty martinis with names like "Panties Off!" and "Horny Ape," and ordered a single malt whisky.

Penny contented herself with slurping a martini roughly the same color as her hair until the waitress departed with my order. Then she rolled her eyes.

"Blessed are the cheese makers?"

My withering look had no apparent effect on her. I'd never been able to decide if Penny possessed some strange immunity to my power or if she was simply oblivious to everything. I'd tested her extensively during her interview. Hiring someone with a high tolerance to glamour avoided the potential for annoying personal entanglements and uncomfortable questions.

Even during these last six months, dear dense Penny merely saw the outward manifestations of my power surges—the errant sprinklers, the power outages—and failed to identify me as the cause. Far more difficult to hide something like the cheese maker debacle.

"My mind wandered. It happens."

"Yeah. More and more frequently."

I accepted my single malt whisky, downed it in one gulp, and handed the glass back to the waitress for a refill. Penny began whistling. "Always Look on the Bright Side of Life," of course.

"Yes. Thank you, Penny. How did we do on sales?"

"Thirty-three copies of the book. Fifty-four CDs. Ninety-eight sets of affirmation cards."

A good haul, but not spectacular. Especially since forty percent of the proceeds would go to my business manager. A regrettable necessity for someone who possessed no official identity. I suppose I could have found a shady lawyer to manufacture the requisite documents, but it was easier to pay Sheldon to handle everything. The fae are notoriously lazy when it comes to such details. That was one of the reasons I valued Penny; in spite of her many flaws, she was good with accounting and travel arrangements and other mundane tasks.

Penny sucked down the last of her grotesque drink—the sound unpleasantly reminiscent of a death rattle—and asked, "So what is it with you lately?"

"I beg your pardon?"

"Last weekend you went off on some tangent about Edmund Booth."

"Edwin."

"Tonight it was Monty Python. I'm just asking 'cause I want to be prepared for tomorrow's seminar in Stamford. What's it gonna be? The Three Stooges?"

"I've been working too hard."

Penny snorted.

"As you might have realized if you bothered to attend any of my recent seminars instead of slinking off to ... wherever."

"Maybe I'll start sitting in again. Your senior moments sure liven things up."

"They are *not* senior moments!"

Penny flinched. The big-haired women twisted around to stare at me. Everyone was staring at me. All conversation in the lounge had ceased. Even the piano had gone silent. And I was sweating. Again.

The soft patter of footsteps broke the appalling silence.

"Everything okay here?" our waitress inquired nervously.

My withering stare proved more effective with her.

She visibly recoiled, trembling. Aware that I was only making matters worse, I suppressed my annoyance and offered her a repentant smile.

"Another whisky, please. A double."

As she retreated, Penny whispered, "Jeez, I was just kidding. Lighten up, will you?"

"Forgive me. I'm a bit ... tired tonight. You have no idea how exhausting it is to say the same things over and over again."

Penny muttered something under her breath. Once, I would have been able to make out the words. Now, I had to ask, "What was that?"

Her defiant glare took me aback. "I said, 'Especially when you don't mean any of them.'"

I mentally counted to ten before asking, "What does that have to do with it?"

"Why the hell do you think I skip out as soon as you start lecturing?" she demanded in a fierce whisper. "It's not what you say. I mean, it's mostly stupid stuff that people should be able to figure out for themselves, but it's not lies or anything. But you don't believe a word of it. And you obviously think everyone in the audience is a sad, lonely, desperate loser."

"They *are* sad, lonely, desperate losers."

"Then you should feel some compassion for them! Not contempt."

I couldn't very well tell her all fae felt contempt for humans. So I merely said, "I do feel compassion."

"Bullshit."

I stared at her, astounded by this unexpected rebellion.

"You don't care about the people who come to you. You don't care that they need your help."

"I help them."

"You don't even look at them. Do you have any idea how many are coming back two-three-four times?"

Repeat business. That was encouraging. I couldn't understand why Penny was scowling.

"Don't you get it, Finn? It wears off! For a little while, they think they're on to something. And then that good feeling just . . . vanishes. Some of them notice as soon as you leave the dais. For others, it probably takes days."

Well, that was only to be expected. Some humans were more susceptible to faery glamour than others.

"And they're so desperate to recapture it that they come back again and again. Don't you see anything wrong with that?"

On the contrary, it seemed ideal. But clearly, that was the wrong response.

"I see that they haven't fully absorbed what I've attempted to teach them and are eager to try again."

"Why don't you just shill your self-help crap on the Home Shopping Network? At least that way, I wouldn't have to watch what you do to them."

If only I could. Unfortunately, faery glamour tended to interfere with the operation of cameras. The photographer who had shot the glossy headshots that adorned my merchandise had spent a full day retouching them before he'd managed to remove the rainbow of light obscuring my features.

Mercifully, the waitress's arrival gave me an excuse to avoid a response. I sipped my drink, enjoying the heat that blossomed in my belly. For all their failings, humans did have a few gifts. Distilling whisky was one of them.

Penny regarded me with a stony stare, arms folded across her meager chest.

"If you disapprove of me so much, I wonder why you remain."

"Because I'm stupid. I keep hoping you'll change."

Another thing to which the fae could not aspire. Oh, we made minor accommodations to pass in this world, but the only genuine change we underwent was the one that had begun draining my power and my life force.

Penny's head drooped, affording me a view of her blonde roots. I'd seen her with so many different dye jobs that I'd forgotten her real hair color.

Summoning a magisterial calm, I told her that we were both tired, that the schedule in recent months had been arduous, that next week would give us a much-needed break during which to review our options.

In the middle of my monologue, Penny's head came up. To my astonishment, tears glistened in her eyes.

"Fuck you, Finn. I don't need to review my options. I quit."

She fumbled in her belt pouch and produced a red-and-white brochure that she slapped onto the table. Then she hopped off her stool and clumped out of the lounge.

Heaving a long-suffering sigh, I picked up the brochure. It was a train schedule for the Metro-North New Haven line. Did she actually expect me to take a train to Stamford? When she knew that riding on trains and planes made me queasy? And what about my merchandise? How was I supposed to lug five enormous boxes on public transportation? Her selfishness was simply unbelievable!

My power began to roil. The shot glass trembled in my clenched fist. Before it could shatter, I bolted the whisky and signaled for the waitress. I scrawled my room number on the bill and scrambled off my stool, shooting a murderous glance towards the lobby when I recognized the strains of "People" coming from the gay boy's piano.

People who need people are *not* the luckiest people in the world. They're as sad and lonely and desperate as the ones who attended my seminars.

Spying another exit, I veered away from the lobby, grimacing when I noticed a short flight of semi-circular stairs carpeted in faux tiger skin that led to some sort of "jungle room." The young couple seated in the rattan armchairs gaped at me as I stormed past, but I didn't care. I had to get out before my power shattered every window in the lounge.

I flung open the glass door and darted onto a brick patio, where I forced myself to slow lest some passing human notice my otherworldly speed. A walkway lined with tall, ornamental shrubs offered a modicum of privacy. I followed it away from the covered entryway of the hotel and picked my way into a small patch of pachysandra.

Earth below me. A haze-shrouded moon above. A cool breeze—redolent with the salty spray of the sea—kissing my face. The embrace of the elemental forces of nature allowed me to slough off the unpleasantness with Penny. The proximity of the spring equinox helped me regain my sense of balance. A few deep, cleansing breaths and I was calm again.

Then I felt them. The same fae I had sensed earlier. Only much closer now.

The energy seemed to be coming from that tall building a block away with the words "The Lofts at New Roc City" emblazoned in white neon. An apartment complex, perhaps? But if memory served, New Roc City was some sort of indoor amusement park. A perfect spot to troll for humans. And so easy to lure them away from such mundane forms of recreation as movies and mini-golf and bowling.

Their energy pulsed with excitement; clearly, they had sensed me, too. I hoped they were merely curious. If they considered me an interloper, there would be trouble. I was still strong enough to defend myself from a lone at-tacker, but against a gang of young fae . . .

My only option was to scurry back to the hotel. Hu-miliating to flee, but I would be safe there; even they would never cause a scene in public. This little garden was just dark enough to represent a challenge.

I turned toward the hotel entrance and drew up short when I discovered Penny trotting down the walkway. I groaned aloud and hurried towards her.

"We need to talk," she said.

"Not here. Not now."

"Yes, here. Yes, now."

I seized her arm. She planted her feet like a recalci-trant mule.

"Penny, please. . . ."

But it was already too late. A shadowy figure flitted across the patio. Another eased between the shrubs. I whirled around and spied a third mounting the stairs that led down to the parking lot.

Theatre critics had compared me to the greatest ac-tors throughout history. Women and men alike had wept and cheered at my performances. All show, of course. No substance. Like my seminars. The fae would sense that. But show was all I had.

Penny stiffened, finally noticing their presence. They closed in slowly—two boys and a girl hovering on that dangerous cusp between adolescence and adulthood. In spite of my fear, I had to admire their ineffable grace and beauty. Even their grungy clothes and carefully maintained glamour failed to conceal it completely.

A wave of longing suffused me—for my youth, for Faerie. It had been so long since I had encountered any of my kind.

The taller boy grinned at me. The other one scowled. The girl simply maintained a watchful distance.

I offered them a brief nod of greeting, but placed my hand over my heart in token of my peaceful intent. "Good evening, friends."

The tall boy snickered. "You old guys always have such nice manners."

I merely nodded and tightened my grip on Penny's arm. Of course, the boy noticed; they noticed everything at that age: the smallest gesture, the underlying anger hidden behind a smile.

He nodded toward Penny. "She yours?"

"Yes."

Penny stirred restively, and the boy grinned. "She doesn't seem to think so."

"Suppose we leave her out of this."

"Suppose we don't want to."

"I'm not looking for trouble."

"I don't expect you are."

"We're only here for the day. We'll be leaving in the morning."

"Maybe."

He rocked casually on the balls of his feet. The girl sidled a little closer. I retreated into the pachysandra, pulling Penny with me.

"Penny," I said without taking my gaze from them,

"why don't you go back to the hotel? I'll join you in a moment."

"No."

"Penny . . ."

"I'm staying with you."

I risked a glance at her. Her pointed chin was thrust out defiantly, but I could feel the tremors coursing through her arm.

"Can't control your girlfriend?" the shorter boy taunted.

"You know how it is with these old guys," the taller one replied. "Control's the first thing to go."

Penny bristled like an angry cat. "Go fuck yourself, asshole."

"You're not helping," I muttered between clenched teeth.

"Maybe we'd rather fuck you," the tall boy said, still smiling pleasantly.

"Maybe I'd rather fuck a duck."

My breath hissed in. If they were merely human adversaries, it would have been foolhardy to provoke them. But to antagonize three young fae looking for a little sport on a Saturday night . . .

Thank all the gods in this world and the other, they seemed more amused than angered by her truculence. But that, of course, could change in a heartbeat.

"Maybe we should fuck a duck and then fuck her," the short one suggested. Rather unimaginatively, I thought. Even the fae had lost some of their cleverness over the centuries.

That helped calm me. I even managed to infuse my voice with a hint of boredom. "Maybe we should all just go our separate ways."

The tall boy shrugged. "Not much fun in that."

"Or this."

"For you, maybe."

He darted toward us, and I yanked Penny away so abruptly that she gasped. Too intent on the boys, I failed to notice the girl until Penny gasped again.

The girl snaked her left arm around Penny's waist and pulled her close. Her right hand came up to caress the spiky magenta hair. Penny's face contorted with anger and then relaxed as those green fae eyes ensnared her.

"Pretty," the girl said, tweaking a spike.

The boys chuckled, content to watch—for now.

"Let her go."

"Soon."

Penny's terror battered my senses, but her gaze was wide and trusting, her mouth curved in a hesitant smile. The girl's lips brushed Penny's temple. Her tongue flicked out to lap against Penny's cheek. Her hand slid down that slender throat to cup a small breast.

The flood of emotion took me by surprise. Fear. Rage. Possessiveness. Humiliation. And something else I failed to identify as my control snapped and my pent-up emotions coalesced into a wave of power that knocked the fae girl backward and made the shorter boy wince. I heard the crack of shattering glass as the lamps illuminating the patio exploded, the icy tinkle of the shards pattering onto the bricks, and my voice thundering, "That's enough!"

I sensed more than saw Penny's legs buckle and flung my arm around her waist. If I'd had enough power, I would have given her calm and reassurance, but all I could do was hold her.

The girl's lips curled in a feral snarl. The shorter boy

radiated astonishment. The tall one merely seemed . . .
interested.

"Is this what we have sunk to?" I demanded. "Once,
we were the shepherds of this world, living in harmony
with the earth and all her creatures. Even after we retreated behind the mists, we remained beings of beauty
and grace and majesty. We instilled awe in those who encountered us. Inspired generations of poets and writers,
composers and artists. Offered mystery and possibility to
a world mired in the grinding crush of reality. But look at
you. Pranksters. Mischief makers. Soulless seducers."

The words reminded me of my contemptuous delight
at suckering the audience, my calculated decision to se-
duce Elena/Helena/Something.

"Look at *us*," I corrected in a trembling voice. "We've
allowed cruelty to become a habit that hurts us as well
as innocents like this girl. It must stop. *We* must stop. We
are better than that. We have the potential for so much
more. We have to unleash that potential. We have to . . .
we have to . . ."

"Manifest," Penny murmured.

"Yes! Manifest the possibilities! Change may be difficult, but surely every being is capable of it. We need to
change. To transform. To affirm that transformation to
the world. Right here. Right now. And nurture the new
selves we have brought into being!"

A wild excitement filled me, a reckless urge to throw
back my head and fling out my arms and embrace the
whole world. The feeling warmed me like single malt
whisky even as it cooled the sweat beading my brow. It
set my nerves tingling one moment and soothed them
the next. I felt alive and strong and more powerful than
I had in years. Decades.

And the fae understood. More importantly, my kin-folk felt these same emotions. Their beautiful green eyes grew impossibly wide as they contemplated the possi-bilities. When they burst into laughter, I laughed with them, carried along by their pleasure, giddy with my own delight. If not for the need to support Penny, I might have rolled in the pachysandra with them, too. Instead, I just watched, relishing their joy.

It took several minutes for them to regain control. They lay on the ground, staring up at us, still shaking with silent chuckles.

"Manifest the possibilities!" the tall boy wheezed.

That started them off again.

"Affirm the transformation!" the other one cried, drawing whoops of laughter from his comrades.

"Nurture our new selves!" the girl gasped.

By then, my smile had faded. It vanished altogether when the tall boy dragged himself to his feet, wiped his eyes, and announced, "You should do stand-up, Grandpa. That was the funniest shit I've ever heard."

The other two rose, still giggling. The tall boy sketched a mocking bow to me and another to Penny. "Sir. Madam. It's been a rare treat."

They strolled off in the direction of New Roc City. Now and then, one would exclaim, "Have you started manifesting your possibilities?" or "Don't make me come over there and unleash your potential!" And they'd all stagger with helpless glee.

So much for transformation.

Belatedly, I realized that I was still clutching Penny. I eased free and peered at her anxiously, but she was watching the fae.

"Who *were* those guys?"

"Those guys," I replied, "were assholes."

Penny responded with a most un-Penny-like giggle. Then she regarded me so intently that a new wave of anxiety rippled through me.

"You were great," she finally said.

I shook my head, embarrassed by my ridiculous display and my failure to correctly interpret the reactions of the young fae.

"I mean it," Penny insisted. "I'd have bought the CD in a heartbeat."

That won a very small smile from me. "Ah. But would you have sprung for the affirmation cards, too?"

Her nose wrinkled as she grimaced. "The book, maybe. But not those stupid cards. No offense."

"None taken," I replied. And was surprised to discover that I meant it. "Well. I suppose we should—"

Penny stopped my words by throwing her arms around my neck and kissing my cheek. Before I could react, she stepped away and shoved her fists in the pockets of her jeans.

"That was just . . . you know."

"Yes."

"I wasn't coming on to you or anything."

"No."

"Anyway. Thanks. For protecting me."

Protectiveness. That was the emotion I had been unable to identify. Imagine feeling protective toward Penny. The mind boggled.

"I could have killed that bitch. But somehow . . ." Penny's hands fluttered wildly; clearly, she was still experiencing the after-effects of our run-in with the fae.

I snagged one flailing hand and tucked it in the crook of my elbow. Then I guided her up the walkway toward the main entrance. Her eyes widened when she saw the shards of the shattered lights littering the patio. Fortunately, the hotel's windows and doors appeared to be intact.

"Did you do that?"

I hesitated a moment, then said, "I think so."

"How?"

"Let's just say it was another senior moment."

I prayed she would let it go at that. I was exhausted, utterly drained from the events of this tumultuous day. I felt . . . thinned, as if my flesh had grown translucent over my bones. One day, it would. But the hand I held in front of my face merely looked a bit paler than usual.

"That's kind of cool," Penny said.

"What? Oh. The lamps."

"Scary, but cool. I just hope you don't ever get pissed at me. Really, really pissed, I mean. I don't want my eyeballs popping out or my guts exploding."

"I wouldn't want that, either. Very messy."

She stuck her tongue out, and I smiled. Dear gods, the resilience of the young.

"This has been some weird fucking night, huh?"

"Very."

"You know, if you did that . . . what you did with them . . . in front of an audience . . ."

"I would have to find another source of income."

"No. It would be awesome."

"Really?"

"Totally."

The glass entry doors slid open to admit us. Penny's forehead creased in a puzzled frown as I urged her towards the piano and leaned close to the boy to whisper my request.

She laughed when he launched into "Always Look on the Bright Side of Life." Then she began to sing. I filled in the whistles. We were still singing and whistling when we entered the elevator; after all she'd been through tonight, she didn't need to trudge up four flights of stairs.

Her smile faded as she hesitated outside her room. Yesterday, I might have feared she intended to invite me to spend the night. Tonight, of course, I understood the source of her hesitation and the shivering that wracked her body.

It affected all humans differently, an encounter with the fae. But after the glamour wore off, shock inevitably set in.

I plucked her key card from her fingers and inserted it into the lock. I grimaced when I gripped the steel door handle, but that was mostly habit; I felt little more than an unpleasant tingling in my palm.

She waited for me to turn on all the lights and pull the drapes closed before stepping inside. "Would you mind staying?" she asked in a small voice. "Just until I fall asleep?"

"Of course not."

She emerged from the bathroom in a pink-flowered flannel nightgown that looked two sizes too big for her slender frame and a pair of purple socks with a hole in one toe. I felt an absurd tug of fondness for her, coupled with an unexpected flash of fear, and recognized it as the same protectiveness that had swamped me earlier. Strange that one emotion should encompass both fondness and fear. Stranger still that I should feel it.

I tucked her into bed and impulsively bent down to stroke that impossible hair.

"Try and sleep. We have to be up early tomorrow if we want to reach Stamford by 8:30."

Her smile lingered long after her eyes closed.

I left the light on in the bathroom lest she awaken in darkness and become frightened, but I snapped off the others and cracked open the drapes again before settling myself in the armchair by the window. The man reflected in the narrow rectangle of glass stared back at me. He looked oddly unfamiliar and unbearably fragile. Almost . . . human.

Then his lips puckered in a silent whistle and—after a long moment—he smiled.

HOW MUCH SALT

April Steenburgh

The world had gotten smaller, and no one had seen fit to tell him.

Dylan peered out at the gaggle of humans picking at carefully arranged bits of food balanced on plates that seemed fated to spill. His favorite summer basking spot was taken up by a young dandy and a woman he appeared to be failing to woo. Her eyes were on the gulls, dipping and whirling overhead while calling out their aggravation at the intruders.

The humans made pretty pictures, true, but when had they started to appear scattered through his favorite haunts? The dry calls of irritated seals mixed in with the eternal shouting of the surf, most likely lost on the humans. Dylan's gaze was pulled back to the ill-fated couple on his rock, the indelicate way in which the man was pressuring her, the resignation twined with unhappiness in her expression. It made his blood run hot, urging him to haul out of the surf and lay his head in her lap, to slip his skin and kiss the salty tears from her eyes.

The sight of a selkie male would ruin that woman forever; no human man would be able to measure up in her eyes after. Why then did they all hover in the surf, glaring at the interlopers?

It was the unexpected aspect of the situation. Humans were supposed to skulk around the same fishing and washing spots they had always appeared in. There was no precedent for finding them wallowing around on selkie beaches.

Dylan added a confused, angry huff to the mutterings of the colony of selkies scattered through the waves around him. This was his territory, and this . . . invasion would not be tolerated.

A bull seal charging up onto the rocks was not intimidating enough, no matter how he barked and called, posturing and puffing in aggression. The humans were startled, but instead of sublimating into satisfying fear, they seemed to settle into . . . doting. Nature was quaint, if one went by their inane chatter. Dylan suffered their cooing and cajoling with ill grace, settling on his preferred spot with something very close to a sullen air. He closed his eyes, taking comfort in the way food had slithered and slipped from plates at his disruption.

His family was slower to respond, slipping onto the shore only as the humans grew apparently bored with his inactivity, and started gathering the scattered evidence of their intrusion as the sun slipped towards evening.

He heard her before he saw her as she settled beside him, slipping out of her sealskin with a sigh that begged elaboration. He glanced over at her where she sat, expression inviting. "Where did they all come from?" Aine was the splendor of the young sunset rolled into a casually human form, red gold hair whipping around her head in the evening wind. Her dark eyes were wide in a face just a little too lean and perfect to belong to the girl she posed as. Clutching her seal skin she sniffed daintily, catching the smoke and sweat smells that the humans had left behind them.

Slipping his skin was always easiest just as the sun was setting. The evening air tickled, leaving startled goose flesh in its wake as he carefully set his sealskin beside him on the rocks. Dylan frowned, the expression spreading across chiseled features. He exhaled in a very seal-ish huff, nostrils flaring. "I'm not quite sure . . ." All across the shore, seal maidens settled onto their favorite spots, brushing tangles of seaweed from long hair with sharp fingernails. Dylan watched them, their grace soothing, their beauty rivaling the most elegant shell at the bottom of the sea as the moon rose and lit pale skin. He didn't remember there being so many humans before, but time was a tenuous thing to an immortal.

Dylan pulled Aine near, pressing his face into her hair and inhaling deeply of brine and musk. "Don't worry. They can't stay forever."

He had faint recollections from last season of the feel of a human woman soft and warm beneath him, her gaze gone unfocused with a heady dose of sensuality and roiling waves of magic, the morning sun warm with the new summer above them, the flavor of her sweat reminding him of the sea with its roiling surf and magic-riddled depths. The taste of her, salty and sharp on his tongue, added that dangerous tenderness and fascinating intensity to the seduction selkie lovers were infamous for. He could hear the wails of her menfolk as she drowned herself trying to slip beneath the waves after him, but that should have chased the humans off, not drawn them near. It was a warning that had always worked in the past.

The selkies drifted off with the morning tide and, as always when they were surrounded by nothing but the sea and each other, the human problem seemed less pressing than it had before.

When next Dylan came to shore he balked slightly before creeping up the beach alone at night to slip his skin and stare at a rather changed shoreline. The dwellings had been unexpected. They definitely had not been there on his last visit to this particular shore, settled in amidst rocks and weeds, connected by roads. Never before had his shores been so full of human habitations. Habitations that looked dauntingly permanent. Everywhere looked the same, an oppressive and overwhelming wave of humans. Dylan sat on the beach alone, head cupped in his hands, seal skin carefully hidden. Every now and then someone read, remembered, and believed old stories about stealing seal skins to gain a fairy wife.

Or husband.

Dylan reflexively checked the skin he had stashed in the bag at his side. He had an air about him that reminded folks of an actor or musician down on his luck, bag over his shoulder, clothing just this side of artfully worn, soulful eyes in the middle of a face too handsome to easily forget. At least that is what they told him, humans who took his contemplative expression for depression and offered conversation and the odd handful of coin or cash.

His family had drifted apart—wandering up rivers, into lakes, and into human beds. Some willingly, some following their skins as they must. Aine had been the last, casting an almost apologetic expression over one shoulder, her right arm linked around that of the young man who had been flying the kite that had caught her eye and imagination.

What an awkward situation. Dylan had no interest in giving in and moving on like so many of his people. He scratched the side of his face, allowing himself to be amused by the way people passing by made a point of not paying attention to the slight webbing the action exposed between his fingers.

Standing with a sigh, Dylan turned his back on the sea and, ignoring the way he wanted nothing more than to whimper and run back to let the waves swallow him he started to walk inland. Desperate times called for desperate measures, and there was no surer sign of desperation than a selkie walking away from the sea.

He had never thought the smell of salt and seal would tantalize his nostrils a mere day's walk from the shore he had so resolutely turned his back on. It had taken some practice, and some patience, walking along the side of loud roadways, nose wrinkling against the bitter fumes of human transportation. He honed in on and followed the familiar smells like a hunting hound on the trail of a deer.

Dylan followed a bit of road that turned to the right, made his way across a wide stretch of asphalt filling with cars and the excited shouts of children. He allowed the current of excited humanity to pull him towards what looked to be sea cliffs rising from the ground.

"This . . . is strange." Dylan ran a hand along the concrete that had been shaped to mimic a wave-formed tunnel through rock. After walking through the tunnel a woman asked him for money. Dylan scrounged a collection of coins and cash out of one pocket and into her hand, only half paying attention as she stamped the back of his hand, and then wandered in through the excited mass of humans that gathered just inside, adjusting hats and rubbing lotion on faces and ears.

It was a jumble of sights and smells, predator and prey all jumbled together in a way that could never be natural but was so very fascinating. Seal, polar bear, gull, penguin, fish. . . . Nostrils flaring in an attempt to take in every subtle hint, eyes looking everywhere but where he was going, Dylan felt the woman he ran into more than saw her.

She stumbled back with a startled *oomph!* and he reflexively threw a hand out to catch her, tendrils of magic twisting in a net of pheromone and suggestion. She was a cute girl, all wide eyes and freckles, younger than his usual prey but he was off center and she was enticing.

"I am so sorry about that." Dylan was the model of outdated concern, offering her a steadying hand before stepping back. "Are you all right?"

She had the slightly muddled look of a human brushing at the edges of fairy charms, but she nodded. "I'm fine. Really. Should have been looking where I was going."

"My fault." Dylan smiled apologetically and wandered off into the crowd. But not too far. He set his backpack at his feet as he leaned against the penguin viewing area, hands in his pockets, smile on his face.

Dylan watched his freckled girl settle on the bench, the oddity of the setting carried away by the familiarity of an ancient ritual. Selkies were picky about their prey, took their time watching and selecting. He could taste the loneliness of the young adult as she recovered from her embarrassment at having run into a stranger in public—salty and sweet and oh so enticing. . . .

A throat was cleared near to his ear, distracting him. Lips curled up in displeasure, Dylan turned away from his pretty girl, intent on telling the intruder to go elsewhere. His snarl twisted to horrified dismay as he took in the woman standing before him, his backpack over one shoulder. Oh, a selkie's worst mistake, taking his attention away from his skin. It had seemed safe, sitting on the ground at his feet. It had seemed secure as he watched his pretty girl. "That's mine. Return it."

The interloper's eyes were narrow, and more importantly *knowing*. Somehow she knew what prize she held in her hands, and was all the more dangerous for it. The muddled young girl across the way forgotten, Dylan stood still, hands clenched into fists at his sides and heart pounding.

Human park-goers looked up in concern as clouds gathered in the sky, a chill wind slinking through the previously warm afternoon, threatening a storm. There was very little of the charming, unassuming young man left in his expression as he stared down at the woman who held his freedom in her hands.

She bared her teeth in the feral cousin of a proper smile, fearlessly meeting Dylan's eyes, inspiring the hair on his arms to stand at attention. "Come with me." She gestured with her free hand as she turned her back on him, unconcerned with the storm roiling in his eyes, and started to walk.

Selkie. The recognition tumbled through his fear and fury. She was a selkie, and she had stolen his skin. It was unthinkable, a selkie stealing from another. The sun crept out from behind a cloud as Dylan turned thoughtful and followed after. He had no other option.

"You want me to do . . . what?" Her name was Ilane, and she was tired of running the seal show. Dylan's tongue fumbled around his mouth. Here the woman who had brought him to the small office had tossed him his bag as she shut the door behind them, shutting him in with the smell of salt and seal, brine and musk and everything he missed from home. Clutching his bag to his chest in a way that was sure to have embarrassed him had he noticed, Dylan stared at the sleek, tiny selkie seated at the cluttered desk.

Ilane snorted in something close to amusement. "Did you just beach yourself? How sweet. I run the seal show here. There are two other selkies in the tank—an old bastard called Carrick who I swear has been here since the park opened, and a young girl I picked up last year called Murel—a straggler, like you. Her family dispersed and she went a wandering and wandered her way straight into me. Sound familiar?"

"But what *is* all this?"

Ilane smiled broadly, revealing teeth a little too pointed to pass closely for human. "This is a sea park. Humans pay to wander through and gawk at the things that they have dragged out of the waves. For my little band, it is a nice, comfortable vacation. All the humans we could want, and all of them already primed for loving us. It is as close to perfect as one can get these days. Carrick retired when he took me in—we even had an actual grey seal back in those days. She was the sweetest little thing. I am handing you my job and retiring. Technically, you will have to speak with the park manager, but I will give you a good word, say I called you, let you know I was retiring and there was an opening. You will bring with you a little seal you have decided to name after me and huzzah. The show is yours and I get some tank time."

"It seems so undignified . . ."

Gathering her hair into some sort of tie, Ilane stood. "It's about time for the two o'clock. Let me show you what you will be doing."

Caught, just as surely as any woman he had dangled at the edge of his magic, Dylan followed in Ilane's wake.

After walking through a short series of hallways, Ilane deposited Dylan in a chair looking down over a tank of water and sculpted shoreline. An old bull seal barked a sleepy greeting from his place at the edge of the manufactured shore, rolling over slightly in the sun, dislodging the smaller female that had been using his side as a cushion. Dylan recognized them, tasted their briny magic in the air. Selkies.

They both rolled into the water as Ilane approached. She made a fuss over placing some balls and buckets while the seats around Dylan filled with chattering humans.

Ilane moved to center stage, a smile on her face. "Good afternoon, everyone. Welcome to the seal show!" She raised a hand and Carrick pulled himself up onto the stage with a dry bark, rolling and lifting fins on command as the audience cheered.

Dylan had to admit, it was an elegant solution. Nestled in the middle of the human sea park, their territory protected and preserved, the selkies held court. Sure, they carried on like new pups, rolling and barking and begging for the amusement of their audience, but in the soft smile of a woman watching her young child clap and shout in glee, Dylan felt it all come together. There was salt enough, glittering in laughing eyes, pleasure enough to get his pulse pounding. He was off center in this world that kept changing, but here, there was a chance to settle in. Theirs was a symbiotic relationship, human and selkie—it may well be this was the better option as opposed to skulking from shore to shore, carefully guarding his seal skin and still unable to stay away from those who would take it.

Ilane made her way through the emptying stands after the show, stopping for bits of conversation here and there before reaching Dylan where he still sat. "Well?" Her teeth flashed white and sharp in her quick smile. "Perfect, isn't it?"

"I'll consider it." He wanted to answer her wide smile with one of his own. There was an obvious, easy companionship between the selkies, one that made him almost itchy with the need to be a part of it. But he could smell the harsh tang of automobiles and unidentifiable bits of food that were too close and too strong. It made him want to back up a bit, slip into the water and reassess the situation. "Are you sure I couldn't just join the tank side of things?" Still the center of attention, inspiring salt and smile, but safe in the water—that would be easier to get used to, to deal with.

"No way. I get my bit of retirement if you join up. Who knows when the next selkie will chance through?" Ilane snorted, plopping down into the chair next to Dylan.

"Exactly. If I agree to this, what happens when I decide I've had enough?"

"Selkies are immortal. I am sure one will snatch back

a skin, or get bored of slipping around the shore and hoping for the best. Someone will come through, skin clutched, but not quite close enough, and you can have your chance at making a deal."

"Stealing a skin seems so . . ." Dylan floundered around for a word that had enough disgust and discomfort in it to express the sinking feeling in his stomach, the way his lip wanted to curl.

"Better another selkie than a human." Ilane shrugged. "It's a good life, brother. It's just been long enough for me. For now."

There had been so many people in the stands. They had stared at her, at them, entranced. The air had been thick with happiness, adoration, exultation. . . . It had been enough to keep him from remembering the look on Aine's face as she left, the feeling of waking on lonely stones, the snorting and snoring of his family missing from the night.

Ilane had a flush to her skin and a glitter to her eyes that Dylan had not seen gracing a selkie in a long time. It was the poise of a Seal Maiden positioned perfectly on the shore, catching every stray moonbeam in her hair. It was the assurance of a selkie male cresting a wave, hands outstretched toward the human woman grasping after him. It was a confidence Dylan didn't remember losing, but having had that little epiphany, he couldn't bear being without.

Humans were meant to be enthralled by selkies. Dylan inhaled, tasting the salt in the air, holding it before exhaling and meeting Ilane's raised eyebrow with a crooked smile. "I will give it a shot."

Dylan would put on a seal show they would never forget.

*   *   *

Carrick sprawled across some concrete masquerading as a bluff, dark eyes open only a sliver to acknowledge Dylan's entrance as he soaked in the afternoon sun, fins spread to maximize his basking. Ilane had settled beside him, distinctive nose propped on his back, mimicking his half-nap. Only Murel seemed restless, swimming circles around the deep tank, much to the delight of the crowd that gathered at the lower viewing area watching her lithe movements through a pane of glass set below water level. The attention of the seals was always on him, at least a little, visible in the way nostrils flared occasionally, whiskers twitched, and eyes rolled ever so slightly beneath lazy lids.

Ilane's nose worked and one eye cracked open. With a stretch and a snort Ilane rolled herself off of Carrick and into the water. She joined Murel in her laps around the tank and Dylan indulged in his own stretch as park patrons started to gather in the seating area positioned to give them a good view of water and demonstration area.

The children were his favorites, leaning as far over the railing between themselves and the seals as possible, eyes and mouth wide open in the thoughtless joy they had not yet learned to suppress. The parents had their cameras, and often a hand on the more exuberant of their offspring, just in case. They couldn't fall in, not with the additional wall of glass between rail and water, but it was a reflexive gesture, and one Dylan approved of.

Making his way from demonstration area to bluff, Dylan whistled quietly at Carrick. "C'mon, old man. Let's earn our keep." He rubbed a hand along Carrick's speckled side, ending with a pointed push as Carrick's eyes seemed intent on sneaking back shut.

Carrick huffed in irritation, admitting Dylan was more likely correct. He wriggled to the edge of the bluff, mouth open as he gave the distinctive wheezing bark before sliding down into the water.

Dylan took a minute to be envious of his charges, gliding effortlessly through the tank, touching here and there with fin and nose, holding lengthy conversations that the audience missed, before moving back to the center of the demonstration stage. He smiled at Karen, his show partner, as she entered through the well-hidden staff entrance, and turned on his microphone.

"Good morning! And welcome to the seal show." Ilane, familiar with the routine, made her way up into the shallow water at the edge of the stage.

Dylan lifted a hand and Ilane mirrored the gesture with a flipper, rolling on her side to accommodate the motion, mouth gaping open in a mocking grin. Dylan tossed her a fish, ignoring the amusement glittering in her dark eyes as she swallowed and wriggled off the stage and back into the water.

So clumsy on land, the seals were a delight to watch in the water. The crowd gathered to see them perform; sliding up onto the stage like Carrick was doing in response to a practiced gesture from Dylan. But the real show was in the tank where the girls swam complex patterns around each other, enjoying the feel of the water, exulting in the way the audience gaped at them in amazed enjoyment.

Dylan kneeled down as Carrick hauled himself close, moving like a sort of aquatic caterpillar as he propelled himself with rippling muscles. The bull seal was old, and his size impressed the crowd. "This here is Carrick." Dylan bent close, allowing Carrick to press a wet snout against his cheek. The audience clapped and laughed, but none laughed harder than Carrick, a dry rolling cough as he backed away, teasing and taunting with his expression. "Carrick is our old man, and quite taken with little Ilane." A scatter of chuckles from the adults in the crowd greeted that statement as Dylan tossed Carrick the anticipated fish and watched as he carried it back into the water before turning his attention back to the crowd.

"Ilane, unfortunately, appears to be rather taken with you, sir." Dylan picked a young man standing near the edge of the audience, and as close to the glass dividing them from the seals as possible. He had been back every day for some time now, staying as long as possible each time, eyes glued to Ilane's sinuous swimming. There was something twisting behind his startled expression as Dylan addressed him, enough of the Old World in that one to be caught in the glimmer of Ilane's magic as she danced through the water.

"You, sir, what is your name?"

The young man blinked wide eyes twice before answering. "Nick."

"Karen, if you could bring Nick over to the stage here, I think Ilane wants to give him a kiss."

Dylan was afraid for a moment that Nick was going to suffer an unfortunate bit of heart failure before he made it to the stage, the way his eyes went wide and he fumbled every other step, but Karen delivered him in more or less one piece. Dylan patted him in what he hoped was a reassuring fashion, trying to keep a toothy grin from breaking across his face.

Gesturing for Ilane to come, Dylan waited until she had slipped up into the shallow water at its edge before coaxing Nick to kneel. It was a familiar scene—every seal show played it through daily. The audience member kneels as the seal, at a command from its trainer, moves forward to press its nose against a cheek—a whiskery, fishy kiss that never failed to bring the crowd to a frenzy of applause. Ilane carried through with the expected, and then brushed her face across Nick's, catlike in her attempt to mark territory, before slipping back into the water. The audience let out a collective whoop of excitement and applauded.

Nick wobbled, looking like his foot had fallen asleep as he tried to stand. Dylan reached out, not to steady him, but to keep him from lurching into the water after Ilane. Smitten, bewitched, Nick's muscles flexed, considering breaking free of the interloper.

"Jump in now, and the park will surely throw you out. Permanently." Dylan whispered the warning into Nick's ear as he pulled him to his feet.

It was an ancient game in which Nick found himself a player. Dylan watched him fumble his way back to his former place by the glass, eyes tracking every twist of Ilane's body in the water. Only the setting had changed, not the rules. But behind the play was the dedication that made a seal wife so desirable, in all the old tales. Beyond the unearthly beauty was a fierce, fae loyalty. Yes, she had him—but Nick just as surely had snared her with his shy smiles and evident adoration. Dylan wondered just how long it would be before he was short a seal, before Ilane wandered off on two legs the way Aine had, to live with her human in a house by the sea.

It was a fishbowl they were living in, Dylan and his hodgepodge little family. But for every concession made there was a gain. There was salt enough in their filtered tank, salt enough falling from human eyes. Nick's eyes shimmered with the unshed tears of having seen the sublime. A young girl in the crowd laughed so hard she cried as Carrick knocked a ball around the water with his nose.

It was tribute enough, the tears of joy, love, and worship that greeted them each day. Gone were the moonlit shores with their selkie maids brushing out their long hair, perfectly placed to catch wandering human eyes, the selkie men beckoning from just beyond each wave.

But in the evenings, when his lover's taste was still strong in his mouth, slightly salty with sweat, and he gathered his seal skin from where it was carefully folded in the closet of his small office, it seemed the niche they had settled into was nigh unto perfect.

The shoreline was fake under his feet, the water not quite the right temperature, but he had to agree with Ilane, curling his seal skin around himself in the moonlight and slipping into the water, that it was good enough.

HOOKED

Anton Strout

"Leannán?" the stranger asked, his eyes filled with caution, the same as all those who had come across her doorstep before him. He was handsome enough, for a human—black hair, eyes as blue as the bright sky over Central Park itself, but he carried himself with a swagger that spoke volumes. He stood there, hands shoved down into the pockets of the knee-length wool coat he wore against the early sudden chill that had crept into September.

"Yes?" she asked from behind her partially opened cottage door. She pulled her short emerald colored robe closer around herself, letting the green of her eyes hold him in place on the dirt pathway that led back through the trees to the more travelled areas of Central Park. She couldn't help but grin as he stepped back a little. She twisted the power of her eyes along with her smile, strengthening her hold on him. She gave a toss of her head, her short, shaggy blonde bangs swaying as the tip of her swept up ponytail swung wildly back and forth. Leannán fought back the urge to giggle. "I see you found my little home here among the trees."

The stranger looked down as he fumbled through his pockets looking for something. She had seen his kind before. Wall Street maybe, she guessed. Probably liked it rough, and that was okay with her. The thought of it only quickened her heart, even though she was simply watching him search his pockets now.

The man lifted his head and waved a tiny slip of paper no bigger than one of the candy wrappers she occasionally saw blowing down the path past her cottage.

"I'm here about your ad," he said, his eyes showing lust behind them. "It was on the base of one of the statues over by Conservatory Water, kinda near all those miniature sailboats the kids play with."

Leannán took the slip of paper from his hand, but not before letting her pointer finger draw slowly across his palm as she pulled away. "Did you recognize him?" she asked.

"Him?" the man asked, looking over his shoulder with wariness in his eyes. "Him who?"

"The statue," she said, letting out a soft laugh. It sounded like chimes in the wind.

The man relaxed at the sound and turned back to her. "No. Who was he?"

"Hans Christian Andersen."

The man's face lit up with recognition. "The father of the fairy tale? Makes sense now."

Leannán cocked her head. "Does it? How so?"

"Your ad," he said, pointing to the slip of paper. "'Making your once upon a time a happily ever after . . . one encounter at a time . . . ?'"

She smiled. "Yes, I suppose that is true then. It does have fairy tale written all over it, doesn't it?"

He looked over his shoulder again, shoving his hands down deep into the pockets of his long coat. "Do you mind if I come in?" he asked. "Not for nothing, but this isn't the type of thing I want people to spot me out and about for . . ."

Leannán kept the door firmly in place between them. "That depends," she said, coy. "Do you have the payment, Mr . . . ?"

"O'Farrell," he said. "Alan."

She smiled. There was a great power in the knowing of names. "Very well. So, do you, Mister O'Farrell?"

"Of course," he said, digging to the bottom of his outer coat pockets. When he pulled his left hand out, the objects in it shone like miniature suns as daylight hit them. "Although I have to say gold is a bit hard to come by. Wouldn't cash be easier?"

Leannán took the coins from his hand, feeling the weight of them, loving the familiar heft. "Currencies come and go, but gold, well, that's eternal. . . ." She pulled the door open, waving him inside the darkened cottage. "Don't try anything funny. This place is charmed. . . ."

He laughed, following her in. Like most mortals, he probably took it all as part of the role-playing act, but the laughter soon stopped. She turned back to look at him. He was still following, but his eyes were trying to take in the interior of the cottage as he slowed to a shuffle behind her.

The walls were bright white pine, the woodwork around all the interior doorways and shuttered windows carved with intricate mythological figures. Sprites, pixies, naiads, and fairies flew and flittered up and down the wood, so well rendered that they almost looked alive. Throughout the space, tables, sideboards, chairs, and benches sat, cushioned in bright fabrics that resembled the near-cartoonish exaggeration that one would expect straight out of a fairy tale. At the center of it all stood an elaborate four-poster whose sheets looked like a shagged green swatch of moss. The man's eyes worked their way around the main room all the way up the carved beams that reached high overhead. He looked back down after a moment.

He whistled. "Am I allowed to sit on the furniture? It's not made out of candy, is it?"

She gave a bitter laugh of disgust. "That's Hansel and Gretel . . . they're more of a tag team duo. Not really my thing."

He laughed at that. "What is this place?"

"This?" she repeated, twirling around. "They used to call it the Scottish Cottage."

He raised an eyebrow. "You're Scottish, are you?"

"I'm a lot of things," she said.

"I can see that," he said. "Has this always been your home?"

"Not exactly; they built this cottage for the Centennial International Exhibition in 1876, but that was in Philadelphia. I remember them moving it here after, along with several of the other cottages, but I think the only other one that still stands is the Swedish one . . . they turned it into a marionette theatre, I believe."

He cocked his head. "You *remember* them moving it here? In 1876? That's over a century ago . . . you mean you remember someone telling you about it, yes? Your grandmother, perhaps . . . ?"

"I stand by my words," she said, giving a smile. "Fae, remember?"

"And this Disney-fied pastiche was all part of the attraction?"

"No," she said with pride. "This is all of my own making." She twirled around on point in her robe, the bottom of it rising, pulling his eyes to it. "You know, most men don't come here asking me about my family. They don't seem to like thinking of me as someone's daughter." She crossed to the lavish bed at the center of the room and sat on the edge of it, making her face doe-eyed and innocent. "Unless you're into that sort of thing. . . ."

His face washed over with lust, but there was still some reluctance in his eyes. "Don't you worry about getting caught?" he asked. "I mean, leaving flyers out for chrissakes and running your operation right here in the middle of Central Park?"

"Don't worry about that," she said, standing back up, laying the slip of paper off to the left of the room on a sideboard next to a decorative ball. She tapped at the slip with one of her polished nails, looking down at it. "That ad does not catch the eye of everyone." She narrowed her eyes at him. "You ask a lot of questions. Are you an officer of the law?"

"Me?" he laughed, shaking his head. "No."

"Too bad," she said with mock sadness as she walked off toward the enormous bed, pouting out her lips. "Some of my best clients have been men in uniform."

He held up both his hands, like he was being held at gunpoint. "Not me," he said. "I'm definitely not a cop, although I'd be down for the handcuffs, if that's one of your things."

She gave a small seductive laugh.

"But believe me," he continued. "My job is the last thing I want to think about right now." He walked over to the little slip of paper on the sideboard. "I came here for the theme you listed in the ad." His eyes shifted to the decorative ball sitting next to the piece of paper, then his right hand drifted towards it.

Leannán jumped up from the bed and ran over to the sideboard, blocking him from it, driving him back a step.

"What is that thing?" he asked. The light of the room danced across the orb, soaking into it, looking as if it was filling it.

"It is nothing," she said, but the man didn't seem convinced.

"It must be something," he said. "Or else you wouldn't have it placed here in your little fairy cottage set up."

"Remember when you walked in and what I said about this place being charmed?" she asked. He nodded. "Well, this is the source of that, a source of power for me, if you will. We fairies are bound by certain laws, such as this remaining out in the open to keep my fair cottage looking so fair." She twirled around on one foot, laughing. "A fair fairy in her fair cottage."

He laughed at that as well. "You are truly a wonder," he said. "Tell me your tale then, oh fair one."

She stopped her spinning and looked at him. "You might not like me so much if I tell you," she said, coy and pouting.

"You're right," he said, giving her a devilish smile. "I might like you more. Indulge me."

Another hardcore role player, she thought. *Fair enough. Let me give him what he came for then. Let him think my truth a lie.* Playing that game would only add more mischief to this whole event, something that spoke to the dark core of her very being.

"Very well," she said, scooping up the orb, dancing it

along the top of her fingers. "You know those happy stories people tell about fairies? The kind they make movies of, with songs and dancing and ever so much fun?"

He nodded.

"Well, mine is not such a tale," she continued. "Those stories are an insult to our origins. Many fae tales are born in, of, and about death—an omen of such things, and you see, I've been a very wicked little pixie."

"How so?" he asked, enchanted as he watched the ball drifting back and forth across the back of her hand.

"I am known as the Betrayer of my people, one with a hunger for humanity that my kind found . . . distasteful. They do not like the manner in which I dabble in mortal affairs, not caring for my reckless disregard for humanity. I've done what many of them consider dark deeds in the fairy world, crimes against mankind for which they wish to punish me. When taken to task, I fought for my freedom, and even killed several of my own kind escaping their judgment." She flipped her hand over, grabbing the orb, stopping it. She held it up. "The powers of this ball are many, you see. Not just a charm over my home. Its power is what saved me, transported me, allowed me to escape."

"I do see," he said, his eyes coming to life again now that the ball was no longer in motion. Leannán could tell by his face that he wasn't quite buying the tale, but it was no matter. That wasn't what he had really come here for now, was it?

"Anyway," she said, replacing the orb on its stand with a wicked grin. "I don't think you came here for a history lesson on the fae."

"You could say that." He looked down at the slip of paper under his hand on top of the sideboard, then up again at her in her robe. "Can I see them?"

She gave a slow nod of her head, her eyes locking on his as she undid the robe, shrugging her shoulders and letting the garment fall to the floor. Underneath she wore an outfit she knew most men found familiar, a short green strapless dress that left little to the imagination. She tossed her blonde ponytail to the side so the tip of it flipped just over the front of her right shoulder.

"You really did go for Tink —"

She held a finger up to her lips. "Shh," she said. "I am most definitely not like the Disney version of that fairy at *all*." A soft whisper came from behind her back and two opaque wings rose up, fluttering open to their full expanse, standing almost two feet higher than her shoulders. They pulsed with a gentle rhythm that matched her breathing, shimmering in the low light of the cottage.

"They look so . . . real," he said, raising his hand out towards her to touch them, but she stopped him, taking his hand in hers.

"I *do* strive for an authentic experience here," she said, backing him over to the bed. She twirled around once again, spinning like a ballerina, before she wrapped her arms over his shoulders and around his neck, finally dropping the gold coins onto the bed. Her heart raced with excitement as her lips touched his and their tongues met, knowing what was coming next.

She pushed him back onto the bed, his body giving at the joint of his knees, and she threw herself on top of him. She felt his body reacting to her touch as he elbowed his way further up onto the bed. Her wings fluttered as she ground herself against his body, opening her eyes to look at him as he grabbed her hips. His eyes were open as well, looking over her shoulder as he fixated on the wings, marveling at them. She leaned down, his breath hot on her skin. She raked her teeth along his neck, and then bit down.

He let out a grunt of pleasure, but as she pressed her teeth harder against the skin—breaking it—the sound turned to pure pain. He tore his hands off her hips and shoved them between their bodies, forcing her up by her shoulders.

As Leannán sat up, a warm trickle of salty blood ran down the corner of her mouth. "Not the strongest of humanity I've tasted," she said, a bit disappointed, "but it will do."

His eyes locked on it, widening. "What the hell?"

"Too rough?" she asked, sweet and coy, running her finger along the corner of her mouth, working the blood up to her lips. Her wings vibrated with delight. "I warned you I wasn't the Disney version."

"Get off me!" he shouted, anger and disbelief in his plea.

Leannán remained where she was, pressing down hard against him before dropping the glamour she had held in place. All around her the interior of the cottage wavered, then faded away. The cozy confines were gone, replaced with the worn down abandonment of a dark, dirty house in ruin. The bed beneath them became a cold stone slab with tatters of blood-soaked sheets underneath them, some of it still tacky to the touch. Three of the walls were barely visible in the surrounding shadows of the main room, piles and piles of stacked skulls and bones obscuring them. She herself became her true gaunt, wiry form, dressed in tattered, stained remnants and blonde hair crusted with blood and dirt.

"What *are* you? What is this place?" he screamed, increasing his struggles.

"Why, it's my home," she said, running her hands along the cold slab, "and this is your final resting place." She raised a hand, her fingers stretching open like a cat getting ready to strike. "As to what I am, well let's just say there's truth in advertising."

"You're an *actual* fairy?" he shouted. "What the hell kind of fairy acts like this?!"

She let out a laugh that turned into a growl. "Not the good kind, unfortunately for you." She licked at the blood on her lips again, the taste . . . it wasn't just that the humanity was weak in this one. There was something else about it she couldn't quite put her finger on.

"Let me go," he said, interrupting her thoughts. "Y–you can keep the money." His eyes darted around the room, no doubt looking for hope among the horrors.

"Let you go?" she repeated. She reached down to the slab and scooped up the gold coins lying there. "I'm afraid I can't do that."

"Why not?"

"Because I've already been paid . . . and in *gold*."

"So?"

She let out a laugh, this time less like wind chimes, more like broken glass. "A man who pays in cash, well, that's worthless now, isn't it? But a man who pays in gold . . . well, that's a man who put some effort into his bargain, isn't it? That gives our arrangement power, one that sticks, one that binds. As I said, there are rules for the fae."

He shook his head, blubbering so hard she could feel it in her hips. "But I didn't know that's what I was bargaining for!"

"Incorrect," she snapped loudly, venom full in her voice. "You came here hoping for corruption like the mortals from ages ago . . . therefore your soul is forfeit to me."

"But—"

"Enough," she shouted, both hands still raised—one with the coins in it and the other one poised like a claw. "The deal has been sealed."

Without another word, she plunged her hand down, digging into the man's chest.

He cried out in pain and writhed beneath her like a trapped animal, but like all the men—and women—before his visit, she knew how to hold him down as she pulled at his life force.

Leannán basked in the power she felt. The sensation never got old, not even centuries later, but something felt not quite right. She tried to place what it was, and it eluded her, until a strange sensation coming from her other hand drew her full attention.

The coins she held were shifting, transforming in the same fashion as the walls around them had moments before.

"What—"

The gold faded, replaced by thick round discs of bread that filled up her hand and spilled out of it. She followed one of them as it hit the slab, cracking in half, crumbs spreading everywhere. She was so focused on them that she didn't notice the searing sensation in her hand until it was too late. She cried out and slid off the man, trying to stand, but instead tumbled to the worn wooden floor.

The man himself still screamed in pain as he sat up clutching his chest, but it gave way to another sound—a joyous laughter. She looked up at his face. He gave another scream—mocking this time—then let go of his chest. Trickles of blood were still there but they were already fading.

Leannán pulled her fist close to her, the intense burning

growing as the bread fell from the palm of her hand. "Ginger cakes!" she hissed. She hadn't felt a sensation quite as painful as this since . . . she couldn't remember.

"I've never understood it," the man said, standing up, composing himself as he brushed himself off and straightened out his clothes, "but bread always seems to do the trick. Maybe it's because baked goods are something unnatural, something you *make* by converting elements of the natural world, a symbol of home and hearth."

Her eyes widened, the hint of panic at their corners. "How do you know of this? Who are you?"

He shrugged off his coat and a scratching sound rose from the back of his shirt, followed by a soft tearing of cloth. Wings rose up behind him, taller and pointer than hers, more angular. "You do not know me, but I know of you, *Leannán Sluagh*."

She let out a pained hiss, weakening at the sound of her full name. She moved to stand, but couldn't quite get her feet under herself. "Who *are* you?"

"I was raised Alan O'Farrell, the name I told you," he said, "but my true name is Cillian, once—and soon to be once again—of the Seelie Court. Your crimes against them have not been forgotten." He looked around the room in disgust, eyeing the piles of bones. "I see you have added to them since your vanishing."

She looked the man over. "I do not recall you," she said.

"Nor would you," he said. "For I was barely born of the court."

He pulled a length of thin, black chain from within the edged lining of his coat. Leannán's eyes flew open, the coldness of the metal already reaching her from where he stood.

"Iron," she shrieked, and then looked down at his bare hands. "How is it that you can handle such a thing?"

"My time among the Seelie Court was not long," he said, moving toward her. "I was a mere infant. I am more than just of the fae. I was raised as a human child."

"*Changeling* . . ." The word fell from her mouth dripping with venom. That explained the strange taste of his blood. Weak in humanity, but so rich with fae she hadn't been able to place it at first.

He held up his hand, the palm of it crisscrossed with red streaks from where the chain had touched it, but other than that, he seemed unharmed. "I was given to humans, raised by them because my fae parents were no longer among the living. They died in your struggle to escape from the punishment for your crimes against the mortal world and fairy folk alike."

Her face calmed, her eyes shrinking to thin slits. "So *that* is what this is about . . ."

"Queen Nicnevin knew you were crafty, that you would run rather than face your crimes."

She let out a dark, icy giggle. "Well, we fae *are* known for our mischief . . ."

"Mischief?" he laughed. He walked around the room. "Is that what you call all of this? My dear lady . . ." He bent down and lifted her head with his hand, looking her straight in the eyes, the light in his going dark. "This is pure abomination. Turning milk sour, making masters fall in love with their servants, twisting a mortal's hair into tangles, these things are mischief . . . but this?"

Leannán stared at the floor of the ruined cottage, her voice thick with disdain. "Well played, *changeling*," she said. "Acting the common, lustful human to strike my fancy, to reel me in. I should feel more anger toward you than I do, but the trickster in me cannot fault you for your well-planned snare. All the more foolish, me, for falling for it." Her eyes darkened, becoming a more sinister shade. "Still, I will not have you judge me."

The man stood, his hands still holding the loop of chain. "It is not my place to judge you. No, the Seelie Court will do that, and hopefully bringing you to them will secure my place there. I cannot take all the credit for ensnaring you, however. Nicnevin knew what she was doing, putting me amongst the humans. She thought you might have fled to the new world the humans had discovered but she knew the chances of finding you would be hard, given your mastery of deception. She also knew of your hunger for humanity and that it would take someone susceptible to your charms—a human, or at least someone raised as human—to eventually find you. And, well . . . here we are."

He threw the loop of chain over her, pulling it tight. The cold iron burned against her flesh, her wings crumpling under its touch, turning a worn brown. Leannán could barely move, but found the strength to struggle toward the half-decayed remains of one of the men nearby. She wrapped one arm around its torso, and with the other grabbed its jaw in her other hand, staring into its hollow empty eye sockets, cocking her head back and forth. "How can you stand to have been raised by them? To live among them?"

"Actually," he said, pulling the body away from her and laying it against the other remains. "I have found them quite delightful to live amongst. They really are remarkable creatures, full of imagination . . . hopes . . . dreams." He laughed. "Do you know what they say of us? They call us the 'middle nature between Man and Angel!' Isn't that delightful?"

Leannán held up the fringe of her tattered green dress. "And they make an amusement out of us," she countered.

Cillian rose up *en pointe*, spinning in his human clothes. He stepped into a light dance with enough joy in it that Leannán could not help but feel the hint of tears rising at the corners of her eyes.

"My dear dark twisted soul," he said, with a low, sweeping bow as he finished that was just as poetic, "what are we but creatures of mirth and magic?"

"So kill me then," she said, thick with misery now, letting the tears fall. "End my life as I ended those of your parents."

"As I mentioned, that is not for me to judge," he said, walking over to the sideboard, which now looked rotten and worm-ridden with age, all save the decorative ball that sat atop it. He picked up it, rolling it back and forth across his hand. "The very 'good' that drives my wish to once again be part of the Seelie Court is the same thing that prevents me from acting like the same monster that you are. I will not kill."

He pulled the chain tighter, her wings browning and crumpling even further. She cried out but made little effort to resist as he forced her to stand.

"Come," he said. "It pains me to see even you in this state for very long."

"Where are you taking me?"

He held up the small orb from the sideboard, its insides glittering like a thousand stars. "I think you know."

"The Court of the Unseelie will not stand for this!"

The man's face scrunched up. "The dark mischief makers? Even their kind frowns upon what you have done here. There is mischief, and then there is this."

"I can pay you better than the Queen," she pleaded, falling back on her knees, crawling away from him.

"Your liar's gold means nothing," he said, pointing to the broken crumbs of bread scattered across the slab that had once been the bed.

"No," she said. "Not gold!" Leannán changed direction, crawling back to the pile of bodies off to her left. Frantic, she picked through the dried out and not so dried out husks of corpses, pulling trinkets, wallets, and billfolds out of the remains of the clothes they had worn in life. "Cash, coin, jewelry . . . the currency of the modern world! I care not for it myself, but after many years living here in solitude, I have amassed quite a fortune from my visitors. Take it. Take *all* of it, but leave me be. Forget you ever found me. Surely your services can be bought, bounty hunter."

Cillian shook his head. "You may call me a common bounty hunter, but I've been promised a place in the court for my service," he said. "I cannot be bought."

Leannán fell back to scrabbling among the bodies, turning from him, but he tugged at the chain, spinning her around as he forced her to her feet. As she turned, she raised her hand, blowing a handful of fairy dust into his face, willing her glamour over him. *Forget*, she thought as the dust settled. *Release.*

His face remained stoic, unchanged, and then he began to brush himself off. "Your charlatan tricks hold no sway over someone of your own kind. Enough bandying of words."

He jerked at the chain, the iron digging into her numbing flesh. He raised the orb high overhead, and brought it down hard against the stone slab of the bed. The glass erupted, the light of a thousand stars pouring out, filling the room. The voices of countless souls cried out into the night, rising up through the structure as it shook, the night sky filling with them. The pulse of power from it shook through Leannán's body, and the interior of the building tore itself apart, collapsing in on itself, dust and debris raining down into the center of the main room. She raised her arms in a defensive posture as the great vaulted ceiling caved in on the main room.

By the time the rotting beams of the Scottish Cottage struck the ground, there was no sign of anyone other than the centuries-old accumulation of corpses, coming to a final rest beneath the fallen remains.

CRASH

S.C. Butler

"**Y**ou stole my trade!"

Janet resisted the urge to conk Schlegel over the head with the nearest handset as the man sighed patronizingly and swiveled his chair away from his desk to face her. Hundreds of bids and offers blinked on the computer screens behind him.

"What are you talking about?" he asked.

"You know perfectly well what I'm talking about. The euro trade was my idea."

"Not my fault I found a buyer before you did."

"I've been pushing that trade to Tiger all week. They'll never pull the trigger now someone else has done it."

Schlegel shrugged, and turned back to his screens. The fact that he didn't think he'd done anything wrong infuriated Janet even more. The entire trading floor was staring at her, but she didn't care. She hadn't come to Wall Street to make friends. Just money.

She picked up the handset. Even if she smashed it

against Schlegel's desk instead of his head, it would still get his attention.

"Janet, can I see you for a moment?"

Halloran had come up quietly behind her. Barely five feet tall, he was hidden completely by the banks of computer screens whenever he prowled the floor, despite his shock of frighteningly red hair. He motioned toward his office.

No one had ever seen Halloran actually smoke, but the smell of nicotine in his office was overwhelming. His permanently flushed cheeks worked furiously as he chewed his anti-smoking gum.

He nodded to a chair. Janet crossed her legs as she sat. Halloran had been known to be distracted by her legs.

"I heard you all the way in here," he said.

"Schlegel stole my trade."

Halloran's bushy eyebrows twitched.

"We're a team here, Janet. You know that. We share our ideas."

Janet clenched her jaw. These chats with Halloran were always the same. He loved to talk about how the trading floor was a team, but that only worked if you were a partner like he was. Everyone else at DBJ was compensated according to individual performance, not overall results. Janet hated the hypocrisy of it, but knew she had to play along. Someday she'd make a really big score and kiss the hypocrites goodbye.

She smoothed the hem of her skirt. "I understand, Mr. Halloran. It's just that the firm could have made a lot more money if Schlegel had waited to pitch the idea till after I'd sold it to Tiger."

Halloran rubbed his enormous nose with a thumb. "Maybe. And maybe Tiger was stringing you along while they put the trade on with someone else. It's the trades you make that matter, Janet, not the ones you think up. You have to be a salesman, too. And you can't be a salesman unless you're part of the team. If you aren't . . ."

Halloran shrugged. He knew, even better than Janet, that he held all the power.

She left his office angrier than when she'd gone in. What she really needed was a good Mega Millions jackpot. Or making the final table at the poker world series. Money cured everything. A lot of money. How she made it didn't matter. Just as long as she made it.

She made a little that afternoon when the market tanked, which calmed her down. The market had fallen sharply the last few days, and she'd set up a few shorts. It was March, the millennium had passed without incident, and most people believed stocks would go up forever. But not Janet. Greed was good, but you had to be lucky, too. And nimble. The guys on the wrong side of the day's big selloff had already lost enough in the last few hours to consider throwing themselves out a window.

After work, she hooked up with Buzz and several other friends, which calmed her down some more. They started the evening with dinner at the Union Square Café, then moved on to an artist's opening in Chelsea, bowling on West Street, and finished the night at a friend's band's CD release party in Tribeca. By the time that was over, it was five-thirty in the morning. Janet had to be at work by seven, but she'd pulled all-nighters before. Going home made no sense: she'd just have time to shower and dress before she had to come back downtown. Nights like this were why she kept a suit at the gym across the street from the office. She was a trader, wasn't she? If she couldn't stay out all night to unwind, what the hell was the point?

Convincing Buzz to come downtown with her was easy; Buzz worked only when he wanted. But it was raining hard and they couldn't find a cab, so, halfway to the gym, in order to get out of the rain, they ducked into a pub Janet knew on South Street that opened early for breakfast.

"I know this place," Buzz said as they slid into a booth. "I used to come here with my grandfather."

Janet snorted. "The founding partner of Dedham, Benz, and James, in a dive like this?" She nodded toward the bum slumped over his arms at the next booth. "No way."

"We used to come here when I visited him for lunch. I think a lot of the partners used to come here."

"Well, they don't come here anymore."

The waitress who poured their coffee dimpled when Buzz asked if the place served fresh orange juice. Buzz was cute, even if you didn't know he was rich.

The bum looked up when the waitress left.

"Excuse me," he rasped in a low voice like paper ripping in the next room. "Did I hear you say your grandfather worked at DBJ?"

Buzz gave the old man his best New York stone face. "No."

The bum scratched the back of his head. "I could have sworn I heard you mention Dedham, Benz, and James."

"You shouldn't have been listening to our conversation."

"Sorry. But my ears still work, you know. I used to be a trader at DBJ. Cliff Dedham hired me over a drink in this very bar."

Buzz's face softened. "You knew Clifford Dedham?"

Uh-oh, Janet thought. Time to intervene.

"Come on, Buzz. Let's go. I'm not sure I have enough time for breakfast after all."

"Go on if you have to. I want to hear what he has to say about my grandfather. It'll only take a second."

"Cliff Dedham was your grandfather?"

The surprise must have been too much for the old man, because he began to cough before he could say anything more. Wiping his mouth on his sleeve, he came around the front of the booth and perched on the bench at the other side of the table.

Janet grimaced, and moved into the back corner, as far from Buzz and the old man as possible.

"You knew my grandfather?" Buzz asked.

"I was one of the first people he hired."

"That was like seventy years ago. You don't look that old."

"Well, I am. It's one of my curses. I'm nearly a hundred and one."

Janet found it hard to believe that anyone who'd done so obvious a job of pickling himself could still be alive at a hundred and one. He probably hadn't worked for DBJ either, and thought he could cadge a free meal by pretending he had after hearing her talk about the firm.

Buzz didn't seem to doubt him. "So you were there from the start?"

"Yeah, but I didn't last long. Like a lot of traders, I thought I was smarter than everyone else."

"She's a trader." Buzz nodded toward Janet.

Janet could have smacked him.

"I never heard of a woman trader," the old man said, "but then I've been out of the business a long time. I wouldn't think a woman would be able to handle it."

"Things have changed a lot since your day, grandpa,"

Janet said. "You can't just sign up your college buddies for a couple hundred shares of General Motors any more. Now you have to have ideas."

The old man laughed, which started him coughing again. When he was finished, he said, "I take it back. You'd have fit in on our desk just fine. But you're wrong if you think it was easy. We were selling stocks and bonds to people during the Depression. I don't care what it's like now, it was worse then. And I was impatient. That's why, when I met a fellow right in this very bar sixty-four years ago, and he started talking about someone he knew who could call the market, I got interested. I should have known better, because I'm Irish. But then, I suppose that's why he told me his story in the first place."

"Janet's Irish," Buzz said.

Janet kicked Buzz's shin hard under the table.

The old man turned his attention to Janet. "Then you'd better pay special attention to what I'm about to tell you, or you might find yourself where I am."

"I doubt it."

"Maybe. But, if you're like most of the traders I knew, you won't be above taking a shortcut when it's offered. When this fellow told me what happened to him before the Depression in 1929, you can believe I listened. Even if it did sound more like something out of a fairy tale than anything that could happen in New York.

"He didn't come right out and say it, of course. We were Americans, not a couple of boghoppers too stoned to find our way home in the fog. But I knew what he was talking about. I didn't really want to—but I knew. You don't find market tips at the end of the rainbow. Just leprechauns."

Buzz laughed. Janet rolled her eyes.

"I know you don't believe me," the old man said. "But

it's true. You see if it isn't. The day after a big move in the market, at least five percent, go down to the bottom of Wall Street and look for a rainbow. If there is one, follow it. It doesn't do any good to try on a day when there hasn't been a big move or there isn't any rainbow. You have to have both."

"Give me a break." Janet poked the top of the table with her forefinger. "If you found a leprechaun, why is it you're an old drunk and Cliff Dedham was the big success? Leprechauns give you wishes, right?"

"They do. Unless you take the pot of gold. The guy I talked to took the gold. That's what I should have done, but it was 1937, and the leprechaun didn't actually have a pot of gold. Just a lot of old bearer bonds that weren't worth five cents on the dollar. So I thought I was being smart when I took the wishes. Ha.

"Never take the wishes when you meet a leprechaun. Always take the cash. Even if it isn't as much as you'd hoped for."

"So what did you wish for?"

"Long life. You can see that came true." The old man tapped his chest, and went into another fit of coughing.

"What else? You must have gotten some money."

The old man nodded. "I thought I was being clever. Instead of asking for a hundred million three year treasury notes, I thought I'd go for the whole hog. I wished for the ability to call the market."

"That's a pretty good wish."

"I thought so, but the leprechaun spotted the catch pretty easily. I can call the market, all right: I just can't time it. Even now, I can tell you the next big move will be down. But I can't tell whether the bear will start tomorrow or eighteen months from now."

"Everyone knows the next move will be down," Janet scoffed. "The Dow's gone up for twenty years. By definition, the next move has to be down."

The old man nodded. "Exactly."

"What was your third wish?"

"That was the worst. And what happened then should have warned me what was coming. You see, my girl and I had just broken up, and I was feeling pretty bad, so I wished she'd change her mind and marry me."

Buzz frowned in sympathy. "I'll bet I know what happened next. A month after she married you, she ran off with your best friend."

"It was worse than that. She got hit by a bus getting out of a cab the night of our honeymoon. I killed her."

"Jesus." Despite her certainty the old man had made up the whole story, Janet was horrified. But if there was a kernel of truth anywhere in the tale, it was probably the part about his wife. Something awful must have happened to the guy or he wouldn't be such a wreck.

Her cell phone rang. Not knowing how to commiserate with a bum, Janet was glad for the interruption, but it was only her regular alarm, set to warn her she needed to be at work in half an hour in case she'd overslept.

She turned to Buzz. "I have to go."

Buzz took two hundred-dollar bills out of his wallet and handed them to the old man. "Get yourself a good meal and a new coat," he said.

The old man folded the bills deftly. "Your grandfather was a fine man," he said.

The rain had stopped when they went back outside. Dawn had risen. A rainbow bloomed over Brooklyn, its colors vivid. Janet shaded her hand against the sunrise, and followed the arch over the elevated part of the FDR and the tops of the buildings behind her. The rainbow's peak disappeared in gray clouds, but the bottom looked like it came down somewhere near Wall Street. The Stock Exchange, perhaps, or the Twin Towers.

"Did the market have a big move yesterday?" Buzz asked.

"Six and a half percent. Down." Janet frowned as she realized why Buzz was asking. "You can't be serious."

"Why not? Let's have some fun."

"What, wandering around Wall Street at six-thirty in the morning is your idea of fun? I have to be at work in half an hour."

"Come on, Janet. I don't think we're actually going to find a leprechaun any more than you do. But when was the last time you saw a rainbow in New York? We'll never get a chance like this again."

She followed him reluctantly. They climbed Wall Street with the arch looming high above their right shoulders. Turning onto William, they hurried three more blocks to Maiden Lane. More splendid than the entrance to the most magnificent casino, the end of the rainbow splashed brilliantly over a shoe outlet one more block away.

"Jesus." Janet pointed at the stone building running the length of the block on the left hand side. "That's the Federal Reserve."

Buzz's eyes widened. "I thought the Federal Reserve was in Washington."

"There are twelve branches of the Federal Reserve, all over the country. This is the one with the gold."

"The gold?"

"Five million tons. More gold than anyplace else in the world."

"Wow. It really is the end of the rainbow."

He was off down Maiden Lane before Janet could stop him. This time she didn't even think about not following. The coincidences were starting to enter the far reaches of probability, and Janet was too good a trader to let luck like that pass her by, no matter how absurd the odds.

Buzz had stopped to look at a subway grate standing wide open in the sidewalk in front of the shoe store when she caught up with him.

"Something else you don't see every day," he said.

Janet peered into the darkness under the street. "You want me to go down there?"

"You see anything else around here that might lead to a leprechaun?"

Janet looked up and down the walls of the long stone building. Black bars as thick as her calves covered the windows. Really, there was no way there could be leprechauns in the Federal Reserve, but they would have to go inside if they wanted to find out.

"You first," she said.

Buzz descended gallantly. Janet followed, finding a handrail just below the street. The metal steps ended in slick stone.

"Which way?" she asked.

Buzz pointed toward a faint light glowing down the tunnel about half a block away.

They went from light to light. When Buzz offered Janet his hand, she took it. She found his grip uncomfortably reassuring in the ick and dampness.

She couldn't pinpoint the moment exactly, but at some point the world shifted. The smell was different. Earthy, rather than disgusting, like a hole in a garden rather than a city sewer. Still, when something long and thin brushed the top of her head, she shrieked. But it was only a root hanging from the roof.

She saw more roots ahead. Lots of them. But where had the roots or the dirt come from? The nearest trees were in City Hall Park, five blocks away.

"This is weird," Buzz said.

"We must have come the wrong way."

But they had already come far enough to see that the next light wasn't a bare bulb at all. It was an iron sconce, with a warm, flickering candle.

Janet couldn't help herself. Maybe there really was a leprechaun on the other side of the wooden door just beyond the candle. It sure as hell wasn't the Federal Reserve. And if there was a leprechaun, Janet was certain she'd do a much better job trading with it than the old man had. There was a saying on Wall Street, bulls win, bears win, but pigs lose. The old man had been piggish, and had lost. Janet had no desire to be piggish at all.

She let go of Buzz's hand and walked toward the door.

"Janet, are you insane?"

"I'm going in."

The door was short, not much taller than she was; Buzz would have to stoop to get through. The knob was on the left side, large, and carved to look like a small head. As Janet reached for it, it craned away and fixed her with an iron eye.

"Oi! What d'you think you're doin'?"

The knob's brogue was as pure as Thomas Mitchell's. No, this definitely wasn't the Federal Reserve or City Hall.

"Can't I go in?" she asked.

"O'course you can go in. But what's that got to do with pawin' at me?"

"I thought you were a doorknob."

"I am a doorknob. D'you take me for a spittoon?"

"How can I turn you, if I can't touch you?"

"You might try askin'. Politely."

"May I go inside? Please?"

"T'would be my pleasure, lass."

The door opened into a cozy living room like something out of a book Janet might have read as a child. A pair of armchairs faced a cheery hearth; a bright fire gleamed on the grate. A small side table between the chairs sported a large glass half filled with what smelled like stout. The ring of foam on the rim of the glass suggested it had recently been sampled.

"What is it?" a strangely familiar voice asked from one of the chairs.

"You've a guest, Jacko," the doorknob answered. "Two, p'raps, if the other musters the stones to follow the lass."

A man's face looked around the side of the nearest chair. Given that she'd almost recognized the voice, Janet shouldn't have been surprised that she recognized the face. But she was. Halloran was the last person she'd expected to see. The bushy red eyebrows and gigantic nose were unmistakable, even if he was smoking a pipe that looked like an ornate table leg, and wearing small square glasses.

He was just as surprised as she was, but caught his pipe before it hit the floor.

"You!" they exclaimed simultaneously.

Halloran jumped to his feet. Janet found the sight of the cold-blooded bastard in his undershirt and slippers, his pants held up by suspenders, almost as unbelievable as the fact of where she'd found him. At least the paper in his hand was the *Wall Street Journal*.

"You're a leprechaun?"

"How the hell did you find me?"

"I met a guy in a bar."

Halloran snorted. "It's always a guy in a bar."

"You're a leprechaun?" Janet repeated.

"No, I'm a selkie." He shrugged huffily, and snapped his paper, which he then folded and put in his chair.

"What are you doing here?"

His temper worsened. "Where else would I be? This is my home!"

"Aren't leprechauns supposed to be out in the woods somewhere? In Ireland?"

"I emigrated."

"To Wall Street?"

"What, you think I'd come all the way to this country so I could be a shoemaker? Lots of Irish on Wall Street. I'm right at home."

"And you're really a leprechaun?"

"I already answered that question. How'd you find me?"

"I followed the rainbow."

"It stopped raining? I guess the weekend's not going to be a total loss after all. Maybe I can get in a full eighteen holes."

"You know him?"

Janet looked behind her. Buzz had finally followed her inside.

"He's my boss."

It sounded absurd. Here she was in an underground living room next door to the New York Fed with a guy she saw, and hated, regularly. Taking his gold would be easy.

"*Was* your boss," he said. "Consider yourself fired.

Barging in on me at home like this. Where are your manners?"

Janet smiled. "Being fired won't matter if I have your gold."

He looked at her slyly, a fox peering out through the shrubbery of his eyebrows. "You know about that?"

"Of course I know about it. You're a leprechaun. That's how it works."

"I could grant you three wishes instead."

"I don't want wishes."

"You sure?"

Halloran tilted his head to one side, thumbed his suspenders, and winked. A tourist might have been fooled, but Janet was enough of a New Yorker to recognize when she was being conned.

"Just give me the cash," she said, looking around the room for pots of gold.

With a sigh, Halloran pulled back the rag rug that covered the floor and opened a trapdoor. A sturdy wooden ladder led to the cellar below.

Janet couldn't make out anything in the darkness.

"I don't see any gold," she said.

"I'm not Fort Knox, you know."

"Yeah, but you are living right next to the New York Fed, which is even better."

Halloran beamed. "It is, isn't it? Prime piece of real estate I've got here. Better than the damn bogs my cousins still call home back in the Old Country. Nothing like a little gold nearby to keep out the damp and warm the cockles of your heart. But that doesn't mean I can lay my hands on it. I have to work for what I have, just like anyone else."

"Do you have a flashlight?" Janet asked.

Halloran smiled around his pipe. "Nope."

"How am I supposed to see what I'm doing down there?"

"That's not my problem."

"I have an idea," Buzz said.

He went out into the hall and came back with the sconce and candle. Janet held out her hand.

"I'll carry it." He hefted it like he was doing curls. "It's heavy."

"You're coming with me?"

"Sure."

Since Buzz had the light, he went first. Janet couldn't get a good look at what was in the cellar until she was already below the floor, her normal caution buried under a rich loam of cupidity.

She had to stoop, the ceiling was so low, and Buzz had to crouch. Halloran would have fit just fine. Her shoes scuffed against solid Manhattan schist as Buzz turned slowly, holding the sconce before him, so they could see the entire room. There was no pot of gold. Just metal filing cabinets along one wall.

Janet yelled back up the stair. "Where's the gold!"

Halloran's face appeared in the rectangle above. Janet's heart jumped. A quick kick, and the leprechaun could bury them forever. Though Buzz was big and strong, and the chairs hadn't looked heavy enough to weigh down the trap door against them.

"There isn't any gold," Halloran said.

Janet was indignant. "You said there was gold."

"No, you said there was gold."

"What's in the cabinets?"

Halloran shrugged, and sucked on his pipe.

Janet remembered what the old man in the pub had said about bearer bonds, and turned back to Buzz. "Let's look in the cabinets."

What they found was better than gold. The cabinets were full of stock certificates, which were a lot easier to carry without a truck. IBM and General Motors and Microsoft and AOL. Intel and Yahoo and InfoSpace. Amazon and Cisco. Every blue chip and high-flying dotcom Janet had ever dreamed of owning.

She held up a double fistful of paper. "Jesus, Buzz. They're all bearer certificates. We can just take them!"

"That's a good thing?"

"Yes! They're as good as cash. Whoever has a bearer certificate in his possession owns it. If these were registered certificates we could take as many as we want, but it wouldn't matter unless Halloran transferred ownership to us. With these, all we have to do is walk into a brokerage house and sell them. For cash."

Buzz began grabbing certificates by the handful.

"You'll never get enough that way. Do you think we can lift one of the cabinets?"

They couldn't. Halloran had bolted them to the wall. They tried stuffing certificates into their pockets and inside their coats, but that ran the danger of wrinkling or ripping them. In the end Janet went upstairs and, with an attitude that dared Halloran to stop her, dragged the rug down to the cellar. Then she sorted the certificates into piles according to the largest face value, mostly the high-flying Nasdaq names, and rolled up as many of those as she could in the rug.

With each of them carrying an end, she and Buzz struggled up the ladder. On their first and second attempts the rug split open and everything fell out on the floor. Janet was forced to do another sort before they were finally able to carry the load up to the den without spilling any of it. And the hardest part was still to come, lugging the carpet through the sewer.

"Think you have enough?" Halloran asked.

Janet blew a loose lock of hair away from her face. "If I could get a truck down here, I would. Don't think we aren't coming back."

"It only works once. You'll never find this place again."

"I can follow you after work."

"I won't be showing up for work."

"That reminds me: thanks for firing me. Now I don't have to bother to resign. Not with this nest egg." She patted the rug.

Buzz was gloating, too.

"How much do you think we got?" he asked.

"I don't know. Thirty, forty million."

"I believe you have about forty-seven million there." Halloran eyed the girth of the rug. "That is, assuming you only took the highest priced shares. I know you have no qualms stealing from me, but would it bother you to know that a leprechaun's gold is a metaphor for his country's capital base? That's why Ireland was always so poor—people kept stealing our gold. The same thing will happen here."

"What do I care about other people? You think I'm a liberal or something? I'm a trader. Besides, forty-seven million isn't even an ink stain on the capital base of this country."

"I said the relationship was metaphorical, not nominal. The last time someone stole my securities was 1929."

Janet patted the rug. "As long as I've got mine, what do I care?"

"No, I suppose you wouldn't."

"You wouldn't, either."

"That goes without saying. I'm a leprechaun. Watching humans screw up is my favorite pastime."

"Well, I'm not screwing up. Not unless these are forgeries."

"I assure you, they are the real thing. You are a wealthy woman."

"That's all I need to hear. Come on, Buzz. Let's get these to a brokerage."

They had some trouble getting their loot out through the sewer tunnels. The lights that had led them in had gone out, and Buzz had to hold the sconce with one hand to show the way. The last they saw of Halloran, he was watching them from his doorway, puffing at his pipe. For someone who'd just lost forty-seven million dollars, he looked remarkably cheerful. Then Janet lost sight of him as a corner of the rug flipped opened and a couple thousand Microsoft and Apple shares fell out before she could grab them. She nearly dropped her end of the rug trying to keep the certificates out of the sewer, but remembered not to be too greedy just in time.

The sun was well up by the time they made it outside, late enough for the markets to be open. Maiden Lane churned with people on their way to work. It being New York, few people cast a second glance at them as they lugged the rug down the street. Suddenly a man buying a cup of coffee from a street vendor shouted, "Look out!" and pointed above their heads. Janet had no time to react. The rug was jerked violently down out of her hands. There was a loud thud, like a bundle of newspapers being tossed out on a curb, and stock certificates burst up into the air out of the carpet and fluttered around her.

She looked down. A man lay motionless on the ground, the rug squashed beneath him. Blood oozed from his face.

She looked up. A man and a woman leaned from a window nine or ten stories above. The woman held her face in her hands.

A crowd gathered. Even Wall Street stopped for sudden, violent death.

"He must have lost a fortune."

"To be sure, the market's taking it on the chin again this morning. It's just like October 1929 all over again."

Janet hadn't thought she'd hear that voice again. Halloran stood at the front of the crowd, looking like any other man in a dark suit and not something out of a fairytale.

His eyes twinkled.

"Let's just hope the Depression that follows isn't as bad as the one we had back then."

On her hands and knees, Janet scrabbled at her shares.

FIXED

Jean Marie Ward

There were lots of advantages to being a part-time cat. Being chased by a Rottweiler named Bitsy through Holcomb Creek Park wasn't one of them.

Heart pounding, chest heaving, Jack Tibbert raced down the bike path, insensible to the late November cold, the people on the path, or anything except escape. Bitsy's heavy grunts grew louder as she closed the gap between them. His imagination added the heat of the dog's breath on his neck as her massive jaws closed in for the kill. He had to take cover—high where her crushing teeth couldn't reach. But where? To his right the ground dropped sharply to the creek. The leafless saplings masking the fall were barely up to Jack's feline weight. They'd never survive the dog. The only trees worth climbing grew on the left side of the path. To reach them he'd have to cross a field of dead grass set with exercise equipment too low to fend off a Chihuahua. It was gonna be close.

He feinted right. With a triumphant *woof* and the

crackle of dead weeds, his pursuer plunged into the brush. Jack veered left, gaze locked on the outdoor balance beam. If he could run the dog into the log ...

"Look out!" a female voice screamed.

He turned just in time to see a bicycle twice his height tearing up the center of the path. Instinctively, he jumped. The wheel clipped his shoulder. He tumbled across the pavement and kept rolling until one of the saplings knocked all the wind out of him.

It took him a minute to put the world back together. *Had to get up. Dog. Too close. Yelping?* He shook his head.

"Are you all right?"

The light girlish voice seemed to come from heaven, which had dropped to a few feet overhead. The angel kneeling beside him had a perfect oval face, almond-shaped eyes, and windblown black hair streaked with rusty brown. She looked about sixteen, maybe a year younger than him—the kind of girl you see in all those dumb TV shows set in high school but you never meet in real life.

Small teeth raked her plump lower lip. "Don't scratch me, okay? I need to touch you to see where you're hurt."

Sugar, you can touch me wherever you want.

Somewhere in the background, Bitsy started to whine. Her owner wailed, "But it's the cat's fault!"

"Not if Bitsy was off her leash and chasing him," Jack's vision shouted over her shoulder. *Foxy chick was a cat person, too.* He purred, arching his back into the hand she trailed along his fur.

"Spine and hips, good," she muttered to herself. She found his tail. He flicked the tip playfully. "All right. Anything else we can fix."

She flinched at another blast from the Rottweiler's

owner. "Just keep her calm, Mrs. Saar. It'll be okay. I've got my phone.

"It's not like it hasn't happened before," she added under her breath.

She couldn't keep her hands off him. Swearing at the hit-and-run cyclist, dialing her phone—the whole time, one of her hands was stroking him or scratching the sweet spots behind his ears and between his shoulders. He rewarded her by turning the baby blues on high. They worked their usual magic. Her bright brown eyes and pretty pink mouth got all soft. She forgot the phone pressed to her left ear. When the call connected, she bounced in surprise. *Ev-er-y*-thing bounced.

With a grin as wicked as feline lips allowed, Jack rolled his shoulders and hauled himself to his feet. Joints popped. A dozen different muscles and tendons hummed with pain. He tottered a couple steps, wincing at his scraped fore pads, and collapsed dramatically across her jeans. He wasn't hurt much—nothing broken, anyway. Roughed up, yeah. Sore, definitely, and he'd be stiff tomorrow. But he had hopes for tonight.

"Oh. Oh, hi, Wes," she gasped. "Um, it's Rika."

High hopes.

"No, it's not that. I'm coming in, but we've got a situation here in the park. You need to send somebody to help Mrs. Saar."

"If I ever find the idiot who approved that adoption, I'm going to strangle them with a choke collar and throw the body to the ferrets!" Wes bawled loud enough for Jack to hear.

Rika jerked the phone away from her ear and giggled. "Relax. We got off easy this time: no police dogs. But there is a cat."

She scooped him up one-handed and cuddled him between her jacket and the nubbly sweater underneath. Jack was in heaven, and he hadn't even died.

"Has the vet been there yet?"

Vet! The only place nearby she'd find help with a dog *and* a vet was the Madeleine Humphrey Animal Shelter. Jack's hind paws shoved against her thigh, but his front end went nowhere. His left arm was caught between her fingers, and her thumb pressed behind his right shoulder. Time for claws or teeth, but he couldn't. He just couldn't.

"Great. I think he's okay, but he needs to be checked out. I'm bringing him in now."

It could be worse, he told himself, as Rika hurried toward the cinderblock building at the intersection between the bike path and the overpass. Madeleine Humphrey had the longest "hold time" in the area—one of the reasons he picked Holcomb to rough it. They wouldn't try anything right away, and it'd be nice to have a warm bunk for a change. There'd be food in the break rooms, aspirin, showers with real soap. He might even get online. With a pathetic mew, he rubbed his head against a sweet-smelling breast. She laughed a little breathlessly. He could play along for a couple of days; beyond that, well, they hadn't invented the cage that could hold Jack Tibbert, with or without thumbs.

Wes was the biggest vet tech Jack had ever seen—as in defensive lineman big. He escorted them to a gray room lined with a row of elevated steel cages he called the "Isolation Ward." As far as Jack was concerned, it wasn't isolated enough. The cage next to his held a pair of motor-mouthed kittens with enormous ears and even bigger egos. The other cats moped over their paws like they hadn't napped in hours. To add insult to injury, his nose told him the little monsters were the only ones who rated canned food, and he was hungry enough to eat a squirrel. He stared reproachfully at Rika while Wes secured the door to his cell.

"Don't look at me like that," she pleaded. "It's not that bad."

It wasn't. Jack had inherited his human mother's immunity to iron, and the cage was large enough to hold his human form—if he positioned himself right. He didn't think he'd need to shapeshift, though. The lock was a simple drop-handled latch. Not that he planned to let her off the hook. The guiltier she felt, the more petting he'd get.

"It's only for a couple days, until we're sure you're okay, then we'll move you into the big room. The cages are seven feet tall, and you can climb all the way to the top."

Wes shook a finger the size of a sausage in front of her nose. "Don't you fall for that pitiful act. He's just softening you up so you'll be easier to train once you get him home."

Rika crouched next to the cage, stroking the bars. Jack inched toward her.

"Uh huh," Wes said knowingly.

She shook her head and straightened. "My parents'll never let me have a cat. Besides, he's somebody's pet: he wasn't wary at all. And his fur's so soft, like a bunny. Somebody out there is going crazy looking for this little guy."

Not that little, Jack bristled.

Wes snorted. "You'd think, especially considering he looks like a purebred Snowshoe. Do you know what they cost?"

"Wes!"

Wes raised his hands in surrender. "All right, all right, I'll check him for microchips and post his picture in all the usual places. That'll give you ten days to wear your folks down."

"It's not that simple."

"Sure it is. Tell them we'll give you a good deal on fixing him, too. He should get it done soon. He'll be healthier, happier, have fewer behavioral problems. He'll never miss it."

Like hell! Spitting, ears flat, hair spiked, Jack leapt back, kicking his water bowl and splashing the kittens. They shrieked. Cats all down the line hissed and snarled. The humans gaped. Then Wes sputtered, "Hee. Hee. Hee," like an asthmatic bird. Rika, the traitor, doubled over and howled until her face turned red.

"That must've been some joke."

High heels clicked against the cement floor as the newcomer stalked into the room. Tall and slender, with the face of an aging supermodel, the woman wore a fur hat and belted wool coat even Jack could tell were expensive.

Wes gulped, "Dr. Kellas!"

"It was more of a visual," Rika burbled, "We were talking about . . ."

"Not now, dear. Where is everyone?"

Without waiting for an answer or removing her gloves, the doctor grabbed a clipboard from the rack next to the door and began a slow circuit of the cages, comparing notes to cats. She moved like a model, too. But something smelled off. Jack couldn't say what, only that it didn't jibe with the normal stew of people, animals, disinfectant, and soap.

"We've got three volunteer dog walkers working the

kennel—soon to be four." Wes waggled his eyebrows at
Rika. His big hands made little shooing motions where
the vet couldn't see them. Rika smiled and stayed put.
"Enid's car broke down while she was at her sister's, so
she won't be in this weekend. Flo and Bobby Ray ought
to be along soon. They're in the park with Mrs. Saar.
Bitsy slipped her leash again and managed to get herself
tangled in the only briar patch between here and Library
Bridge."

"You'd think she'd learn from the vet bills," Dr. Kellas
said softly. "Obviously, she needs more."

It should've been an observation, but it sounded like
a threat. The atmosphere in the room changed, like a
wind shift in the savannah carrying the scent of lion to a
herd of unsuspecting gazelle. Suddenly Jack was very
aware of the songbirds tweeting in the cages at the front
of the building and the dogs complaining in the other
wing. Even the kittens shut up, pressing their bodies to
the wet plastic floor of their cage.

A chill brushed his spine, lifting fur that had just
begun to relax. Jack's ability to sense magic was no better than human. The difference was he knew it existed
and taught himself to read the warning signs in other
animals. This one was lit up in neon. He hunkered down
and tried to think cat thoughts; the last thing he wanted
was to attract any kind of magical attention.

"Amen, sister—I mean, doctor," Wes corrected himself. "I told the adoption counselors Bitsy was too much
dog for a little woman like that, but did they listen?"

Dr. Kellas didn't answer. Black wool replaced Rika's
jeans in Jack's field of view. Paper snapped beneath
leather-gloved fingers. *Not good.* "Where are the notes
on this one?"

"Oh, he just arrived. That's the boy Bitsy got herself all worked up about. I've asked Rika to write him up." His hands clapped Rika's shoulders. "It was love at first sight. I think our little volunteer's about to become a mother."

Rika started to object but Dr. Kellas cut her off. "Did the dog bite it? Is it injured?"

"We don't know that he is," Wes said. "We'll run the usual tests, but he seems fine. Well, he scraped his paws, but a little ointment'll take care of that."

"No," Dr. Kellas growled. This close, her odor was inescapable. Beneath layers of perfume, peppermint, and coffee, her breath stank of blood and spoiled meat.

Cat instinct screamed at him to hide. He didn't need magic to know he was chum in a shark cage, and she was a Great White *Something That Wasn't Human*. Shockwaves of magical energy pounded his senses, stretching his nerves until he thought he was going to shake apart.

"Just as I thought," she said. "Prepare this animal for surgery. I need to operate immediately."

His head shot upward. Backed against the steel bars, he couldn't help seeing past her glamour. The lines scoring her forehead and bracketing the corners of her wide, lipsticked mouth floated like a painted veil over a pale, ageless face as perfect as a marble Madonna. Black eyebrows and lashes set off eyes the color of green apples. Cat eyes as hard as jade, with oval slits peeping through round human pupils. She was a true cat sidhe, one of the Celtic fae who could work magic as well as shapeshift. And every feature of her terrible, beautiful face twisted in loathing.

"*Mrow!*" *No!* He turned somersaults in his cage. There wasn't anything wrong with him! He was fine! Perfect!

Rika's gaze darted from the cage to the vet. Her shoulders pulled back as if she was trying to distance herself. He yowled in frustration.

Wes pressed a hand to his cheek. "With all due respect, Dr. Kellas, I don't think you can. Flo wants you to look at Oscar's abscess first thing. Then there's the K-9 clinic. How about this: I'll see he gets into X-ray as soon as Bobby Ray gets back. If things are as bad as you say, I'm sure Flo'll find a way to work him in."

"We can't wait that long. He's already showing signs of extreme agitation. If you don't take care of concussions and spinal injuries immediately, there could be permanent damage. You wouldn't want that," she crooned, lasering the humans with her gaze. "It could lead to intracranial hemorrhage, convulsions, ischemia."

What the hell was she up to? Jack pressed his face against the bars of his cell. Most fae races had no problems with iron, but for pureblooded Celtic sidhe, it was worse than kryptonite. It burned them on contact, disrupted their spells and let anybody who knew what to look for—human or otherwise—see through their illusions. Even so, most people would've dismissed what he saw as hallucination. The doctor's aura crackled with the green static of rising magic. The kittens in the next cage whimpered, further tainting the air with their piss.

"I'd have to put him down." She sang, and her crystalline soprano transformed a statement into a spell. "But I can fix him. I'll operate and neuter him for free. When I'm done, he'll be the perfect pet."

"*No!*" Jack screamed. She wanted to castrate him! Lobotomize him! "*No! No! Noooooo!*"

Rika wrenched her gaze from the fae and slammed both hands against his cage, almost knocking him over.

Her fingers locked around the narrow bars as if she knew their power. He held his breath.

"He doesn't have a concussion," she panted. "His pupils are the same size."

The sidhe's nostrils flared, but her tone remained mild. "That's a human marker, dear."

"Rika, honey, you're upset," Wes said. "But you got to listen to the doctor. She's only got the cat's best interest at heart."

"She wants to destroy me!" he howled, ramming the cage door.

"See, he wasn't acting like that a minute ago," Wes said. Beneath her concerned-doctor disguise, the sidhe's eyes blazed with triumph. Pureblooded Celtic fae couldn't lie outright, but all her misdirection and medical mumbo jumbo led to a single conclusion—and the harder he protested, the more it looked like she was right.

"He's scared," Rika objected. "He can tell something's wrong."

"There is something wrong—with him. Look at him," Wes said. "How could you live with yourself if something bad happened to that boy because you thought you knew better than the doctor? But that's not going to happen, because the doctor's going to operate, and you're going to be right here waiting for him when she gets done."

It was a hell of an exit line. Dr. Kellas didn't try to top it; she left. Wes hurried after her. Jack wanted to scratch him. Why'd he have to put that thought in Rika's head? Jack didn't want sympathy; he wanted her to run after them, delay them, not stand in front of his cage chewing her thumb.

"I don't understand. Nobody just goes in and operates. This isn't a TV show. You need X-rays and blood tests . . . all that stuff."

He needed to get out of there. He rolled onto his back and shoved the wire latch with both front paws. White hot pain jolted his arms. "mmOWWW!"

"What're you doing?"

What's it look like? Damn thing was stuck. He should've expected it with giant vet techs smacking it around all day. He positioned his paws closer to the base of the handle and gritted his teeth. His paws slipped— the handle was too slick. What now? Oh.

"You're bleeding!" she keened. Grown cats covered their ears. Dogs on the other side of the building bayed in response. But nobody came running, not Wes, not the other volunteers. Had the sidhe enthralled them all? *Shit.*

He licked blood and lymph off his fore pads. He would've given anything to do a partial shift—thumbs to clench, palms that were only fractionally hamburger. But for half-breeds like him, it was all or nothing—never a good idea with humans around.

"Dr. Kellas should be taking care of your poor paws, not, not—"

Humans always got hysterical. At least he didn't have to worry about iron unmasking him. Shapeshifting was in his DNA; no spells or glamour required. When he was a cat, he was a cat in everything but mind. Unfortunately. More strength would've been a plus. He bellied up to the door, hooked his claws on either side of the handle and pulled. This time he saw red stars, but the hook was free of the bar, and he was pretty sure he still had all his claws.

"You popped the catch," Rika gasped, dropping to her knees. *Blocking the door.*

Snarl later. Right now he needed to free the bolt. He pushed his muzzle through the bars on the far side of the latch and tried gnawing it. Bad idea. Scratching didn't help, either. He was too close to focus on the bolt, and his human brain couldn't compensate for distance the way it did for color, but from its position relative to his whiskers, it was as warped as the rest of the handle.

"You're problem-solving! I knew you were special."

He nodded. *Got that right.* Carefully, he fitted his right paw to the hook. Pushing it was like grinding a broken blister over the head of a nail.

"Do it again," she demanded. "Nod if you understand what I'm saying."

Sure.

"Omigod, are you a . . . ? No!" She jumped to her feet and paced like she was the one in the cage. "Don't go there. Remember what happened the last time you thought you found a *bakeneko* — and that was your mom, not Cruella de Vet."

He got Cruella, but *Bach E. What*?

"Latches and nodding — they're just tricks. He can't do magic, or he'd have blasted the door. He's got one tail, he walks on four legs, and he can't talk. Face it, he's only an animal." She whirled. Her forehead knotted and mouth strained. She kicked the floor. "But that doesn't give her the right to cut him up."

So save me! "Me-e-ew."

Nobody did pitiful like Jack Tibbert. She practically melted over his cage. "Don't cry, baby. I won't let her hurt you. I'll turn you loose first."

Yes!

"No. They'll crucify me over a *cat*. They'll strip my

community service credits. My grade point'll tank and . . . oh God! I put the shelter on all my college applications!"

His jaw sagged. *Fate worse than death here, and you're angsting about grades?* Hissing in disgust, he checked his hind legs. The pads weren't as raw as the ones in front. He dropped to the cage floor and poked his right leg through the bars.

"It's my word against hers, and she's the vet of the day. Wait, that's it—get another vet." She pulled out her phone and mauled the screen. "C'mon, Dr. Vygotsky, be home. Be home. *Noooooo*," she moaned. "Don't transfer me to the answering service!"

Not enough leverage. He needed a better angle.

One of the kittens chirped.

The zombie filling the doorway had a fluffy towel slung over his left arm. He was dressed like the surgeons who had operated on Jack's mom. A blue smock covered his scrubs and layered latex gloves extended past his thick wrists to clasp the ribbed ends of his sleeves. A shower cap was pulled low on his forehead, and a blue paper mask stretched from ear to ear. The dark eyes between had forgotten how to blink.

Rika's eyebrows drew together in a frown. "What's with the gown, Wes? It's not sterile in here."

Wes ignored her. Under the sidhe's spell, he couldn't tell her the point wasn't hygiene; it was making sure he wouldn't touch iron, even by chance. As if Jack'd leave it to chance. He hunched in the center of the cage and extended his aching claws.

"Stop, Wes, listen to me. We can't do this. This cat is special."

"Yes, it is," he rumbled in tones much deeper than his

usual fluting drawl. He would've walked over her if she hadn't stumbled out of his way. She grabbed his towel arm. He shoved her aside. She staggered into the corner cages. The bars rang, and cats *mrow*-ed in alarm.

"Wes?" her voice wobbled. "What's wrong?"

Six feet away.

"No!"

Four feet. Two. Wes jerked the latch. Jack sprang.

Right into the towel. He twisted, trying to escape, but somehow that made it worse. The more he struggled, the tighter the towel wrapped around him, binding his legs to his body.

"Wesley Ernesto Perez, put him down!"

Ponderously, without ever easing his hold on the towel, Wes turned. "This cat needs immediate surgery."

"He does not." Rika reached for him but flinched before connecting. "Please," she begged, "Dr. Kellas made a mistake. He's totally okay."

"Stop deluding yourself, dear," he said in a ghastly echo of the fae's human voice. "You're a child. She's a doctor."

"So was Frankenstein!" Rika yelled at his back.

It didn't have any more effect than Jack's efforts to wriggle free. He snapped at Wes's fingers, but he couldn't turn his head, and the spell on Wes's mind hadn't affected his reflexes. Panic stole Jack's breath. His cat form didn't stand a chance against Dr. Kellas and her pet thrall. He needed to shift, but he couldn't, and rolled up tighter than a burrito, his bones would be crushed, his organs pulped inside him. He'd seen what happened to his brother.

Calm down! They wouldn't kill him like this. Dr. Kellas had to at least pretend to operate, if only because of

Rika. *Who'd insist on a second opinion.* A sick chuckle sputtered from his throat, and he could breathe again.

His timing sucked. The surgical prep room greeted him with a nose-burning rush of wintergreen. Inside was an unholy hybrid of doctor's office and operating theater, complete with built-in desks, rolling stools, and pole-mounted machines with dangling wires and menacing robotic arms. Thick translucent plastic covered the rectangular table in the center of the room, obscuring the gray surface beneath. Steel, and a lot of it. That was something, at least.

Dr. Kellas wasn't wearing a mask—nothing to get in the way of her voice. The rest of her was as iron-proof as her thrall. She had no trouble tapping the enormous syringe in her gloved right hand.

Wes set him on the table. Jack tensed, sweating the milliseconds until the towel loosened. Dr. Kellas couldn't inject him blind: the needle might miss. But the vet tech's heavy hands never lifted from his back. The syringe homed in on his flank, growing larger as it approached like some cheesy special effect.

The double doors to the hallway crashed into the wall and scrub sink with teeth-jarring clangs.

"Dr. Kellas," Rika trilled, "I brought the towels you asked for."

The doctor whirled, hissing denial. Her hold on Wes wavered. Jack flailed free of the towel, shifting to his human form as he fell behind the table. He landed cat-like on all fours and yanked the plastic free.

"Don't let him escape," the sidhe ordered.

Wes had him in a wrestler's bear hug before the plastic hit the floor. Jack was five-foot-eight and a hundred forty pounds of lean muscle and dirty tricks, but hoisted a foot off the ground with Wes's meaty fists locked under his ribs, none of it mattered. He kicked, elbowed, and strained against the table—he tore at Wes's gloves and the back of his neck. He tried everything short of eye-gouging, but it was like beating on a tree.

"Leave, Rika," Dr. Kellas thundered. "Shelter volunteers aren't allowed in surgery."

Her voice resonated with power. The sound and the giant needle in her right hand—not to mention the naked guy dangling in midair on the other side of the operating table—should've sent Rika running. Instead, she stood transfixed. Her gaze trailed from his shaggy seal brown hair, past his blue eyes and the beard he was trying to grow, past the darkening bruise wrapped around his left shoulder, to lock on the white, palm-shaped birthmark bleached into the permanent tan of his chest. It was the same white and light brown he wore in feline form, if not in the same places.

"*Bakeneko*," she breathed. "You're a *bakeneko*. Why didn't you say—"

Dr. Kellas grabbed Rika's chin in her left hand. Pointed claws strained her latex gloves. "Erika Nakamura, hear me. That isn't human; it's a cat; a pretty little cat that needs an operation right now."

"Rika, don't listen!" Jack cried. "She's trying to hypnotize you!"

"Let go of me!" Rika shrieked the same instant. She slammed the towels into the doctor's right arm. Syringe and towels dropped to the floor. Before the vet could react, Rika grabbed her wrist in one hand and chopped the inside of her elbow with the other.

Spitting fury, the fae retreated. She hadn't drawn blood, but the sound magic of the Celtic fae didn't need it. Her voice soared, producing notes and harmonics that couldn't, shouldn't flow from a human throat. "He's a cat who needs fixing. Fixed, he'll be the perfect pet. Docile and friendly, he'll never roam or mark or claw."

Rika's perspiration grew musky with fear. Jack shouted, "Grab the table! Iron breaks the spell!"

Rika shook her head, not listening. Soon she'd succumb, and there'd be two humans against him, as well as the fae. The big artery leading to his legs pulsed beneath Wes's fist—another shift-killing hold. Jack needed a weapon. Where were the damned instruments? They were steel. If he could just reach one . . .

"Stop it!" Rika's scream knifed through the fae's song. She snatched a metal tray off the drain board and swung it into Dr. Kellas's side. "He's a person, not a pet!"

Dr. Kellas screeched. She grabbed the red plastic hazmat bin from the floor next to the sink. Wielding it like a shield, she thrust and dodged. Her poisonous music swelled once more. "Cat, little girl. Little girls love cats. Cat, cat, caaaat . . ."

"Don't patronize me!" Rika slammed the bin, grazing the doctor's jaw on her upswing. Jack flinched at the smell of seared meat. Dr. Kellas stumbled, dropping the bin. The burly arms around Jack's waist trembled, but not enough. The sidhe caught herself on one of the rolling machines, and her lips parted on a deadly, expanding pearl of sound.

"Let them go!"

The tray swept down. The fae ducked. Her sleeve snagged on a protruding knob, and when she tried to swerve, her foot caught in one of the trailing cords. She fell into the gap between the sink and the built-ins. Her head struck the side of an overhead cabinet and the counter beneath it. She crumpled to the floor.

With a soft grunt, Wes flopped forward, pinning Jack against the table. He weighed as much as a tree, too.

"Help," Jack wheezed.

"Are they dead?" Rika blubbered. "Did I kill them?"

Here it comes, the freakout we've all been waiting for. Resigning himself to the inevitable, Jack crawled out from under the vet tech. He slumped against the table, amazed he was still in one piece and breathing. Breathing was vastly underrated.

Cold air on unfurred skin—not so much. "Where do they keep the scrubs?"

"You didn't answer." Rika glared at him, clutching the warped tray to her chest.

"They'll be fine." As a precaution, Jack stripped Wes's cap, mask and gloves. The more places he was touching iron when he woke, the better.

"How can you tell?"

She didn't need to know he could hear their heartbeats. There was a slim chance she'd suppress the whole cat-to-person thing. "His chest's moving. So's hers."

"Breathing. Right." Speaking of breathing, hers sounded ragged.

"Scrubs," he repeated firmly.

The tray landed beside the sink with an angry clank. "I just saved your skinny butt. Would it kill you to say thank you first?"

"Thank you, with hearts and flowers and whatever else you need. Now can we get back to clothes? *Hel-lo*— naked guy here."

She *ooop*-ed and covered her eyes. Her free hand

pointed over her shoulder. "Tech station. Bottom drawer."

"Thanks." He kicked the plastic ahead of him. He didn't want to step in the splinters of the doctor's hypodermic, or anything else on the floor, not with red smudges marking his trail. At least they had scrubs his size. He couldn't help a sigh of relief as he pulled the pants over his junk. He was going to have nightmares about this for years.

"How long before they wake up?"

"How should I know? I'm not a doctor." *I'm just trying to look like one.*

"Oh God, I hit a doctor," Rika moaned.

Jack pulled the top over his head. It felt like he'd strained every muscle in his body, and now they were straining back. He'd better steal a full bottle of painkillers.

"I could be arrested! Go to jail! I'll be grounded for life! I might as well quit school and apply to McDonald's right now. I'll never get into college."

"Enough with the drama already. Say she attacked you. Bandages? Booties?"

Her hand dropped. The expression on her face was tragic. "But Wes . . ."

"Won't remember a thing. He wasn't himself when he hit you."

Rika swallowed, nodded. Tears spiked her lashes. He wished . . .

He'd wished a lot of things since his mom died.

He pulled bandages and antibiotic ointment from an overhead cabinet. He was taking too long—Sleeping Behemoth was already starting to twitch—but he needed to deal with his feet. His boots were on the other side of the park, hidden in the restroom building with the rest of his gear. If he doubled up on the booties, he should be able to make it. He just had to find them. He kneed a small rolling stool away from another set of drawers.

"Why'd Dr. Kellas go after you? Do you know each other?"

"I don't associate with mongrels."

The fae's words sizzled with contempt. She inched up the wall. Her cap disappeared, and thick, inky tresses poured past her hips. Her glamour had dissipated, baring the inhuman symmetry of her features, the raw burn on her chin, the sharp facets of her cat-green eye.

Jack blinked. Her right eye glittered green around a cat's slit pupil. Her other eye was nothing but pupil. *That's a human marker, dear.*

"Rika, run!" Jack upended an IV pole, and thrust the wheels at Dr. Kellas's chest. The base was heavy enough for steel. If he could surround her with iron, maybe they could escape. The fae snorted, lips drawn back in a lopsided sneer.

"Stay!" she commanded. Dissonance spread from the word like blackness from the abyss. "I need to sterilize this abomination before he pollutes the clowder. Curs like him can't be allowed to breed. I became a veterinarian to stop this kind of filth from spreading."

Sweat popped on Jack's forehead and dribbled chills down his back. Not lying wasn't the same as telling the truth. Hitting her head must've short-circuited something in her brain. She was saying what she felt without any filter or control. If that happened to her magic . . .

Behind him, Wes groaned, "Dr. Kellas, is that you?"

"Finally," she said. "Seize him, thrall."

"What did you call me?"

"Thrall, slave—what does it matter? Do it!"

"Slave?" The question ended an octave higher than it began.

"Wes, she hit her head," Rika said. "She's not herself."

"Stop talking, you two. Get help. She's dangerous!"

The fae laughed, and even with skinned palms on a cold steel pole, silver bells rang inside Jack's head, tearing through his brain until it was leaking, warm and wet, out his ears. Eyes slitted against the pain, he jabbed her with the wheels. She arched her back, daring him to hurt her. He didn't want to hurt anybody. He just wanted to get out of there, but he didn't know how. He couldn't explain the real danger to Rika and Wes, so he stood there like a dork while the fae rubbed her shoulders against the wall. Static lifted a fan of fine black hairs from her gown. A few strands brushed the pole's axles. To Jack's shock, they caught fire, red gobbling the black as if he held the ends to a candle. No wonder pureblood sidhe never cut their hair—not with steel scissors at any rate.

With an irritated sniff, Dr. Kellas smothered the cinders between her fingers. "What's wrong with you proles? Get this filthy mutt off me!"

"Who are you calling a mutt?" Wes boomed.

"She's sick," Rika said.

"Where are your eyes? Look at him!" She pointed at Jack. Disgust twisted her features into a black-furred muzzle. "He's *brown*, like some dirty underground gnome. He's not even human!"

"That's it," Wes snapped. "Not another word. I'm calling 911, and you're gonna sit your crazy ass down and behave until the EMTs get here, or I won't be responsible for my actions."

The fae's lips curled back from her fangs. Her throat

corded and her gown lifted as she filled her lungs with air. Jack shoved the stand hard into her chest. Steel met hair with an electric snap and flames spurted from the wheelbase, igniting a fiery halo around her face but leaving her clothes untouched.

She bellowed, flinging the pole back. Jack went with it, skidding on the plastic, and landed between the counter and the table half under a rolling metal basket. He pushed it aside. It rammed back into him with the partially shifted fae on top. She was as big as a cougar, roaring, tearing at him with smoking claws. Gagging on the stench of burning hair, he grabbed her arms and flung himself to the side. Her back struck the base of the table and her hind claws yanked the basket from between them. She threw her weight against him. He shoved back with all his might, desperate to keep her smoldering claws pinned against her shoulders.

Foam erupted out of nowhere. One minute fire wreathed her lion's face; the next, she was covered in weird-smelling chemical goo. She squawked and batted it with her oversized paws, but the foam continued to hiss over her.

Jack lurched to his feet and grabbed a stool, ready to bring it down on her head. A whoosh of icy water from the other direction cut him off. Rika aimed the high pressure nozzle of the scrub sink down the length of Dr. Kellas's body. The fae squalled like a cat at bath time. She shot from under the table and exploded out the doors to a chorus of barking dogs, shrieking birds and a host of animal sounds Jack couldn't begin to identify.

The fire extinguisher in Wes's hands coughed a final puff of foam. "Rika, honey, could you turn off that water? I'm getting soaked."

The cavalry arrived a minute later. The doors flew inward with another syncopated crash, framing a no-nonsense blonde in a shelter-branded hoodie like a gunfighter at the entrance of an Old West saloon. A tiny old woman with a red leash draped around her neck and another super-sized vet tech propped the panels open behind her.

"What the hell is going on here?" the blonde demanded.

Wes opened his mouth. Closed it. Rika chewed her lip. Jack lowered the stool, straightened his shoulders and stuck out his hand.

"Hi, I'm Jack Tibbert, from Rika's homeroom. She's told me so much about the shelter, I had to check it out." Jack didn't have any problem with lying.

Neither, apparently, did Rika. "Jack!" She picked her way through the jumble of equipment and carefully laced her fingers in his. "Flo, it was awful. Wes and Dr. Kellas were taking care of the cat I brought in, and something happened. Wes got shot full of anesthetic, and then Dr. Kellas hit her head. She went crazy. Somebody needs to find her. She could hurt herself."

The old lady sniffed, "I told you that cat was a menace!"

"Yes, Mrs. Saar, you did." Flo's gaze dropped to the fire extinguisher. "Good God, that foam-covered freak in the parking lot was Dr. Kellas?"

"I don't know who else it could be. Speaking of which"—Wes pursed his lips and took a deep breath before continuing—"we need to talk. That woman's crossed the line for the last time."

"Can it wait 'til Monday?" Wes looked at her. Flo rubbed her face. "Fine. You can tell me about it while we put this place back together. Bobby Ray, get Mrs. Saar and Bitsy settled, then call the other vets. See if anybody can cover emergencies for the rest of the weekend. I'll reschedule the clinic." She turned to Jack. "I don't know what to say, kid. This isn't our normal." She examined him more closely. "You okay?"

He managed to shrug without wincing. "Mostly."

"I can take care of him in the break room," Rika said brightly. "I got my Red Cross certificate this summer."

He was doomed. Even though she wasn't pressing his sores, he'd break his paw if he tried to shift with her fingers threaded in his. She didn't let go until they were locked inside the break room. Leaning against the door handle, she studied him from under her bangs. Hell. After all that talk about magic and Bach-E-Neckids, he should've realized she was one of *them*.

"I guess you want to know if what you saw was real."

"No, I want to know how long you've been living in the park."

He stiffened. "Who says I have?"

She crossed her arms under her breasts. He gulped.

"Up *here*. Indoor cats have hair between their pads. You don't."

He started to say that didn't mean anything, but her scowl told him she knew better, and the prickly little pheromones scenting the air between them said he'd used up all his freebies staring at her boobs.

"Three months."

"Why?"

"Why else? No money."

"But your parents . . ."

"Mom died in August. Dad's been gone so long I don't remember what he looks like, and before you ask, everybody I've ever met from his side of the family takes after Psycho Sidhe."

"You can't stay there."

"No kidding. It's the first place she'll look."

She flicked her fingers as if it didn't matter. "No, I meant it's no way to live. You should be in college."

"College?" he yelped. "I haven't even graduated high school."

Big mistake. Her eyes and mouth turned hard.

"Forget it. Social services stuck me with a pair of holy rollers who thought Harry Potter was the Herald of the Apocalypse. I'm not going back. It's only for a couple months." Well, less than a year. "I can always get a G.E.D."

"On the run from Dr. Kellas and everybody else? Like that's a plan with a future." She cocked her head to the left, where a sagging curtain divided the break area from a half wall of cardboard boxes. "You need dry clothes. The shelter keeps extra sweats and flip-flops here for emergencies. I think this qualifies."

Only one way to deal with her. Deploying his eyelashes for maximum effect, Jack slowly lifted his raw hands. Being dragged to the kitchenette sink wasn't the reaction he'd expected, but her mews of distress were encouraging, and the liquid bandage she sprayed over the cleaned scrapes did dial down the sting a few notches.

"Give it a minute to set, and you'll be good to go until we get home."

"Home?" He jerked his hands from her grasp. "With you? Your parents won't even let you have a cat."

"This is different. Trust me, we'll have you fixed up in no time."

He groaned, "Please, don't use that word."

An impish grin lifted the corners of her mouth. "Yeah, that could be a real buzzkill. But it doesn't change the facts. People like us need to stick together. We can help each other."

"To an early grave. Look, Rika, I appreciate everything you did, but I gotta split, and you gotta let me. That vet wasn't the forgiving type before she hit her head, and now—shit, I don't know what'll happen now." He leaned in close enough to kiss. He learned early to always leave them with a thrill. "Keep something iron or steel with you all the time. Will you do that for me?"

She giggled. He would've been insulted if he hadn't been so scared. Didn't she know what a full-blooded cat sidhe could do to her and her family? He whined in frustration. Chick was crazier than Dr. Kellas.

"You're so cute when you're clueless," she cooed. Her face shimmered and morphed into a pointed black nose and white furry chin. Red fur rolled down the rest of her features as pointed ears poked through her hair. She was a fox. For real.

"What? You think cats are the only people around here with tails?"

A PEOPLE WHO ALWAYS KNOW

Shannon Page & Jay Lake

Hestia ai Morning Glory ten'Amber, High Lady of the Goldhelm Family of the Westernmost Fae and formerly queen of their realm, peered into a begrimed window of the 30 Stockton bus as it pulled up to the stop on the corner of Columbus and Union. She wasn't actually looking for anyone—her magical senses had told her before it had even pulled up that there were only humans aboard—but she had been searching for so long, and finding so little, it was hard to lose the habit.

The changeling situation was entirely out of control.

With a sigh of hydraulics, the bus closed its doors and pulled out into the stream of traffic on Union. Hestia took an involuntary step back and wrinkled her perfect nose against the diesel fumes. Horrid! That the humans could stand to live amid such ugliness.

She noticed that a few people were glancing in her direction. Had she let her glamour slip? Hestia took a quick inventory of her person. No, she was still clad as an ordinary matron: pale linen shirtdress, buttoned down the front; matching pumps, sensibly low at the heel for daytime; a smartly contrasting handbag that snapped at the top. As she looked more closely at other women, though, she realized that they were all dressed in a far more slovenly fashion. And not accessorized in the least. Was that a cloth sack that young woman carried?

Oh, by the Tree. Had styles changed yet again? It had only been a few score years since she'd been over on the human side. People never would settle on anything, would they?

Lifting her chin and meeting the boldest of the humans' gazes with a strong, haughty expression of her own, Hestia began to walk down the sidewalk towards Stockton. This would take her farther from the Hill and the doorway back to Faerie . . . but she wasn't ready to return just yet.

Not until she had found the little miscreants who were making such a mess of the situation, anyway.

Iannon, untitled youngling of the Ferrishyn Family of the Westernmost Fae, laughed aloud as he ran down another vertiginously steep San Francisco street. Rex, Lucas, and Gardenia trailed behind him, not quite daring to lose control as Iannon did. Magic worked sporadically at best here in the human realm; it was all they could do to hold their appearances steady to something resembling human. This was easier for Iannon than for the others, with his delicate ears and blue eyes. Gardenia might as well dress up as a clown and be done with it.

"Can't catch me! I win!" Iannon sang as he darted into a cross-street, jumping over cars as they swerved to avoid him. He made the opposite sidewalk and stopped abruptly, turning to face his pursuers.

They were on him in a moment, Rex grabbing high as Lucas aimed low. The two fairies tumbled Iannon to the ground, where they were leapt upon by Gardenia. All four fairies rolled and shrieked and scrabbled and grabbed at one another, until the whole pile of them barreled into the side of a building and came to a stop.

By now everyone was laughing just as hard as Iannon. He picked himself up out of the fray and flicked a spot of dirt off his trousers. "Well! That was invigorating."

Lucas was the next to rise. He'd received a splash of mud across his pale face; Iannon reached over and wiped it clean. "You shouldn't do that," Lucas said, trying for a serious tone but not quite achieving it.

"You were a mess. It was unsightly."

"Not that." Lucas rolled his bright eyes. "The roughhousing."

"Why not? They can't see us."

"Then why is that car on the sidewalk?" Rex, now standing, pointed to a small red convertible across the street.

Iannon looked over at it, then cocked his head and looked from a different angle. Yes, he would have to admit, that didn't look entirely intentional. "I don't know," he shrugged. "Carelessness?"

"You aren't trying hard enough with the misdirection," Lucas said. "You know what the Lady says . . ."

Iannon snorted. "The Lady loves me. She doesn't mind. Besides, what do we care? They're only human."

Lucas gave him a most annoyingly grown-up look.

"Oh, all right," Iannon said, before his friends could

nag at him further. "I just wanted a bit of exercise before we get started. I'm ready now."

"Good. Shall we start with the girl?"

Loretta Sinnette left the office late. Again.

When she'd taken the job, she'd been promised occasional overtime. "Once a week at the most," Mr. Clarkson had said. "Unlike most investment houses, we want our young staff to have personal lives."

It was a nice thought. Would have been even nicer if it had been true.

At least most of her overtime was paid, if she chose to report it on her time sheets. But what was she supposed to do with all the money? She was too exhausted and too busy to spend it. Pile it up in the bank, she supposed. Her children could spend it when she was dead.

Assuming she ever had time to have children. Which would mean having time to find a husband. And that got back to that whole quaint concept of a "personal life."

"Ha," she muttered as she let herself out of the building, into the foggy San Francisco night. "Personally falling asleep in front of the TV again."

The Financial District was quiet at this hour. She'd have to walk up to Market Street at least to get a cab, maybe even up closer to the Civic Center. At least she could afford a cab—the Muni at this hour would be depressing indeed.

Gathering her coat more tightly around her, Loretta strode toward the lights of Market Street.

Suddenly there were dark shapes to either side of her. Someone grabbed her right arm as a young man appeared before her. He had dark curls, bright blue eyes, and a mad, feral look. Loretta needed only an instant to take all this in, before she could even gather breath to scream.

The young man put a gentle hand over her mouth, moving almost too quickly for her to perceive. "No, no, none of that," he whispered.

Her terror fell away, though she could not have said why. Something in his voice ... it was gentle and bewitching. She let her breath out through her nose, as his hand still covered her mouth, and relaxed into the grip of whoever held her arm.

Dark, it was so dark! Why could she not see who held her?

The man before her dropped his hand. "There, you see? Nothing to be frightened of. Walk with us." He gave her a dazzling smile. Loretta smiled back at him, still not understanding. Wondering where her fear had gone.

There were two people behind her as well; she could sense that even though she could not see them. And though they were on Sansome Street, in the heart of the Financial District, there was not another soul about.

The dark-haired man took her left arm and turned her around, walking back in the direction of her office. "Here we go," he murmured in her ear.

Loretta walked numbly. She felt encased in a bubble, a safe and mysterious cocoon. As they approached a streetlight, she glanced over at the one to her right. He was another young man, also peculiar looking: bright blond hair and very pale skin. Almost luminescent, though that had to be a trick of the light.

She looked away, back towards the one who had spoken. "Where ..." she started, but stumbled over her own words. The whole thing felt like a dream.

"Hush for now, you're safe with us," he murmured.

They walked on, to the sound of light footsteps behind her.

Hestia walked aimlessly until she got to Telegraph Hill, then decided to climb to Coit Tower. Many fae, when they came topside, avoided heights with the reflexive discomfort of creatures who spent their lives underground, but Hestia had always been unique. Unafraid. She welcomed the giddy freedom of the open air and the brilliance of the stars above.

Though not many stars could be seen, here in the middle of the city, with all its polluting, glaring lights. How different the world had become! Every time she came over, it seemed to have become more crowded, more complex. Brighter, faster, noisier.

Hestia made her way to the top. At least it was a bit darker and quieter up here, though she still had to avoid humans—in pairs, in groups, and a few solo night wanderers. She stood in the shadows behind a couple who were holding hands as they gazed at the view of downtown in the middle distance. The woman leaned her head on the man's shoulder. After a minute, he kissed her.

Very sweet, Hestia thought dispassionately. She felt distracted and out of sorts. Should she go back under the hill and try again later?

The younglings had gotten such a head start. And they had covered their tracks well once they came across. Both of these things had taken Hestia by surprise; she would not underestimate them again. Somehow, they had gained access to the records of all the recent changelings, and then set out on their reckless task before anyone realized something was amiss.

It had been foolish of her not to see this coming. But

how had they even arrived at the idea in the first place? Younglings should not be so involved with fae politics. Youth was a time of play and growth and learning.

The wind shifted; Hestia snapped out of her reverie and stared down at the street below. It wasn't a scent, precisely, but she suddenly knew that the pack of younglings was nearby.

She stepped out of the shadows to peer more closely at the world below. Her keen fairy eyes picked up movement, a small group . . . not four, but five. Her inner senses confirmed what she saw. They had captured another one.

"By the Tree," Hestia whispered, before slipping over the low wall that separated Coit Tower's observation platform from the shrubbery on the hill below.

It had been so easy for them to find and glamour the poor unfortunate. She had no idea she had magical powers of her own, so she fell under the influence of the fairies without a murmur. Iannon held her arm anyway as they walked down the darkened street; Rex and Gardenia kept the streetlights and stores obscured, at least while they passed. A careful human observer might wonder at the small moving cloud of darkness, though it was more likely the misdirection would turn their attention away as well.

"Where are we going?" the changeling girl murmured, at last finding some semblance of her voice and reason though she was still lulled by the fae presence that surrounded her.

"A nice quiet place to talk," Iannon said, patting her arm gently. "We want to tell you a story."

"I like stories." Her voice was dreamy and unconcerned.

"Excellent." Iannon drew her a bit closer. The girl breathed deeply and sighed. *Probably the biggest hit of fae pheromones she's ever received,* Iannon thought, smiling to himself. At least since she was an infant, anyway.

He led his little band to the shelter they had been using this trip, at the base of Telegraph Hill, on the bay side. It had once been a corner grocery store, now long vacant. As they approached the door, Gardenia stepped forward and, with a few murmured words, brushed aside the wards that guarded the entrance. The door swung open and the five went in.

Iannon led the party to a room in the back, where the fairies had set up their camp. Glamour lay heavy in here, infusing the space with light and loveliness: comfortable sofas and mattresses in the corners; a few small tables laden with dishes of grapes and strawberries, perfectly fresh; and low tinkling music coming from everywhere and nowhere.

The girl sighed again, with obvious pleasure. Iannon took her to a bright red sofa and sat her down. She leaned against a thick pillow and grinned up at him.

"Are you hungry?" Iannon asked her. She might well be fae, but she surely had human habits of eating at regular times. He had learned this the hard way the first time they'd come over to help the stolen ones return home.

"Oh, yes, please," she said, but did not move.

"I'll do it." Rex brought her a dish of fruit.

She blinked a few times and then slowly reached for it. After another pause, she began feeding herself the grapes, one at a time, chewing each one thoroughly and swallowing before taking another.

Gardenia started to giggle, but Iannon silenced him

with a quick glare. It was cruel to mock them. They didn't know any better.

"Let her eat her fill, then we shall get started," he whispered to his friends.

"Of course," Gardenia said, nodding impatiently. "We know."

Iannon shook his head and stepped over to the window, staring out into the night. He could, he supposed, have chosen a more reliable crew of assistants, but these were his friends. Nothing had ever gone seriously awry. Nothing they couldn't fix, anyway.

He was about to turn back to the room and see how the girl was doing when a small movement outside caught his eye. Iannon sharpened his vision and peered out. It wasn't a cat, or some other night creature; it wasn't a human either. The movement was too familiar. And a minute later, his magical senses told him what he had already suspected: *she* was out there.

She had found them.

Loretta sat on the most comfortable couch imaginable, eating the most delicious fruit she had ever tasted in her entire life. No food would ever again taste so good, not for the rest of her days. She already ached with the sadness of the time when she knew she would have to stop eating, when she would have to put the bowl down, when her belly would be full or when the grapes would run out; but the sadness was washed away anew with every new bite.

A vague and infinitesimal part of her awareness understood that there were other beings in the room with her, and that she had some confusion as to what this was all about. That concern fluttered at the very edge of her senses and was easy enough to ignore. So she did, instead putting another grape in her mouth.

All too soon the grapes were gone. Loretta wanted to sob at the loss, but her hand found a huge, red, luscious strawberry instead. She put it to her mouth.

At once, the memory of the grapes vanished. The strawberry! She had never before tasted anything so delightful. Her life would now be devoted to eating these strawberries. She had achieved nirvana, perfect happiness, utter satisfaction.

After a sweet and formless time, Loretta understood that someone was sitting beside her on the sofa. It was the odd but very beautiful young man who had come to her in the first place. She gazed over at him, the memory of his gentle hand over her mouth now filling her. Loretta put a finger to her mouth, feeling the sticky-sweetness of the strawberries still there.

"Are you satisfied?" he asked.

"I . . ." She started to answer but had no words, so she glanced down at the bowl in her lap. It was empty. Again, the despair of loss and abandonment threatened to overtake her, but it quickly faded into a sense of fullness, of happiness. Of, yes, satisfaction. "Thank you," she said. "Yes."

The man, boy, whatever he was, smiled. "Wonderful. Now we shall tell stories."

Oh yes, stories. Loretta liked stories. She had forgotten all about that part. How funny! She had forgotten so much, so quickly. It was still like a dream. A really, really wonderful dream.

"I am Iannon." The boy put his hand out formally.

She took it. It was cool, and soft. "I am Loretta."

"I know." He grinned at her. His beauty was breath-

taking. She fell in love with him, pell-mell, in that moment. She would love him forever; she would bear his
children; she would hold his hand from this day forward,
never letting go.

Then he let go. "And this is Rex, Lucas, and Gardenia," he said, pointing to other people in the room. There
were other people in the room! Loretta had forgotten all
about them! She gasped and looked at them all as Iannon introduced them. Each one was so gorgeous, it was
as though they radiated light from their very pores. Her
head almost ached, to hold such beauty, but then the
pleasure of it was so strong, there was no aching.

How did they live with themselves, being so lovely?

". . . will grow less overwhelming soon," Iannon was
saying. She blinked and tried to understand him, to hear
him. "You will get used to it before long, and be able to
put the sensation aside as needed."

"I don't want to," she murmured, even as a part of her
knew this was not true. She knew she could barely think,
could not reason. Yet it felt so good . . . why would she
ever want it to stop?

Now Iannon leaned forward and took her hand once
more, and the bliss enfolded her. "You are one of us."
The words made no sense, except that they did, she knew
it was true, she had never felt so loved, so at home. . . .

Hestia approached the building cautiously. Iannon had
spotted her; she'd seen him through the gap in the
boarded-up window. She always found them sooner or
later, and he knew that.

So what was his game this time?

The maddening thing was, they weren't even funda-
mentally at cross-purposes. Iannon and his band were

capturing changelings and returning them to Faerie; Hestia believed that infants should not be switched in the first place. The difference was that Hestia, as former Queen of all the Westernmost Fae, was respecting the authority of the current king and queen, however she might feel about them personally. She was trying to convince them to change fae policy. It was foolhardy and dangerous to return the changelings ahead of their appointed time.

Iannon was ignoring all this, simply taking matters into his own hands. And the ruler of his rogue family—his be-damned *Lady*—refused to stop him. If Iannon and his gang were not brought under control, the entire delicate balance of power in Faerie could be toppled, disastrously.

Hestia paused a block away from the shuttered storefront. She slipped into deeper shadow, giving herself time to think. Powerful as she was, with four of the younglings there, she would be hard-pressed to overcome them all and wrest their captive from them. And the captive would be helpless, drowning in glamour and confusion.

It was cruel, what they were doing, immersing the poor creatures like this. Yes, Hestia agreed that all changelings should be returned from whence they came. But slowly, gently, with explanation and preparation and plenty of time to adjust to the dramatically different world. As commanded by King Goren.

The Lady had to be behind this, and not for the first time. No youngling, however rebellious, would persist in such blatant disobedience to the authority of the king and queen unless he had the support of his clan mother. Which meant that the Lady was even more two-faced than Hestia already knew her to be. She had stood before the rulers of Faerie and told them her pretty lies, smiling all the while. There was no other explanation.

But this was a larger problem, one that was not Hestia's to solve. Not that she could.

Not today, at least.

The storefront door opened. Iannon slipped out.

So he comes to me, Hestia thought, and stepped from hiding. "Youngling, I am here," she said in a low voice, pitched for fae ears.

Iannon walked toward her, the moonlight casting shadows on his pale face. He had let his glamour slip away almost entirely, but even if a human saw him now, they would only see a far-too-pretty young man. Not for the first time, Hestia wondered how much human blood the youngling carried. He blended in altogether too well here to be pure fae.

"You cannot have her," he said without preamble as he reached Hestia.

"You cannot, either. It is wrong for you to take her thus. Return her at once."

"Too late," he laughed, and Hestia started.

She knew at once what he had done, even before she sensed his confederates darting out the back way. Towards Buena Vista and the doorway under the Hill.

Iannon ran off after his partners in crime. Hestia gave chase even as she knew she would not catch them before they crossed over. They had had too much of a head start, and she was hindered here in the heavy, unmagical air.

Not a problem, though. She'd snare them easily in Faerie. Then she'd drag the entire sorry bunch before the king and queen, red-handed with their new captive. Enough diplomacy: she was fed up and ready to spend some of her own political capital before the problem became even worse.

Thus reassuring herself, Hestia covered the distance to Buena Vista in a few minutes and almost dove blindly into the doorway before she realized it had been shut to her.

"By the Tree!" she shrieked, and flung a countercharm.

The passage home did not budge.

She paused, looking at it more closely. "Why, the little worms . . ." she muttered.

They had somehow gotten hold of a time-charm. The Lady's work again, no doubt; none of the younglings had this kind of power.

But it meant that there was nothing Hestia could do until it wore off on its own. Which would be in seven days' time, by the shape and scent of the charm.

Stuck in the human realm for seven days!

Hestia stood in the dreary woods of Buena Vista Park and slowly shook her head.

Iannon brought everyone through in a jumbled rush of laughter and bruised elbows. Lucas was carrying the changeling; she was worthless now, but not for long. Iannon would begin her reeducation at once. Her powers would grow with every breath of Faerie air she took in, every bite of magical food she ate.

And thus their strength would grow, for she would be grateful to her rescuers.

It could not be soon enough before the Ferrishyns became ascendant in Faerie. Far too long had the weak, peace-loving factions ruled here, endangering all of the fae with their tactics of appeasement, their willful ignorance of the dangers of humankind.

King Goren and his foolish new queen would be taken down.

When he thought about it, Iannon could almost be glad for the changelings. Full-blooded fairies, raised by the enemy, returned home. What more valuable allies could there be?

For now, however, the girl had to be nourished, cared for. Then she could be introduced to the others. After that, she could be told of her rightful place in the world.

"Bring her along gently," Iannon said, leading his group to the Lady. He could see that Loretta was dazed by her surroundings. She tasted the air, savoring it; he smiled to imagine her first breaths here. She would never again be satisfied in the human realm.

This was his favorite part of their reclamation project: the changelings' earliest impressions of Faerie. Here was light and warmth and a golden-green meadow. A large, gleaming house—nearly a palace—was nestled into the trees at the far edge. And her new companions... Iannon could see Loretta realizing that they no longer looked quite so human. Gardenia's ears took their proper shape, and Lucas became feral, though still lovely, his own ears tufted with a golden fur.

"You are one of us," Iannon whispered to her once more. He'd told her several times that she was a fairy, a magical creature, who belonged here, with them. The humans who had raised her were no relation. He knew the knowledge would soak in over time.

Iannon looked down to give her a gentle smile. Loretta gazed at him wide-eyed, and smiled back, clearly in the first stages of overwhelming infatuation.

Ah well. She would learn.

"Welcome home," he told her.

*   *   *

Hestia roamed the night streets of San Francisco, brooding. Her anger had flashed and then dissipated; she was not one to waste energy on worthless emotions. The time-charm was set, and that was that. She was going to spend the next week on the human side.

She could go a week without eating or sleeping, of course, though she'd be far more comfortable if she found a decent resting spot, one where she could release the glamour and be as she was. For a brief moment she considered the now-abandoned store the Ferrishyn younglings had used, but quickly discarded that idea. She wouldn't taint herself with their indecency, their evil energies.

They were boys. No telling how nasty the place must be.

She needn't push herself to hunger, either. She had brought a few morsels of fae food with her, enough to remind her of home if need be.

Her feet grew tired in their odd and confining human shoes as she walked through the night. As the dim light of dawn grew in the east, Hestia boarded a bus, flashing a colorful ribbon at the driver in lieu of fare, and rode where it ventured. The grumbling vehicle carried her to where the edge of the land met the edge of the ocean: a liminal space, a boundary line, a place of great power, though not one the fae generally worked with.

Hestia took this happenstance for its inner meaning and departed the bus. She was not the ordinary sort of fae; she would gladly work with unusual power.

Dropping the shoes by the side of the road, she walked across the damp sand in her proper bare feet. Her confining skirt refused to blow and move in the wind, as skirts should; she shed that as well, and then her foolish blouse after that. The bitter salt-fogged air embraced her unclad body. The morning had dawned cold and gray, and no humans walked the beach, so Hestia did not need to cloak herself in any glamour. She let it all go now, following the uncomfortable human clothes, and became a fae creature of terrible beauty: sharp teeth, twisting hair that flowed to her ankles, pointed ears, golden eyes.

She ran at the edge of the water, chill waves lapping at her ankles, as she let her mind loose to worry at the problem without conscious intent. Hestia passed the end of the sandy beach and onto rocks, barely noticing. Her nimble feet chose her path here as easily as they had done on the softer surface. Soon it was sand again; she noted this with a tiny corner of her mind.

When this stretch of sand ended as well, Hestia stopped. "I have been going about this all wrong," she said aloud, to the gulls and the sand clams and the great gray sky.

One week later, Hestia sat in a small, brightly lit room in the Castro. The beautiful young man across the formica dinette from her sipped his tea and frowned. "Why do you have to go?" The tone could have sounded unpleasant, whiny; yet he was so lovely that it was charming instead.

She reached over and patted his hand, making him smile. "This is only for a short time, my sweet. Trust me."

He lifted his bright green eyes to meet hers. "I do trust you."

"Finish your biscuit, dear."

The boy picked up the last of the fae-made cookie and put it in his mouth. "These are so good."

"Now, remember what to do when they arrive . . ."

Nodding, he said, "Yes, of course: I am surprised, confused, befuddled; I have no idea why they have come for me. I resist, but then relent the moment they glamour me."

"Yes. And when they take you through?"

"I pretend to fall for the Lady's charms. And I wait for you." He beamed at her, like a good student.

"Perfect." She glanced at the window, at the ray of morning sun. "They should arrive soon, and they must not find me here." She briefly considered obscuring his memory just a bit, to help him in his role, but decided to leave him as he was. No sense complicating things further than they needed to be.

Hestia got up and kissed the boy. Then she slipped out into the anonymous, human-filled streets and waited to spring her trap.

So the Ferrishyn younglings thought they could out-maneuver her, did they? Hestia ai Morning Glory ten' Amber would show them the value of long life over youthful daring and impetuousness.

And she would demonstrate to the Lady the finer points of using another's weapon against them.

As the sounds of the laughing, roughhousing fairy boys approached the boy's apartment, Hestia smiled and began to make her way to the newly opened doorway home.

Loretta sat among a field of tiny asphodels, watching the vague, glorious sky above. She'd been here for months, it felt like; or possibly only a few hours. She never could tell. The Lady in her grand house of creamy rose stone and gold and cedarwood had been so kind, everything

Iannon had promised, yet already she was coming to see the entire world of Faerie as she saw the sky.

Back in San Francisco, when you looked up into a clear sky, you knew you were seeing forever. Day's azure brilliance, night's glinting depths—it didn't matter. She could understand why the ancient philosophers had decided that the heavens were a family of spheres nested in one another. Like mountains fading into the distance, the sky went on.

But here in the lands under the Hill, there were never any clouds. Even the shadows were tentative. The world folded in on itself, that vague sky elusive as a shadow at the corner of the eye.

A fairy approached. Pert, freckled, slight . . . Loretta recognized her as Twyla. One of the hundreds she seemed to have been introduced to lately. With or without the ethereal beauty of fairy glamour, the girl was beautiful.

Haunted, too, by some unhappiness that was as covered over and indirectly visible as the sky itself.

Loretta knew a kindred spirit when she saw one.

"Iannon has brought another changeling through," Twyla said, smiling shyly.

No, Loretta corrected herself, not shyly. Sadly. Just a little while ago, she would still have mistaken the set of those pale lips for bliss itself.

"Will the Lady be seeing her soon?"

"Him," Twyla corrected. "A beautiful manchild. She has asked for you to attend upon her meeting, in hopes of easing his arrival that it might be better handled than yours was."

"I will come." Loretta wondered whether that was wise, whether she might have been smarter to stay amid the woods and fields. Everything these people did was political. Everything was theater.

She would never have thought to miss working for Mr. Clarkson.

Giggling all over again, Iannon brought the new lad by winding paths to the Lady's home. No one walked in a straight line in Faerie, except to meet their final doom. Even their feasting tables were set in gentle horns, curved in honor of the beast-aspect of the first powers in the world.

Rex, Lucas, and Gardenia hustled the boy along. He was gorgeous even without glamour. The Lady would be quite pleased. Possibly pleased in an extremely personal and profitable—to Iannon—fashion.

He was happier with this work than he'd been with much else in a long time.

The boy stumbled, smiling foolishly. Fae or no fae, he'd been raised among humans too long. Much like that twit Loretta that they'd rescued about a week ago.

Except this one was a keeper. It was almost as if he had a glamour of his own.

"Quality will out," Iannon sang, to no one in particular.

The boy grinned, and found his footing a bit better on the crushed red coral of this particular winding path.

At the Gate of Horn, one of the side entrances to the Lady's home, Iannon and his little gang were greeted by the old harridan Hestia. *She* was one of the stodgy ones with her head stuck in the past and her heart so closed in on itself she didn't know any more what was good for Faerie and the fae. He still marveled that someone so closed-minded as her had ever been Queen.

"Iannon," she called out. Her voice was like the closing of a steel trap. "How did you find your time among cold iron and foul air?"

He swept an elegant bow. There was nothing Hestia could do to harm him here on his own protector's doorstep. "The night's a delight, your grace, and the place is no worse under broad daylight."

"Went shopping for yourself this time, I see." She nodded at the boy they'd picked up. He grinned foolishly back.

Iannon, struck with a rare, cold moment of self-doubt, shouldered past the elderly fairy. "Bring him in, boys."

Hestia followed close, as if one with their group, right into the hallway lined with ormolu and marble, decorated with friezes celebrating victories past when their kind had still raised wooden lance and bronze sword in the field against grunting men in animal skins.

Iannon realized he'd been had, at least to a degree. She was here under no invitation except his.

The Lady would be less than pleased with him. He counted on her displeasure with Hestia to be much greater. Two creatures of such might never shared willingly.

Hestia strode through the halls of the Lady's house as if they were her own modest cottage. Most of the secret of power was behaving as if it were already yours. Even so, she allowed herself to linger every few paces in admiration of paintings, mosaics, and the cunningly wirebound skulls of various enemies of the Ferrishyns. That would give foolish young Iannon a chance to scuttle ahead and adopt the pretense that he had not swept her past the door wards in his careless haste.

That suited Hestia perfectly. Besides, her young man needed to meet the Lady on his own terms. As it were. Hestia preferred to think of herself as a finale rather than as an accompaniment to the main event.

She approached the silver-bound ebon doors of the Lady's presence chamber just in time to hear the rising babble of voices from within. The frog-faced footmen waiting there, each in his peacock feathered clawhammer coat, tugged at the great, heavy handles and let her pass through onto the pietra dura floor of the room beyond.

The tableau she met there was a feast to the eyes of Hestia ai Morning Glory ten'Amber, High Lady of the Goldhelm Family of the Westernmost Fae.

The russet-haired Lady of the Ferrishyn clan had her hands clasped upon the cheeks of the boy so lately brought from the human world by her favorite, Iannon. The boy himself was shedding glamour like a dandelion sheds seeds, to reveal beneath the withered visage of a barghest—one of the mindless old ones who still trapped and consumed unwary fae in the darker regions of the backlands where no one sensible ever went. An ancient horror of their people, long since hunted nearly to extinction, barghests lived on now in the cracks of the world, or as the twisted pets of the powerful. They could not be slain with either silver or iron, though one who knew the right word could call a barghest to heel.

Simply by entering the dwelling of the Lady in this moment, Hestia proclaimed that she knew the right word. She was one of the few with the power to glamour a barghest so that not even so powerful a fool as Iannon could see the difference.

The Lady should have known better, but she'd been

caught up in the moment. At her side, the changeling Loretta's mouth formed into a shriek of horrified terror. The Lady's own face was a study in concentrated hatred.

She'd fought the barghest to a stop, but was unable to repel it. The dark-furred questing fingers were so close to those copper eyes, that perfect mouth. No one around her had moved close, for fear of breaking the stalemate in the wrong fashion.

"A word with you, Lady," said Hestia just a little too loudly.

Even some Ferrishyn courtiers smirked at the jest.

The Lady's eyes promised bloody retribution, likely with heated iron hooks and starveling ferrets. No one else moved, even to draw breath, except the barghest, who growled.

Hestia continued. "Each of us might call off our dogs, do you not think?"

A blink, then another, that beautiful face still set in terrible concentration.

"I think it best if your dog take mine for a walk in the park above our realm. I am sure a full cycle of the moon in human form, without his glamour, only my poor black dog to look after him, will do Iannon a wondrous amount of good." Hestia could not hope to banish the Lady to the world above, but the embarrassment of being caught out so foolishly would do the Ferrishyn mother great harm in the theater of fae politics. King Goren would be sure to note this ... *misstep*.

Another blink. It was assent, clearly witnessed by the dozens of her faction.

Hestia uttered a word in the oldest language, that spoken by the rivers of fire and the roots of the mountains before the waters first came and brought with them

every green and growing thing. The barghest released
the Lady and dropped back to all fours, nothing now but
a rangy black dog with a bit of blood on his muzzle.

Iannon leapt to speak. "Lady, I—"

His liege-mother cut him off. "I believe you have a
dog to walk, cur." The Lady's eyes when she looked back
at Hestia were hooded once more, even the threat veiled.
"You have made your point, madam. For now."

Stiffly she rose from her throne of oaken heartwood
and dragonbone to leave the presence chamber.

Hestia knew that this was ultimately a petty victory.
King Goren would not allow them to settle the score
further, for such vengeance might promote kinstrife. Not
now, with the problems of time and living space and
population that bedeviled Faerie. Petty or not, it was *her*
victory.

She smiled sweetly at Iannon. "Don't forget to eat
while you're up there," she said in her kindliest voice.
"Not to mention what comes after."

The barghest licked his hand as Iannon stared at her.
He couldn't summon the threat of heated iron in his
gaze, Hestia realized, but give him a few more centuries
of serious mischief and he might.

For that, she could wait. Good enemies were even
harder to find than good friends.

Loretta followed the strange old fairy out of the presence chamber and away from the blighted home of the
Lady. "Ma'am," she said. "Please . . ."

The old fairy beckoned the girl to her side. "We must
away, before even the laws of guesting are tempted to be
broken."

She could see the glamour on this one. So much

deeper than Iannon's, it was like comparing a pine forest to a blackberry bush. "I would go back."

That was met with a small smile. "With that foolish boy of the Lady's on the loose over there?"

"You're sending him as human. He won't know what to do." She giggled, an inappropriate thought popping into her head. "He probably doesn't even know what toilet paper is."

"You plan to watch him suffer?" The old fairy sounded curious. "That is very . . . unusual . . . for one in your stage of development. A vice usually reserved to us old ones."

"No," Loretta said stubbornly. "I'll help him. I have a month to show that beautiful fool what it was he tried to take away from me. I'd like him to learn what it takes to survive up there."

Hestia threw back her head and laughed. It was the mirth of wind and storm, the amusement of water thundering down a mountain. "Oh, you are a subtle one. You already know the lesson of enemies."

"I know the lesson of being human," Loretta said. "We are an uncertain folk. I may not be one of them anymore, but you cannot take my past from me."

"What do you think you can take from Iannon?"

She grinned, knowing how wicked she must seem. "His certainty. That is who the fae are. A people who always *know*. I will break him of that."

THE SLAUGHTERED LAMB

Elizabeth Bear

The smell of the greasepaint was getting to Edie.

"Oh my *god*, sweetheart, and then she says to me, 'Honey, I think you'd look fabulous with dreads,' and I swear I stared at her for ten whole seconds before I managed to ask, 'Do you think I'm a fucking Jamaican, bitch?' I mean, can you believe the gall of . . ."

Nor the mouths on some others, Edie thought tiredly, pressing a thumb into the arch of her foot and trying to massage away the cramp you got from a two-hour burlesque in four-inch stilettos. They were worth the pain, though: *hot* little boots with the last two inches of the dagger heel clad in ferrules of shining metal. When you took them down the runway, they glittered like walking on stars.

She looked in her makeup mirror, still trying to tune out Paige Turner's fucking tirade about fucking Jamaicans, which wasn't getting any more interesting for its intricacy. Edie's vision was shimmering with migraine aura—full moon tonight—and the smell of makeup and scorched hair was making her nauseated. The fucking cramp wasn't coming out of her fucking foot. No way she could walk in flats like this.

She didn't want to go home: there was nothing in her apartment except three annoying flatmates—one of whom had an incontinent cat—and a telephone that wasn't going to ring. Not for her, anyway.

She wanted a boyfriend. A family. Somebody who would help her get rid of this fucking headache, and treat her like a person rather than a side-show. Somebody who wouldn't spout bigoted shit at her. She didn't get that from her father's family, and she certainly didn't get it here.

"Fuck." She dropped her foot to the floor, arching it up so only the ball and toes touched. "I'm fucking fucked."

"Aw, sweetie," somebody said in her ear—a lower voice than Paige's, and a much more welcome one. "What's wrong?"

Somebody was trying to distract Paige by asking her if she was staying up for the lunar eclipse. It wasn't working. Edie wondered if a punch in the kisser would do it.

She looked up to see Mama Janeece leaning over her, spilling out of her corset in the most convincing manner imaginable.

"I gotta get out of here," Edie said. "You know, I'm just gonna walk to the subway now."

She jammed her foot back into the boot. The support eased the cramp temporarily, but she knew there'd be hell to pay all night. *So be it.*

"It's fifteen degrees," Janeece said. "You're going to go out there in high heels and a wig and four inches of fabric?"

"I've got a coat. And a bottle of schnapps back at my

place." Edie stood. She smiled to take the sting out of it, then made sure her voice was loud enough for Paige to overhear as she gathered her coat. "Besides, if I have to listen to any more racist bullshit from Miss Thing over there, I'm going to be even colder in a jail cell all night. Somebody ought to tell her that it ain't drag if you look like Annie Lennox."

She sashayed out, letting the door swing shut behind her. Not quite fast enough to cut short the cackles of outraged queens.

Halfway down the corridor, she realized she'd left her cellphone behind. It wasn't worth ruining a good exit for. She would get it tomorrow. Anyway, she didn't have anybody to call.

The coat wasn't long enough to cover her knees and the cold burned through those hot little boots. After ten steps, Edie regretted her decision. But going back now would be a sure way to convert triumph into ignominy, so she soldiered on, sequined spandex stretching around her thighs with each swinging stride as she click-clacked up Jane Street toward Eighth Ave. Sure, it was cold, but she could take it. Sure, her feet hurt—but she could take that, too. She was probably less miserable than the gaunt black hound with his hide tented over his hip-bones that she glimpsed slinking aside at the first intersection.

The cold deadened her sense of smell. Manhattan's rich panoply of scents gave way to ice, cold concrete, and leaden midwinter. The good news was, it deadened her incipient migraine, too. And in the freezing dark of the longest night of the year, there weren't many people hanging around to hassle her.

Of course, she'd no sooner thought that than the purr

of an eight-cylinder engine alerted her—seconds before the car glided up beside her. Somebody rolled down the window, releasing warm air and the scent of greasy bodies. A simpering catcall floated through the icy night. A male voice, pitched sing-song. "Hey lady. Hey lady. I like your big legs, lady. You want a ride?"

The car was a beige American land yacht from the 1980s, rusty around the wheel wells. There were four guys in it, and the one in the front passenger seat was the one purring out the window. From the look on his face, his friends had put him up to it, and he was a little horrified by his own daring.

Edie turned, flipped the skirts of her coat out, and planted both hands on her snake-slender hips. She drew herself up to her full six-foot-eight in those stilettos. Something smelled mushroomy; she hoped it wasn't the interior of that car.

"I ain't no lady," she said definitively. "I'm a *queen*."

The car slowed, easing up to the curb. The front and rear passenger doors opened before it had coasted to a stop. Three men climbed out—one must have slid across the rear bucket seat to do so—and then the driver's door opened and the fourth man stood up behind the car.

Edie brazened it out with a laugh, but her hand was in her purse. She didn't have a gun—this was New York City—but she had a pair of brass knuckles and a can of pepper spray. And other advantages, but she'd hate to have to use those. For one thing, she'd ruin her blouse.

The throbbing behind her eyes intensified. She kept her hand in her purse, and was obvious about it. *They* wouldn't know she didn't have a gun. And now that they were standing up beside the car, it was obvious that she had a foot on the tallest of them.

I'm not easy prey, she thought fiercely, and tried to carry herself the way her father would have—all squared shoulders and Make-My-Day. Thinking of him made her angry, which was good: being angry made her feel *big*. The car was still running. That was a good sign they weren't really committed to a fight, and she could pick out the pong of fear on at least two of them.

She smiled through the blood-red lipstick and said, "What say we part friends, boys?"

They grumbled and shifted. One of them looked at the driver. The driver rolled his eyes and slid back behind the wheel—and that was the signal for the other three to pile back into the car with a great slamming of doors. Predators preferred to deal from a position of strength.

"Fucking faggot," one shouted before leaning forward to crank the window up. Edie didn't quite relax, but her fingers eased their deathgrip on her mace.

Oh, bad boys, she thought. *You never got beat up enough to make you learn to get tough.*

She hadn't had time to come down off the adrenaline high when a shimmering veil of colors wavered across the width of the street, right before the beige Buick. The car nosed down as the driver braked hard; that mushroomy smell intensified. The veil of light had depth— beyond it, Edie glimpsed a woodland track, the green shadows of beech leaves, the broken rays of a brilliant sun. She heard a staccato, as of drumbeats, echoing down the street. She took an involuntary step forward and then two back as something within the aurora lunged.

A tall pale horse, half-dissolved in light, lurched through the unreal curtain. It stumbled as its hooves struck sparks from the pavement, reins swinging freely from a golden bridle, then gathered itself and leaped. Its hooves beat a steel-drum tattoo on the hood and roof of the Buick. The men within cringed, but though the windshield starred and spiderwebbed, the roof held. It smelled of panicked animal, sweat, and—incongruously—lily of the valley, with overtones of hungry girlchild.

The horse pelted down the street, leaving Edie with a blurred impression of quivering nostrils, ears red as if blood-dipped, and white-rimmed eyes—and of something small and delicate clinging to its back with inhumanly elongated limbs.

The veil still hung there, rippling in the darkness between streetlamp pools. Edie could see the full moon riding high beyond it, and the sight made her migraine come back in waves. She wanted nothing so much as to put her head down to her knees and puke all over the gutter. That sweetly fungal aroma was almost oppressive now, clinging, reminding Edie of stepping in a giant puffball in the Connecticut woods as a boy. The drumming of hooves had faded as the white horse vanished down the street. Now it multiplied, echoing, and over it rang a sound like the mad pealing of a carillon in a hurricane.

Edie dropped her purse and sprinted into the street, so hasty even she tottered on her heels. She yanked open the front passenger door and pulled the abusive one out by his wrist, shouting to the others to get out and run. *Run.*

The thunder of hooves, the clangor of bells, redoubled.

The driver listened, and one of the passengers in the rear—and he had the presence of mind to drag his friend after. The man she was hauling out of the car looked at her wild-eyed and seemed about to struggle. She grabbed the door-frame with one hand and threw him behind her with the other, sending him stumbling to his knees on the sidewalk when he fell over the curb. When she turned to throw herself after him, her heel skittered out from under her. She only saved herself from falling by clutching the car's frame and door.

Edie had half an instant during which to doubt her decision. Then she dropped to the ground and wriggled under the car, aware that she'd never wear these stockings again. She just made it; her coat snagged on the undercarriage a moment before the clatter of dog nails on pavement reached her ears, and she tore it loose with a wince. Then the swarming feet of hounds were everywhere around her, their noses thrust under the car, their voices raised in excited yips. Some were black, a dusty black like weathered coal. Some were white as milk, with red, red ears hung soft along their jowls and pink, sniffing noses. But they sniffed for only a moment before moving on, baying in renewed vigor. Edie was not their prey.

Close behind them came the crescendo of that hoof-beat thunder. Edie cringed from the judder of the car she sheltered beneath as horse after horse struck it, hurtled over, and landed on the far side. The horses also ran to the left and the right, and all their legs, too, were black as coal or white as milk. The car shook brutally under the abuse, a tire hissing flat. The undercarriage pressed her spine. She was realizing that maybe this hadn't been her best idea ever when she heard human voices shouting. Something broke the wave of horses before her, so now they thundered only to the left and the right. The belling of the hounds was not lessened, except in that it receded, and nor was the pounding of hooves—but the stampede flowed around her now, rather than over. It felt like minutes, but Edie was sure only seconds had passed when the sounds faded away, leaving behind the raucous yelps of car alarms and the distant wail of a police siren.

She wriggled against the undercarriage like a worm between stones. The pavement smelled of old oil, vomit, and gasoline, so cold it burned against her cheek. She pressed against it with her elbows, inching forward, kicking with her feet. So much for the hot boots.

Doc Martens appeared at street level, followed by a young olive-skinned woman's inverted face. She was crowned in a crest of black-and-blond streaks and framed by the sagging teeth of a leather jacket's zipper.

"Hi," she said. "I'm Lily Wakeman. You look like you could use a hand."

"Or two," Edie said, extending hers gratefully.

The woman and a slight white guy wearing a sword pulled her from beneath the car. It was pancaked—the roof crushed in, the suspension broken.

Edie shook herself with wonder that she hadn't been smashed underneath. She turned to her rescuers—the punky girl, that slight man, who had medium-dark hair and eyes that looked brown by streetlight, except the right one seemed to catch sparkles inside it in a way that made Edie think it might be glass—and a second man: a butchy little number with his slick blond hair pulled back into a stubby ponytail, who wore a tattered velvet tailcoat straight out of *Labyrinth*.

"Oh, these shoes. Do you know what these *cost*?"

"Matthew Szczgielniak," said the bigger and butcher of the two white guys. She didn't miss his nervous glance in the direction the hunt had run, or the way his weight shifted.

"Edith Moorcock," she said haughtily, smoothing her torn coat.

He stared at her, eyebrows rising. He wasn't bad, actually, if you liked 'em covered in muscles and not too tall. She was waiting for—she didn't know what. Scorn, dismissal.

Instead, the corners of his mouth curved up just a little. "That's rather good."

Edie sniffed. "Thank you."

Then she realized why his face seemed so familiar. "You're that guy. The Mage." He'd been all over the news for a while, after the magic finally burst through in big ways as well as small, enchanting all of New York City. He was supposed to be some sort of liaison between the real world and the *otherwise* one; the one Edie's people came from. The one she couldn't go back to unless she was willing to lie about who she was.

She tried to remember details. There'd been a murder. . . . But if this was Matthew Magus, that meant his companions were people Edie should have recognized too. The woman was supposed to be Morgan le Fay's apprentice. And that meant the little guy was . . . oh *shit*.

Edie stole a glance at Matthew's right hand, but he was wearing black leather gloves.

"From the comic book," she said.

Matthew covered half his face with the left hand, then let it drop. "Guilty. And you're my responsibility, aren't you? You're a werewolf."

"Don't be silly," Edie said, swallowing a surge of bitterness. She dismissed the whole thing with a calculated hand-flip. "Werewolf is an all-boys club. Queens need not apply. Besides, since when was the rest of Fairy ready to write us a certificate of admission?"

Lily and the other man—who Edie also recognized, now that she had context—were already jogging away down Jane Street after the vanished fairy hunt. Matthew turned to follow, and Edie trotted after him in her ruined shoes.

She couldn't let it go. "How did you know I was a werewolf?"

Matthew shrugged. "I've met a few. Never a drag queen before, I admit—" He waved back at the flattened Buick. "That was very brave. Did you stop to think you could have shifted? It's a full moon; it would have been easy."

Edie tossed her wig away, since it was a mess anyway. She wasn't going to tell them that it had been a dozen years since she'd used her wolf-shape. That lupines were pack-beasts, and it hurt too much being alone in that form.

She said, "Turn back into a wolf? Are you kidding? You know we regenerate when we do that? You know how long it takes to wax this shit?"

They were catching up to the others quickly now. "Did you call up that hunt?"

"Just happened to be standing by when it broke through," Edie admitted between breaths. "Lunar eclipse on solstice night. Is it any wonder if the walls of the world get a little thin?"

"That's why we're on patrol," Matthew said. "Solstice night. Full moon. And a lunar eclipse. Let's catch them before they flatten any pedestrians."

They caught up to the others. The little guy favored them with a sideways glance as they all slacked stride for a moment. "You brought the wolf along."

"The wolf brought herself," Edie said.

Lily chuckled.

"Welcome to the party. I'm Kit," the little guy said.

Edie snorted to cover exactly how impressed she was. Him, she still cringed with embarrassment for not having recognized immediately: Christopher Marlowe, late of London, late of Fairy, late of Hell. "Hel-*lo*, Mister Queer Icon. *I* know who you are. Don't *you*?"

"Oh, he knows," said Matthew, breathing deeply. "He just likes the fussing. Edith, I don't suppose you got a look at what they were after, did you?"

Edie remembered the first white horse, the thing wadded up on its shoulders, face buried in its flowing mane. "A little girl," she said. "On an elven charger. She looked terrified."

"Shit!" Matthew broke into a jouncing, limping run. The other three fell in behind him.

The cramp in her foot was back, and now her toes were jammed up against the toes of her boots with every stride. She started to run with a hitching limp of her own, accompanied by a breathy litany of curses.

Here, there were no destroyed vehicles or shattered pavement. It was as still and dark as Manhattan ever gets—the streets quiet and cold, if not quite deserted. The scent pulled her down Washington to West 10th Street, and then she tottered to a stop beneath a denuded tree.

"My feet," she said, leaning on a wall.

"Let me see," said Matthew. He crouched awkwardly, one leg thrust off at an angle like an outrigger, and put his hands on her ankle. She could feel through the soft leather that one of them was misshapen, and did not grip.

"Hey," Edie said. "No peeking up my skirt." She gave him the foot as if she were a horse and he the farrier. When she felt him pressing his hands together over her ankle bone, she glanced back over her shoulder. "You can't see anything with the boot on."

"Hush," he said. "I'm talking to your shoes."

When he put the foot down, it did feel easier. The incipient blood blisters on her soles hadn't healed, but something was easing the cramp in her instep, and the toes felt like they fit better. Matthew touched the other ankle, and Edie lifted the foot for him.

A moment later, and she was offering him a hand up. As he pushed himself to his feet she saw him grope his own knee, revealing the outline of metal and padding through the leg of his cargo pants.

She blurted, "You're kicking ass in a knee brace? Hardcore."

"If the team needs you, you play through the injury," he said. "Ow!"

That last because Lily had thumped him with the back of her hand.

"I need a new knee," Matthew said apologetically, as they limped along a street lined with parked cars and brick-faced buildings. "I'm trying to put it off as long as possible. The replacements are only good for fifteen years or so."

"Ouch," Edie said, even as he picked up the pace. "Ever consider a less physical line of work?"

"Every day," he said.

It wasn't too hard to follow the hunters—the flattened cars and glowing hoofprints pounded in pavement were a clear trail, and there was always the wail of car alarms and police sirens to orient by. The sounding of the hounds carried in the cold night as perfectly as the distant ring of a ship's bell over water. The air still reeked with the scents of hunters and hunted. Before long, Edie was running at the front of the pack, directing the others.

Matthew limped up beside her, the chains and baubles hung from his coat jangling merrily. Despite the awkwardness of his stride, his breath still wreathed him in easy clouds.

He reached out one hand and tugged her sleeve, slowing her. "Can we get ahead of them? Being where they've been isn't helping us at all."

"It's been a long time since I hunted, sugar, and the rest of the pack never thought me much of a wolf." Edie skimmed her hands down her sides and hips as explanation.

Drawing up beside them, Kit said, "You should talk to the Sire of the Pack. Things have changed in Fairy—"

"How much can they have possibly changed? The Pack doesn't want me, and I don't want them." Edie made a gesture with her left hand that was meant to cut off discussion.

A prowl car swept past, its spotlight briefly illuminating their faces, but they must not have looked like trouble—at least by Village standards—because the car rolled by without hesitation. Distant sirens still shattered the night, a sort of a directional beacon if you could pick the original out of the echoes.

Edie saw Matthew's crippled hand move in the air as if he were conducting music—or, more, actually, as if he were plucking falling strands of out of the air. He frowned with concentration. *Magi*, she thought tiredly.

Just out of range of a kicked-over hydrant spouting water that splashed and rimed on the street, Edie paused to consult her mental map of the Village's tangle of streets. The middle and northern parts of Manhattan were a regular grid, but this was the old part of the city, where the roads crossed one another like jackstraws.

Edie raised her head and sniffed to the four directions. "Let's double back and head south on Washington. I think they've headed that way."

"I'm pushing them that way." Matthew fell in behind her, and Kit and Lily followed. Edie's palms were wet inside her gloves: nervousness. The nose didn't lie, but it could be tricked—and it had been a long time since Edie ran with a pack.

Off to the left, Kit cried "Hark!" and slowed his pace to a walk. Edie cupped her hands to her ears. The scent was strong again, and growing stronger. At the end of the block, Hudson Street was still moderately busy with cars, and the noise could have confounded her. But there was the trembling of hooves through the street—

The first horse and rider burst into sight around the oblique corner of West 10th and Hudson. Sparks flew from beneath the hooves. Matthew's hand moved again, and down the street, a pedestrian, distracted by her phone, chose that minute to jaywalk. A panel van swerved to avoid her, cutting off the horse and rider. Edie found herself slowing as the animal raced toward her, running against traffic. She could smell its sweat, its exhaustion and terror.

From behind it, she heard the baying of the hounds.

"Stand aside," Kit said, and took Edie by the wrist to pull her onto the sidewalk, amid the shelter of trees and light poles. Matthew stood firmly in the middle of the street, his back to traffic, his velvet coat catching highlights off the streetlamps. Edie pulled against Kit's grip; Lily was suddenly there beside her, restraining her as well.

"He's the Archmage," Kit said. "If he doesn't know what he's doing, it's his own fool fault."

The Fairy steed bore down on him, and Matthew drew himself up tall. At the corner of a red brick building whose ground floor façade was comprised of grilled Roman arches, the horse reached him. She was going to run him down, Edie saw. She reached out a futile hand—

The horse gathered itself to leap, and as it did, Matthew threw out his arms. "Hold!" he cried, in a voice that shook the windows and rattled the fire escapes against the brick faces of the buildings. "In the names of the City that Never Sleeps—New York, New Orange, New Amsterdam, Gotham, the Big Apple, and the Island of Manhattan—I bid you stand fast!"

Edie would have expected flares of light, shivers of energy running across the pavement—something from a movie or a comic book. But it wasn't there: all she saw was the man in the tatterdemalion dark red coat, his hands upraised.

And the lather-dripping mare planting her heels and stopping short before him. Her head hung low, her throat and barrel swelling with each great heaving gasp of air. She swayed, and for a moment, Edie thought she would collapse.

The girl on her back, all snarled pale hair and twig-limbs, raised her head painfully from where it had rested, face pressed into the mare's mane. Edie gasped.

Here was no elf-child, moving as stiffly as an old woman: just a human girl of eleven years, or twelve.

The hounds rounded the corner in full cry, surging

like a sea around the knees of the running horses. Matthew sprinted forward, arms still outstretched, and put himself between the hunt and the girl. Edie shook off Kit's hand and ran to stand beside him, aware that Kit and Lily were only a step or two back—and that only because Edie's legs were longer. When she drew up, Matthew snaked out a hand and clasped hers, and then she was grabbing Lily's hand on the other side while Lily linked arms with Kit. They stood so, four abreast, and Matthew again raised his voice and shouted, "Hold!"

Edie felt the power through her fingertips, this time, like a static charge. She imagined a barrier sweeping across West 10th from building to building, towering high overhead. She imagined it thick and strong, and hoped somehow she was helping.

Whether she had any effect on it or not, the hounds quit running. They circled back into the pack, their belling turned to whining, a churn of black bodies and white ones dotted with red. The horses drew up among them, harness-bells shivering and hooves a-clatter. At the forefront, on a tall gelding, sat an elf-lord who smelled of primroses and prickles. He had cropped hair as red as his white horse's ears, shot through with streaks of black where a mortal man would show graying. He wore a blousy silken shirt, heavily embroidered, and a pair of skinny black jeans stuffed into cowboy boots.

"Matthew Magus," he said, casting a green-gray eye that seemed to gather light across Edie, Kit, and Lily. His harness did not creak as he shifted his weight, but the bells tinkled faintly—rain against a glass wind-chime. "And companions."

"I do not know you," Matthew said. "How are you styled?"

"I am a lord of the Unseelie Court, and I would not extend my calling to one so ill-met."

Matthew sighed. "Must we be ill-met?"

"Aye," said the anonymous lord, "if you would keep a thief from me."

Now police cars were filling the intersection and both ends of the block. Edie looked nervously one way and another, waiting for men and women with guns to start piling out of the vehicles and charging forward, but for now they seemed content to wait.

New York's Finest knew better than to get between a magician and an elf-lord.

"A thief?" Matthew asked, with an elaborate glance over his shoulder. Edie could still hear the heaving breaths of the horse, smell the sweat and fear of the girl. "I see someone who has sought sanctuary in my city. And as you owe fealty to King Ian, you are bound by my treaty with him. What is she accused of stealing . . . Sir Knight?"

"What's there before your eyes," the Fairy answered, as his companions of the hunt — men and women both — ranged themselves around him. "That common brat has stolen the great mare Embarr from my stables, and I will have her back. And the thief punished."

The mare snorted behind them, her harness jangling fiercely as she shook out her mane. "He lies!"

At first, Edie thought the child had spoken, and admired her spunk. But when she turned, she realized that the high, clear voice had come from the horse, who pricked her ears and continued speaking. "If anything, t'was I stole the child Alicia. And my reasons I had, mortal Magus."

"The mare," said the elf-lord, "is mine."

Matthew did not lower his hands. "Be that as it may," he said. "I cannot have you tearing my city apart—and it is *my city*, and in it I decree that no one can own another. The girl and the horse are under my protection, and if you wish to have King Ian seek their extradition, he is welcome to do so through official channels. Which do *not*—" Matthew waved his hands wide "—include a hunt through Greenwich Village."

The Fairy Lord sniffed. "I have come here, where iron abounds, and where your mortal poisons burn inside my breast with every breath, to reclaim what is rightfully mine. By what authority do you deny me?"

He stood up in his stirrups. His gelding took a prancing, curveting step or two, crowding the horses and hounds on his right. They danced out of the way, but not before Edie had time to wrinkle her nose in the human answer to a snarl. "This is going to come to a fight," she whispered, too low for anyone but Lily and Matthew to hear. The whisk of metal on leather told her that Kit had drawn his sword.

"Why doesn't the girl speak for herself?" Matthew asked.

"Because," the mare answered, "His Grace had her caned and stole her voice from her when one of his mares miscarried. But it wasn't the girl's fault. And I'll not see my stablehands mistreated."

Lily squeezed Edie's hand and leaned close to whisper. "Edith? Shift to wolf form."

Edie shook her head. "I told you, it's been—"

"Do it," she said, and gave her a little push forward from the elbow.

Edie toed out of those boots and stood in stocking-feet on the icy pavement. She ripped her blouse off over

her head and kicked down the stockings and the sequined skirt.

Everyone was staring, most especially the Fairy lord.
Lily, though, stepped forward to help Edie with her
corselet and gaff. She handled the confining underclothes
with the professionalism of a seasoned performer, folding them over her arm before stepping back. Edie stood
there for a moment, naked skin prickling out everywhere,
and raised her eyes to the Fairy lord.

"Well, I'll be a codfish," he said callously. He looked
not at Edie, but at Matthew. "The bitch has a prick. Is
that meant to upset me?"

"The bitch has teeth, too," Edie said, and let the transformation take her.

She'd thought it would be hard. So many years, so
many years of enduring the pain, of resisting, of petulant
self-denial. Of telling herself that if she wasn't good
enough for the Pack to see her as a wolf, then she didn't
want to be one.

Once she managed to release her death-grip on the
self-denial, though, her human form just fell away, sheet-
ing from the purity of the wolf like filth from ice. Edie's
hands dropped toward the pavement and were hard,
furred paws before they touched. Her muzzle length-
ened; what had been freezing cold became cool comfort
as the warmth of her pelt enfolded her. The migraine fell
away as if somebody had removed a clamp from her
temples, and the rich smells of the city—and the horse
manure and dog piss of the hunt—flooded her sinuses.

She snarled, stalking forward, and saw the Fairy
hounds whine and mill and cringe back among the legs
of the horses. She knew the light rippled in her coat, red
as rust and tipped smoke-black, and she knew the light

glared in her yellow eyes. She knew from the look the Fairy lord shot her—fear masked with scorn—that the threat was working.

"So you have a wolf," the Fairy lord said, though his horse lowered his head to protect his neck and backed several steps.

"And your high king is a wolf," Matthew said. "You know how the pack sticks together."

This time, the gelding backed and circled because the Fairy lord reined him around. When he faced Edie and the others again, he was ten feet further back, and his pack had fallen back with him.

"I don't understand why the horse didn't kill you," he called to the girl, over Matthew's head. "They don't let slaves ride."

He yanked his horse's mouth so Edie could smell the blood that sprang up, wheeling away.

"Oh," said the mare, "is *that* why you never dared get up on me?"

As the lord rode off, spine stiff, the rest of the hunt fell in behind him. Edie was warm and at ease, and with the slow ebb of adrenaline, swept up in a rush of fellow-feeling for those with whom she had just withstood a threat.

A veil opened in the night as before, shimmering across the pavement before the phalanx of squad cars. Edie and her new allies stood waiting warily until the Fairy lord and his entourage vanished back behind it. The mare eyed Matthew quite cunningly. *She planned this*, the wolf thought. But the mare said nothing, and Edie would have had to come back to human form to say it—and what good would it do at this point, anyway?

"Well, I guess that's that," Matthew said, when they were gone.

He made a hand-dusting gesture and turned away, leaving Kit to handle the girl and the mare who had stolen each other while he walked, whistling, up the road to speak with the assembled police. Edie went and sat beside Lily, tail thumping the road. Lily reached down and scruffled her ruff and ears with gloved fingers.

"Good wolf," she cooed. "Good girl."

In New York City's storied Greenwich Village, on the island of Manhattan, there is a tavern called the Slaughtered Lamb. A wolf howls on its signboard. In one corner lurks a framed photo of Lon Chaney as the Wolf Man. The tavern is cramped and dark and the mailbox-sized bathroom—beside the grilled-off stair with a sign proclaiming the route to The Dungeon closed for daily tortures—is not particularly clean.

The Slaughtered Lamb (of course) is the favored hangout of Lower Manhattan's more ironic werewolves. Edie hadn't been there even once since she came to New York City. She'd been an outcast even then.

Now she strode west on 4th Street from Washington Square, her high-heeled boots clicking on the preternaturally level sidewalks of Manhattan. Her feet still hurt across the pads, but the worst was healed. She wore trousers to hide her unshaven legs. A cold wind curled the edges of damp leaves, not strong enough to lift them from the pavement.

4th was wider and less tree-shaded than most of the streets in the famously labyrinthine Village, but still quiet—by Manhattan standards—as she made her way past the sex shops, crossing Jones in a hurry. An FDL Express truck waited impatiently behind the stop sign, rolling gently forward as if stretching an invisible barrier when the driver feathered the clutch.

She hopped lightly up one of the better curb cuts in the Village and crossed the sidewalk to the Slaughtered Lamb's black-and-white faux-Tudor exterior. Horns blared as she let herself inside. A reflexive glance at her watch showed 4:59.

Rush hour.

"And so it begins," she muttered to no one in particular, and let the heavy brown nine-panel door fall between her and the noise.

There was noise inside, too, but it was of a more welcoming quality. Speakers mounted over the door blared Chumbawumba; two silent televisions shimmered with the sports highlights of the day. A gas fire roared in the unscreened hearth behind the only open table. Edie picked her way through the darkness to claim it quickly, sighing in relief. It might roast her on one side, but at least it would be a place to sit.

She slung her damp leather coat over the high back of a bar stool and jumped up. She was barely settled, a cider before her, when the door opened again, revealing Matthew Magus and a tall, slender young man with pale skin and black hair that touched his collar in easy curls.

They sat down across from Edie. She shifted a little further away from the fire. "Edith Moorcock," Matthew said, "His Majesty Ian MacNeill, Sire of the Pack and High King of Fairy."

"Charmed," Edie said, offering the King a glove. To her surprise, he took it.

"Edie is a New World wolf," Matthew said. "Apparently,

your grandfather did not find her ... acceptable ... to the Pack."

"Oh, yes," Ian said tiredly. "It's about time the Pack got itself out of the twelfth century." He steepled his fingers as the server came over, and both he and Matthew ordered what Edie had. "I can't imagine what you would want with us at this point, though—"

Edie's heart fluttered with nervousness. "An end to exile?"

"Consider it done. Do you plan to remain in New York?"

Edie nodded.

"Good. The Mage here needs somebody to look after him. Somebody with some teeth." Ian paused as his cider arrived, then sipped it thoughtfully. Matthew coughed into the cupped palm of his glove. "The better to eat you with, my dear," he muttered.

The king regarded him, eyebrows rising as he tilted his head. "I beg your pardon?"

"Nothing, your Majesty."

Ian smiled, showing teeth. If Edie's were anything to go by, he had very good ears. He drank another swallow of cider, wiped his mouth on the back of his hand, and said, "Now, about that changeling girl and the horse that stole her—"

CORRUPTED

Jim C. Hines

If I was going to save this city, I needed three things: one empty detergent bottle, one magazine clipping of Zoe Saldana as Uhura from *Star Trek*, and one stolen child.

The idea of taking the kid bothered me. I hated playing into fairy stereotypes. My partner Larry would give me crap about it for years.

After he got over the fact that I had kidnapped a four-year-old, I mean.

I was working on the detergent bottle when I heard keys rattling in the lock. I set the bottle aside and slid the silver shears into a leather sheath inside my suit jacket, swapping them for a modified Beretta Tomcat pistol. Five inches long, made of brass with a hand-carved oak grip, the gun looked like a toy next to Larry's Glock. But it worked for me, as evidenced by the dead troll in the alley behind the apartment building.

I thought he had been alone, but thanks to the bullet hole in my leg, I had been reluctant to stick around and find out for certain. I gripped the gun in both hands, sighting at a point chest high, about a foot in front of the door. Seven rounds in the magazine and an eighth in the pipe should be plenty for whatever monster had followed me here.

The door opened, and I heard voices arguing. "Why didn't you go before we left?"

"I didn't have to go then!"

The gun vanished into my jacket as Isabel Famosa stepped into her kitchen and tossed her keys onto the counter. Her son Kareem tore through the living room and vanished into the bathroom, not even noticing me sitting in the armchair.

Isabel was more observant. She froze halfway through the process of removing a green windbreaker. "Who are you?"

"Do you have any electrical tape?" I asked.

She backed into the small kitchen. Going for either a phone or a knife. By the time she returned, I had my badge ready.

"My name's Jessica." A lie, but I wasn't about to tell her or the bureau my true name. "I'm with the FBI. Do you know where your husband is, Mrs. Famosa?"

"The FBI? But you're . . . you're not—"

"Human?" She had gone for a boning knife. Nice choice. I hopped down from the chair, clenching my teeth as the movement sent new pain tearing through my leg. Blood oozed through the blue silk tie I had used as a makeshift bandage. Damn troll. I shoved my blonde hair back and hobbled closer, giving her a good look at the narrow pointed ears, the oversaturated blue of my eyes, the deceptively fragile build. "No, I'm not."

I tucked my badge away, keeping my hand close to my

gun. Her knuckles were white on the knife. She wouldn't be the first human to lose her shit when confronted by a fairy. I gave a silent command. With a flutter of wings, a miniature Shia LaBeouf swooped down and swatted her wrist. The knife dropped onto the carpet, and Shia returned to his perch in the spider plant over the window.

"They won't hurt you," I said.

"They?" She stepped back.

I pointed to the curtains on the opposite wall, where a *Playboy* centerfold with gray wings crouched, watching her. "They're pixies. Magically created simulacra. I mostly use them for intelligence and surveillance, but today they're going to help me save your husband's life."

Her son hurried from the bathroom. "Who are you talking to, Momma?" His eyes widened when he spotted me. "Hi! Do you want to play Ben Ten with me?"

"Sorry, kid. I know how I look, but I'm a little old for that stuff." By more than a century. I kept my attention on Isabel, letting Shia watch the boy for me. "Electrical tape?"

"Under the sink in the kitchen." Shock and confusion numbed her words. "What's happened. Where's T.J.?"

"I wish I knew." Crouching to open the cabinet doors beneath the sink almost made me pass out. I locked my jaw and dug through various cleaners, a crusty sponge, and assorted tools, eventually finding a roll of black tape. I limped back into the living room. I wrapped the tape around one end of a straightened industrial staple, one of the big copper ones they use for oversized shipping boxes. I had snatched it from the parking lot beside the dumpsters on my way into the apartment building. "But I know who has him."

I finished cutting the last of four blue ovals from the

detergent bottle, then taped them to the back of the cut-out of Saldana. I used a ballpoint pen to draw a quick circle on her palm, taped the staple into her other hand, and began the spell.

The scent of fresh woodchips filled the apartment. Kareem laughed. His mother grabbed him by the arm, pulling him close, and then—

You know the pain you get when you rip off a Band-Aid? Intense, sharp, but over so quick it's more the memory of the pain that gets to you? Imagine a Band-Aid that covers your entire body, inside and out.

Damn right I screamed.

Fortunately, the pain faded quickly. I sat up, testing my new body. I was stuck wearing the silly red miniskirt and black boots, but I could move without pain. I looked up at my true body, now sitting motionless in the armchair.

I looked tired. Old. We weren't supposed to age, but this job took its toll. Working in the cities, surrounded by steel and iron and rust, facing the worst of humanity and fairy both. My lips were swollen and bloody, and I had a cut on one cheek. I hadn't even felt that one. Shadows circled my eyes, and wrinkles creased my brow, as if worry survived even after the life had been transferred from the flesh.

Kareem was clapping and asking if he could keep me.

I glanced over one shoulder. The plastic ovals had transformed into twin sets of wings, like a dragonfly's. They looked like a cross between stained glass and co-balt blue cellophane. My muscles buzzed as if an electrical current ran through them, and I lifted into the air. "Much better."

"Who has my husband?" Isabel demanded.

The same magic that had animated this body had

changed the staple as well, creating a serviceable copper sword. I preferred my gun, but it was as heavy as my current body, and my magic wasn't up for making a working miniature. "Your husband met some people today. People like me. I don't know what they offered him, but they can be very persuasive. I tried to follow, but they spotted me."

"People like you. You mean . . . fairies."

"As humanity grows, we've been forced into smaller and smaller pockets of this world, but not everyone tries to flee. Some fought, immersing themselves in your cities and your iron and your machines. It . . . warped them. Like drugs in the water supply. It's a darkness you can't imagine, and they hate you for it. They'd kill you all if they could."

"Like terrorists," she said, her face pale.

"Terrorists with magic and centuries of experience." She was about an inch from panicking, and she didn't know anything useful. "I need your son's help."

Her mouth opened, but I didn't have time to argue. Spellcasting was harder in a foreign body, but I managed. Isabel Famosa collapsed in a heap and began to snore.

I flew over to grab a white marble from an open board game. To the boy, I said, "How would you like to go for a ride?"

I was right. Larry Conroy was pissed when he found out what I had done. He was as close to shouting as I had ever heard, his voice buzzing through the miniature fairy ring inked on my palm. "You kidnapped a four-year-old boy?"

"Not all of him." I closed my hand around the marble which hung from a gold chain around my neck. "Just a piece of his soul."

I spread my wings, catching the updraft from the chimney atop the apartment complex. Hot air from the boiler let me circle higher with little effort, until I could see the streets stretched out beneath me. The higher I flew, the more the grating in my bones eased.

I felt it every time I entered a city, a metallic pain, like biting into a ball of tin foil. But the pain of all that iron wasn't the scary part; far worse was when I started to grow accustomed to it, a process that came easier with every passing year.

"Jessie, you're an FBI agent. You can't kidnap kids."

"You'd rather I waterboarded him, maybe?"

Larry's exasperated sigh was jumpy and distorted, like a radio signal in a thunderstorm. Years ago, I had tattooed a miniature ring on his palm, a twin to the one on my own. But a hastily scrawled ink circle was no substitute for the golden tattoo that bound me to my human partner and handler. "You wouldn't have done this twenty years ago," he said.

Sometimes I wished fairy rings came with off switches. "If this works, I'll restore the kid's soul, wipe their memories, and everyone lives happily ever after. If not, there's a good chance this city won't be around long enough to care. Besides, you're forgetting something important."

"What's that?"

My wings twitched, turning me eastward toward the tugging I felt from within the marble. "It's working."

Larry was many things, but he was foremost a damn good agent. "I'll let the team know. What's the location?"

"East. I don't have a distance. Send someone to the apartment, too. Tell them to take care of the troll out back. Oh, and stitch up my leg." Better to do it while I wasn't there to feel the pain.

Shia and the centerfold flanked me as we flew. We were high enough that the people on the street shouldn't notice anything but a trio of birds. Maybe bats, if they squinted hard enough.

"You've been working this case for months," said Larry. "Fairies get annual leave too, you know. When was the last time you went home?"

"I'm fine, thank you, mother." What home? Most of the elder fae had retreated to Fairy centuries ago, before the hills were overrun. There were only a handful of fairy hills left, and none within a hundred miles of here. Even if I did go back, I had been too long among humans. I didn't belong there any more than I did here. "Just shut up and let me do my job, all right?"

"Jessie, I saw the MRI results."

I scowled. Magnetic resonance imaging devices could be calibrated to scan for iron. It was the best tool we had for checking iron toxicity in the bureau's nonhuman agents. "So did I. I passed."

"Barely. And how much longer do you think that will last when every breath sucks particles of rust into your lungs? What if Isabel had cut you with that blade?"

I knew I shouldn't have mentioned that. Before I could answer, a brown shadow tore past my right side, and one of my escorts vanished. I looked down to see paper and plastic fluttering to the ground as a large hawk flapped up toward me. "Scold me later, mom. I've got to go fight bad guys."

Fear sped my wings until my entire body hummed with my efforts to escape. It didn't help. The hawk continued to gain. I darted to one side, trying to beat speed with maneuverability. "They must have left someone to watch the apartment. Shapeshifter, from the size of it."

"Can you end the spell? Jump back to your body?"

"Not without abandoning the kid's soul." Truth be told, I wasn't thinking about the kid. I was thinking about the hawk, and the cloud of twisted magic and toxic iron that clung to its feathers. It was unnatural, an ugly corruption of something once beautiful. "Come on, you bastard."

I dove for the buildings below. If I could find a small enough window or opening—Hell, I'd settle for a gutter I could crawl into. I dropped onto a restaurant rooftop and ducked behind a brick chimney, sending my remaining pixie to slow the hawk. Paper tore, and half a centerfold drifted down onto the hot roof. The hawk landed moments later. I drew my sword and peeked out.

The hawk had vanished, replaced by a fairy who was close to my own true form in size and stature. But she was . . . *twisted*. Her veins were like blue steel, a stark contrast to her pale skin. Her eyes had a strange, shimmering film, like oil on a puddle. Old scars covered her exposed arms and legs, especially the hands. Hair the color of rust hung past her shoulders in filthy clumps. She wore torn-off black jeans and a ragged T-shirt, but it was the steel chain circling her waist that troubled me most. This was a fairy so far gone that she embraced the pain and corruption of iron.

I searched the rooftop. Metal smokestacks huffed greasy steam into the air. Patches of black tar marked old repairs. A small satellite dish was mounted near the northeast corner.

I flew toward the dish, making it there just before the fairy. I grabbed one of the metal legs to stop myself. I nearly tore my shoulder, but my pursuer stumbled past. A human would have fallen off the roof, but she managed to regain her balance at the edge. I stayed low and tugged at the electrical tape on the hilt of my sword until I exposed the end.

"You're different from your companions, little false pixie." Her voice was raspy, conjuring images of poorly maintained factory machines. "There's a true mind in there, and is that a human soul I smell?"

I crouched at the base of the dish, grimacing at the exposed metal. The legs were aluminum, but the steel conduit covering the cables felt like a thousand static shocks jumping onto my skin. I wrinkled my nose at the faint smell of burning paper. Too long here, and my magic would unravel whether I wanted it to or not. "Tell me where you took T.J. Famosa."

Her smile grew. Her teeth had the same oily-metal sheen as her eyes. "Or else what? You'll send another of your paper pixies for me?"

Why couldn't they have sent another troll, big and strong and stupid? I lowered my voice to a whisper. "Larry, I need you to press the barrel of your gun into the ring on your palm."

"What?" I winced and clenched my fist to muffle his words. "Are you insane?"

"It's a fairy ring. I can open it to allow objects to pass through as well as sound." Probably. "For Mab's sake, don't fire until I say the word." I brought my fist to my lips, whispering old words to expand the ring's magic.

The fairy didn't give me the chance. Maybe she felt my spell, or maybe she simply lacked the patience of our kind. She lunged, nails like metal claws gleaming in the sunlight.

I reversed my sword and stepped sideways to where the cable left the conduit and snaked up to the dish. I held the tip of my sword against my stomach. Her palm jabbed the blade through my stomach, directly into the exposed cable behind me. The other end of the sword pierced her skin, and she screamed as electricity ripped through her body.

It shorted out within seconds, but it was enough. I pried the sword free. "Paper doesn't conduct electricity, bitch." I crawled over her spasming body and pressed my palm to her forehead. Before she could recover, I finished my spell and told Larry to fire.

I had survived, but it hurt like hell. A blackened hole passed cleanly through my gut, and a spray of fairy blood covered my body. The sight made me want to vomit, but I managed to quell the urge. The last thing I needed was to start spewing confetti.

"Are you all right?" Larry asked. "Did it work?"

"It worked." My sword was ruined. The remaining tape had melted, and the metal had shed its magic, reverting to a bent staple. I tossed it aside.

Even in death, the fairy appeared angry. Feral. Her lips were drawn back, and her vacant eyes were narrow. How long had she been banished from home, unable to return? How long since the infection had taken her body and mind? Had she realized what was happening at the end, or had she been too far gone to care?

I tested my wings. The steel conduit had melted off the tip of the upper left wing when the fairy pressed me down, but I could still fly. "There's a dead fairy on the roof of Pizza Palace. Corner of Walnut and Fourth. Send someone to clean that up."

"That's two attacks," Larry said.

"Believe it or not, I can count too." I flew higher, trying to concentrate over the pain and noise of the city.

"Both in daylight, in the open? Whatever this is, it's big."

"No shit." I clutched the marble in both hands. Kareem continued to lead me east, toward the edge of the city. I flew in silence for a while, while Larry dispatched people to clean up my mess.

"You didn't even try to question her."

I sighed. "Do you reason with rats?"

"You used to. I know your file, Jessie. Remember the dwarves you brought in back in eighty-six? You spent weeks trying to get through to them."

"And look where it got me." Three dwarves, brothers, had sabotaged a coal mine out east, killing nineteen people. "It would have been quicker to just kill them."

"Execute them, you mean?"

"Spare me. Do you want to save your world, or do you want to worry about procedure and fair trials and all of that human bullshit while they murder your people and mine?"

"How long has it been since you laughed, Jessie?"

My jaw tightened. "There's something ahead." I felt it before I smelled it, and smelled it before I saw it. "They're at the landfill."

Before me stretched the epitome of all things human: a gaping pit, a scar in the earth which housed an ever-growing heap of filth and garbage. A miniature mountain of plastic and steel and decay. A small brick building sat to one side, processing some of the methane stink that filled the air.

"Stay out of sight," said Larry. "We'll have a team there in fifteen minutes."

I ignored him, as he must have known I would. I circled the landfill, joining the seagulls, whose harsh cries made me want to tear off my ears. "There's something strange about this place."

I spied a dozen humans walking entranced around the edge of the landfill, guided by two fairies so far gone I couldn't tell what race they had once belonged to. They had actually incorporated scraps of metal into their bodies, like cyborgs from a bad movie. One might have been a faun, from the odd angles of his legs. The other was larger. An ogre, perhaps?

The humans appeared blurry, almost ghostlike. Had they murdered the prisoners already? If not for the insistent tugging of the kid's soul, I might have missed them entirely.

"What's going on?" Larry whispered.

"They're just walking." Circling. Counterclockwise around a mountain—around a *hill* of human waste. "Impossible."

"What?"

I could feel it now. Beneath the iron and the garbage, its magic warped but familiar. My fists clenched. "They're building a fairy hill."

"Are you sure? I thought that was impossible."

"So did I." But the magic below me was unmistakable. They were using mortals to open a path from this world to Fairy. What would such a hill do to my home? A hill born of steel and iron, its magic shaped by fallen fae. They would loose long-forgotten evils upon this world, and they would warp the beauty of Fairy just as they had done to themselves.

"How long until they finish?"

"I don't know." There were rituals to be followed . . . rituals that culminated with the deaths of those who opened the path. There was a reason humans had for so long mistaken our hills for burial mounds. It was those deaths that opened the way, the passage of their souls from this world to wherever their kind went next, but it had to be done at the proper time. How many laps had they completed? "When will those reinforcements arrive?"

"Ten minutes, according to the GPS."

"That's not soon enough, damn it." I flexed my fingers, looking at the blackened fairy ring in my palm. I grabbed the marble which held Kareem's soul and pressed it against my hand. The ring wasn't big enough, and magic could only bend the rules so far. I felt paper tear as I forced the kid's soul through. I clung to the pain, using it to focus my anger. "Hold on to that. If I don't get back, have someone from the bureau take it to Kareem."

"What are you doing, Jessie?"

"What I have to do." My magic was little use. The lower I got, the more the iron would warp even the simplest of spells. I wasn't even certain I could maintain this body if I landed. So much metal crushed into a single place, pulsing through my mind like static. "They don't know I'm here. We should be able to get off four, maybe five shots before they spot me."

"What if there are others?"

It didn't matter. The metal jutting from the fairies' flesh was both poison and protection, armor against attack. A perfect shot might kill one, but most likely the bullets from Larry's gun would only piss them off. "Trust me."

Magic pulsed through me as I circled downward, stronger than anything I had felt in ages. It carried the scent of home, but . . . burnt. Like the aftermath of a forest fire, the seared-metal smell infused the very air of Fairy.

I flexed my hand. The last two fingers were torn and unresponsive, but the ring still functioned. I gripped my forearm with my other hand to steady my aim.

Larry would never forgive me, but I didn't care. I could taste their magic. It burned my throat and chest. He could kill me, or they could, but I'd be damned before I let them do this.

I studied the humans, wondering briefly which was Kareem's father. Folding my wings back, I swooped toward the front of their line.

I sat in the car, grimacing at the grinding of the engine. The bureau had a handful of vehicles specifically for their fairy agents, with plastic and fiberglass replacing every possible component, but some things required steel.

Larry returned a short time later, sliding into the back seat with me. He was red with fury, his forehead glossed with sweat. "Get us out of here," he said to the driver, his jaw clenched so tight I could barely understand him.

"How's the kid?" I asked.

"Kareem is fine." He wouldn't look at me. "They won't remember a thing about you or what happened."

"And yet you sound like a goblin took a dump in your favorite shoes."

"Five humans are dead," he shouted. "Tell me the truth, Jessie. In the name of God, tell me the fucking truth. What did you do?"

I matched his volume. "I stopped them from opening a hill of iron and unleashing devils you can't imagine into this world, that's what I did."

"You're done, Jessie. When we get back, you're turning in your gun and your badge, and going back to Fairy.

If you ever set foot in this world again, I swear to God I'll—"

"No."

"You murdered those people! Do you feel anything for those dead men and women? T.J. wasn't the only one with family, you know. Just because he survived—"

"*If* I killed them—and I'm not admitting anything—it was because it was the only way to stop the fairies." I knew I should feel something . . . *would* have felt something, twenty years ago. But they were only humans, and their deaths had prevented so many more.

We both knew this wasn't about the choice I had made. It was about the ease with which I had made it. That I had done so without telling him and without regret. That I had ordered Larry to fire again and again until the fairies spotted me and flew to attack me. I had barely managed to end the spell, returning to my injured body in the Famosas' apartment.

"I was the one pulling the trigger, Jessie." His anger had receded for the moment, and I could hear the anguish in his words, even if I didn't share it.

"What did you expect, Larry?"

"I expected you to find another way."

I shook my head. "You know damn well what this job does to us. The price we pay every time we follow our twisted cousins into their havens of rust and iron and death. You monitor our fall, charting every speck of iron that infects our blood, writing your reports as we descend into the same madness we hunt."

"That's why I'm sending you home."

"No," I said again.

"Jessie, if you return now, you might be able to recover. You'll laugh again, and find what you've lost."

"And you'll recruit another fairy to take my place," I said, all but snarling. "You'll destroy them the same way you did me. Maybe not you personally, but you know exactly what will happen to my replacement. So do we. And we do it anyway."

"I told you to get away." Sadness had replaced the last of the anger.

I shrugged. "I can still do this job. Not for much longer, maybe, but I'm not about to let this happen to another of my kin a second sooner than it has to. Someone has to stop them . . . and I trust you to stop me, when it comes to that."

Slowly, he nodded. "The next time you cross the line . . ."

"I understand." I leaned back in my seat and closed my eyes. The fairies had escaped, but I knew their faces. I knew their magic. Human agents were searching the landfill for clues. I might have lost laughter and beauty, but I had this. "Until then, we have a job to do."

ABOUT THE AUTHORS

Barbara Ashford seems to make a habit of cannibalizing her life for her art. She set "How to Be Human™" in the local Radisson Hotel and drew on her memories of acting in summer stock to create the world of the Crossroads Theatre for her first contemporary fantasy novel *Spellcast*. Barbara lives in New Rochelle, New York, with her husband whom she met while performing at the Southbury Playhouse. They have yet to spot any faeries lurking around New Roc City, but you never know. To find out about her latest projects—including the *Spellcast* sequel—visit her at www.barbara-ashford .com.

Elizabeth Bear was born on the same day as Frodo and Bilbo Baggins, but in a different year. This has given her a predilection for mushrooms and speculative fiction. She lives in Connecticut with a ridiculous dog and a cat who is an internet celebrity.

S.C. Butler is a former Wall Street bond trader who has never met any leprechauns, urban or otherwise, and, as far as he knows, never caused a stock market crash. He is the author of the Stoneways trilogy: *Reiffen's Choice*, *Queen Ferris*, and *The Magicians' Daughter*; and lives in New Hampshire with his wife and son.

Jim C. Hines' latest book is *The Snow Queen's Shadow*, the final book in his series about butt-kicking fairy tale heroines (because Sleeping Beauty was always meant to be a ninja, and Snow White makes a bad-ass witch). He's also the author of the humorous Goblin Quest trilogy, as well as more than forty published short stories in markets such as *Realms of Fantasy*, *Sword & Sorceress*, and a number of DAW anthologies. He lives in Michigan with his wife, two children, and half an ark's worth of pets. You can find his web site and blog at www.jimchines.com.

Susan Jett is a graduate of Clarion West and has been writing stories since she could hold a pencil. She's lived and worked all over the world, but most recently, she worked as a teen librarian while living in Brooklyn. She currently lives in an old farmhouse in New Hampshire with her husband Sam, her son Henry, and Nellie-the-wonder-whippet. She is hard at work on her first novel and hopes to publish it before her son learns to read.

Jay Lake lives in Portland, Oregon, where he works on numerous writing and editing projects. His 2011 books are *Endurance* and *Love in the Time of Metal and Flesh*, along with paperback releases of two of his other titles. His short fiction appears regularly in literary and genre markets worldwide. Jay is a past winner of the John W. Campbell Award for Best New Writer and is a multiple nominee for the Hugo and World Fantasy Awards.

Seanan McGuire is a native Californian, and grew up in a town where the annual tarantula migration is a fact of life. This explains a lot. She is the author of two urban fantasy series—the October Daye adventures and In-Cryptid—as well as writing science fiction under the name Mira Grant. She was the winner of the 2010 John W. Campbell Award for Best New Writer. It came with a tiara. Seanan lives with three enormous blue cats, a lot of books and horror movies, and the tarantula migration. She doesn't sleep very much.

Juliet E McKenna's love of fantasy, myth, and history led naturally to studying classics at St Hilda's College, Oxford. After a career change from personnel management to combine motherhood with book-selling, her debut novel, *The Thief's Gamble,* was published in 1999. She has written a dozen epic fantasy novels, most recently The Chronicles of the Lescari Revolution, plus assorted shorter fiction including stories for *Doctor Who* and *Torchwood*. She reviews for web and print magazines and fits all this around her husband and teenage sons. Living in West Oxfordshire, she's currently working on a new fantasy trilogy called The Hadrumal Crisis.

Shannon Page was born on Halloween night and spent her early years on a commune in northern California's backwoods. A childhood without television gave her a great love of books and the worlds she found in them. She wrote her first book, an adventure story starring her cat, at the age of seven. Sadly, that tale is currently out of print, but her work has appeared in *Clarkesworld*, *Interzone,* and *Fantasy* (with Jay Lake), *Black Static*, Tor.com, and a number of anthologies, including *Love and Rockets* from DAW and the Australian Shadows Award-winning *Grants Pass*. Shannon is a longtime practitioner of Ashtanga yoga, has no tattoos, and lives in Portland,

Oregon, with seventeen orchids and an awful lot of books. Visit her at www.shannonpage.net.

Avery Shade is an author of paranormal and urban fantasy of both the adult and young adult variety. Like Autumn, she has a true love of all things green . . . too bad she has a black thumb. She'd like to blame it on the cold, bleak upstate NY winters she endured during both her childhood and young adult life, but even since moving to sunny North Carolina her plants haven't fared much better. Nowadays she is contentedly living her life vicariously through her stories where anything and everything is possible . . . even live plants.

Kristine Smith has spent almost her entire working career in manufacturing/R&D of one kind or another, and has worked for the same northern Illinois pharmaceutical company for almost 25 years. She is the winner of the 2001 John W. Campbell Award for Best New Writer, and is the author of the Jani Kilian SF series as well as a number of short stories. She is currently working on several projects, and wishes she possessed a time-turner.

Kari Sperring has never had a close encounter with any of the fae, although she's been accused of being away with them many times. Rumors that her writing is obsessed with water refuse to go away: her only excuse is that she comes from a family of dowsers. Her first novel, the mildly water-laden *Living With Ghosts*, came out in 2009 from DAW; the second, *The Grass King's Concubine,* contains ferrets, elemental warriors, and a water-stealing clock and is due in 2012. She's British and lives in Cambridge, but hasn't seen the local fae drown any academics to date.

April Steenburgh is a bookstore manager turned librarian who enjoys fire spinning and hunting for dilapidated, forgotten buildings and exploring them with a camera. When not traipsing about the countryside, she can be found around town hunting sweet potato fries or coffee with her partner in writing crimes most creative. She lives with two cats (Phaedrus and Mildmay), three ferrets (Molly, Oliver, and Alexander) and one primordial turtle named Eris. And her partner, who is wonderfully tolerant of the whole operation.

Anton Strout is the author of the Simon Canderous urban fantasy series and *Alchemystic*, book one of the Spellmason Chronicles. He is also the author of over half a dozen tales for DAW Books. Anton was born in the Berkshire Hills mere miles from writing heavyweights Nathaniel Hawthorne and Herman Melville and currently lives in the haunted corn maze that is New Jersey (where nothing paranormal ever really happens, he assures you). In his scant spare time, he is a writer, a sometimes actor, sometimes musician, occasional RPGer, and the world's most casual and controller smashing video gamer. He can often be found lurking the darkened halls of www.antonstrout.com.

Jean Marie Ward writes fiction, nonfiction, and everything in between. Her first novel, *With Nine You Get Vanyr* (written with the late Teri Smith), finaled in two categories of the 2008 Indie Book Awards. Her short stories appear in numerous anthologies. She is also known for her art books, such as the popular *Fantasy Art Templates*. She edited the web magazine *Crescent Blues* for eight years and now writes for other online venues, including Buzzy Multimedia. Her web site is www.JeanMarieWard.com.

ABOUT THE EDITORS

Patricia Bray is the author of a dozen novels, including *Devlin's Luck,* which won the 2003 Compton Crook award for the best first novel in the field of science fiction or fantasy. This is her second editorial tour of duty, having previously co-edited *After Hours: Tales From The Ur-bar* (DAW, March 2011) with her partner-in-crime Joshua Palmatier. She currently lives in upstate New York, where she combines her writing with a full-time career as systems analyst, ensuring that she is never more than a few feet away from a keyboard. To find out more, visit her website at www.patriciabray.com.

Joshua Palmatier is a writer with a Ph.D in mathematics. He currently resides in upstate New York while teaching mathematics at SUNY College at Oneonta. His novels include the Throne of Amenkor trilogy and, written as Benjamin Tate, *Well of Sorrows* and *Leaves of Flame*. His short story "Mastihooba" appears in *Close Encounters of the Urban Kind* and "Tears of Blood" is in *Beauty Has Her Way*. He has previously edited *After Hours: Tales From the Ur-bar* with Patricia Bray, which includes his story "An Alewife In Kish." Find out more at www.joshuapalmatier.com and www.benjamintate.com.

Tanya Huff

"The Gales are an amazing family, the aunts will strike fear into your heart, and the characters Allie meets are both charming and terrifying."
—#1 *New York Times* bestselling author
Charlaine Harris

The Enchantment Emporium

Alysha Gale is a member of a family capable of changing the world with the charms they cast. She is happy to escape to Calgary when when she inherits her grandmother's junk shop, but when Alysha learns just how much trouble is brewing, even calling in the family to help may not be enough to save the day.

978-0-7564-0605-9

The Wild Ways

Charlotte Gale is a Wild Power who allies herself with a family of Selkies in a fight against offshore oil drilling. The oil company has hired another of the Gale family's Wild Powers, the fearsome Auntie Catherine, to steal the Selkies' sealskins. To defeat her, Charlotte will have to learn what born to be Wild really means in the Gale family...

978-0-7564-0686-8

To Order Call: 1-800-788-6262
www.dawbooks.com

DAW 200

Seanan McGuire
The October Daye Novels

"...will surely appeal to readers who enjoy my books, or those of Patrica Briggs." —*Charlaine Harris*

"Well researched, sharply told, highly atmospheric and as brutal as any pulp detective tale, this promising start to a new urban fantasy series is sure to appeal to fans of Jim Butcher or Kim Harrison."—*Publishers Weekly*

ROSEMARY AND RUE
978-0-7564-0571-7

A LOCAL HABITATION
978-0-7564-0596-0

AN ARTIFICIAL NIGHT
978-0-7564-0626-4

LATE ECLIPSES
978-0-7564-0666-0

ONE SALT SEA
978-0-7564-0683-7

To Order Call: 1-800-788-6262
www.dawbooks.com

DAW 142